H
a ...ovels including *My Crim...*
V ...*ut Of Here*. He also co-authored the DS
J: novel, *First Frost*, under the pseudonym James
H ...le is Professor of Creative Writing and Crime
F ...at the University of East Anglia. He lives in
N ...ich with his family.

*Also by Harry Brett*

Time to Win
Red Hot Front

# Good Dark Night

*Harry Brett*

corsair

CORSAIR

First published in Great Britain in 2019 by Corsair
This paperback edition published in 2020

1 3 5 7 9 10 8 6 4 2

A CIP catalogue record for this book
is available from the British Library.

ISBN: 978-1-4721-5274-9

Typeset in Granjon LT by Hewer Text UK Ltd, Edinburgh
Printed and bound in Great Britain by Clays Ltd, Elcograf S.p.A.

Papers used by Corsair are from well-managed forests
and other responsible sources.

MIX
Paper from
responsible sources
FSC® C104740

Corsair
An imprint of
Little, Brown Book Group
Carmelite House
50 Victoria Embankment
London EC4Y 0DZ

An Hachette UK Company
www.hachette.co.uk

www.littlebrown.co.uk

To Rachel

From the dead centre of Breydon Bridge the mudflats and reed banks stretched endlessly. A frozen waste of half water, half land. Mist mingled with the ice, under a thin sky of the palest blue. The sun was rising slowly behind Frank. In front, not so far away from the bridge, were a couple of dredgers – new vessels in a smart dull orange livery. Something else nearby was causing Frank's pulse to quicken.

The dredgers had arrived a month ago, and had barely got stuck in. They were to carve space in the mud for the footings of the new lifting bridge, which would be the third crossing over the Yare to Yarmouth. This was a government-stamped £150 million project.

Another red herring, as far as Frank was concerned. The ballast-laying and concrete-mixing machines were nowhere in sight. The coordination appeared ill considered, wasteful. The way the currents flowed through Breydon Water, the way the mud collapsed in on itself, any hole dug around here would disappear almost before the next tide covered it. Which was how Frank had liked it. He was no engineer, but he'd had plenty of experience digging holes in this mud, burying rats.

Besides, the town needed more than a new bridge to turn its fortunes around. He wanted the dredgers to go away. He was also thinking of the birds, the waders, the reeds, the lugworms, the fragile ecosystem, which needed to be protected, left alone – though he knew it was already too late for that. Too late for most things. His eye caught sight of the forensics tent once again.

He'd pulled over onto what amounted to a hard shoulder. It might have been edging eight in the morning, nevertheless, the traffic was sparse. Rush hour, around here? Yeah, it happened, but most of the traffic flowed the other way. People leaving Yarmouth to go to jobs in Lowestoft, Norwich, and some to the wind farms and platforms on the sandbanks out in the shallow North Sea. Yarmouth was a dark and desperate place at the best of times. Few wanted to hang around for long. Frank was one of the few.

The instrument panel of his Lexus RX, much of which still baffled him, said it was minus two degrees outside. Inside the plush cabin it was a balmy 21.5 degrees. Frank was beginning to sweat. He went to turn the engine off, then realised the engine was already off, because the RX was a hybrid. Yes, he was doing his bit for the environment. Feeding the fishes and birds as well.

He got out of the car and walked over to the thick, chest-high railings. Directly above him were the giant lifting arms. Sunlight was catching the steel, tarnished with seagull shit and a steady breeze of indifference. It was rarely calm, still, in these parts. Desperate voices forever shouting to be heard, and all too soon lost in the wind.

Sunlight was also beginning to stream across the rippled water. The tide was about half in, or half out. There was no sign of anyone attempting to start up a dredger. But Frank was not surprised by this. What dredging might have been going on had been stopped, yesterday. It was all over the news.

Now that he was out of his SUV, leaning over the railings, he could see far too clearly the forensics tent, along with a rectangle of police tape, edging the high-water mark. There was a smattering of vehicles sporting officialdom, though no uniforms in sight. Perhaps they were having a brew, keeping warm, waiting for low tide.

'Fuck's sake,' he muttered, straightening his back and pushing himself away from the railings. There was no rule against sightseeing, and amazingly there were no CCTV cameras on this part of the bridge. Which was why he used to set out from underneath the structure with his various loads, though always at low water.

One of the dredgers had dug up a body less than twenty-four hours ago. They weren't saying whether the body was male or female. What state it was in. How long it might have been there. Frank had yet to contact the assistant chief constable, get her take. He wasn't sure whether any more details would help him, or her.

The traffic appeared to be thickening by the minute – cars, trucks, trundling past him. He wondered whether he could even sense the slightest of sways, the bridge moving, the ground beneath his feet giving way. He climbed back into swathes of leather-studded luxury, knowing he was never going to work out what every button and display did. He was from the wrong century.

He gasped with the creaking effort, breathing in the new car smell, knowing he probably didn't smell so good. Fear did that to you. He'd smelled enough coming off others, one of whom might have been dug up yesterday. Perhaps they'd found more bodies, and weren't saying. Sort of games they played.

He'd probably got lazy as he'd got older. Was less prepared to trek through thigh-high mud, weighed down by all manner of shit. Life was too short.

He pressed the right button and eased the car into drive, saw a gap and pulled out, heading the most circuitous route to the office. *To the office.* The joke of it. In such a vehicle. He'd at least gone for the RX and not the LS. He would have slunk so far into the seat of one of those things that he would never have climbed back out. It even supplied a shiatsu massage. Technology had gone mad.

Soon he was approaching the roundabout, the confluence of two great East Anglian Roads, the A12 and the A47, which then did their utmost to skirt Yarmouth. Not him. He was going to head due east. He'd quickly grown to like his new life and position, his place beside Tatiana Goodwin at the board table. Yes, partners they now were – her idea, her insistence. Now he was a man of stature he could pay others to do the street work, the enforcing, and keep a healthy distance from the dirtiest scum. In his dreams.

A couple of patrol cars were sitting on the edge of the roundabout. The cops huddled inside their rigs, seemingly paying no attention to the passing traffic. They should have been looking a lot harder, and for a lot longer.

It was a rotten, two-faced world, everyone knew that. Frank had only been doing his bit to clean it up, bring back some spark. Credit where credit was due, he thought, flicking on the surround sound, nodding his head their way. They owed him. The town owed him, big time.

'Ben, you don't have to wear a suit every day.'

'You don't like it?'

'Sure, I do,' Tatty said. She was behind her desk. Acres of glass and steel, no paperwork. Her eldest son was standing in front of the desk, an iPad in his right hand. It was his first week working for her, for the business. He was as unsure as she was.

'It's from Boss.' He tapped the breast pocket, hung onto a lapel.

'Of course,' she said.

'Somewhere like that, anyway,' he added.

'Very smart,' she said, picturing Ben's dad, who always wore suits half a decade or so out of fashion. 'It's – I don't know – rather formal.' There was something wrong with the shoulders, and the lapels. The colour wasn't great either – a shiny, dark brown. The suit he'd worn yesterday had at least been black.

'You always dress up. Look at you,' Ben said. Hurt in his voice.

He had a point. She was in suede and cashmere, her favourite fabrics, and designs that couldn't be bought locally. Internet clothes shopping was no fun at all. She enjoyed her trips to Mayfair. She shouldn't have said anything, but it was now Thursday. It pained her to see him in such clothes – reminding her of her husband, his dad. 'Thank you for making the effort to look smart,' she said, trying to turn things around. 'I'm not used to it. Zach always looks like a bloody tramp.' Not that Zach was working for her at the moment, strictly speaking.

'As for Frank, well he has his own style, doesn't he?' she continued, grimacing.

'Sam looks the part, though, doesn't she?' Ben said, his eyes tracing the large, executive loft space. 'She must spend enough on her wardrobe.'

'Yeah,' said Tatty, 'when she gets out of bed.' That was another inappropriate comment. Her daughter, unlike her youngest son, was also meant to be working for her, though she had other issues she was dealing with – more than enough trauma for anyone. She was still not a hundred per cent. Tatty would forgive her anything.

'You're in a good mood this morning,' Ben said, meaning the opposite.

Tatty looked at her eldest, who had remained standing, that silly iPad in his hand, his underdeveloped muscles allowing his considerable frame, draped in such ill-fitting material, to sag. That was it, Tatty realised, unnerved. Ben's suit might have been OK for a dodgy currency trader working in the City, circa 2013 – where his dad had installed him – but it wasn't fine for her smart new office. The Smokehouse was an ocean of taste and restraint, and fancy artisanal workmanship. The latest finishes, following the arson attack, were even more impressive than the first renovation job. There should have been no hint of past incongruities.

She smiled at Ben, mustering all the love and warmth she could. The poor boy couldn't help the fact that he was his father's son. She had to be more accepting. She loved him to bits, of course, was thrilled he'd returned to the fold. Except she couldn't stop herself from shuddering. 'A couple of things have come up,' she said firmly. It all linked, it always would. The past didn't go away.

'Anything I can help with, Mum?'

'Not just yet, sweetheart.' She shouldn't be calling him 'sweetheart' in the office. He shouldn't be calling her 'Mum'. She pushed the chair back, some amazing contraption from a German designer. She'd wanted her kids to work for her, for Goodwin Enterprises, so badly, and now they were all involved – even Zach, by property – she wasn't sure how to handle it. She was not in a good mood this morning, Ben was right. Silence from Frank was not helping.

'I want to run through the presentation with you, before my meeting with the council.' Ben was now holding out the iPad, as if it held the key to the future. 'Keep you in the loop,' he added brightly, tapping the device.

'On that?' She'd walked over to a window. How could she think of new projects? She turned her back on him. Frank had given Ben, and Sam for that matter, the lecture on electronic trails. How computers, phones, devices should be avoided, unless everything was above board,

3

watertight. Weak sunlight was falling faintly on the nearby rooftops. Frost was clinging to troughs, gullies, shady edges. There was a heatwave going on inside the loft. Modern insulation for you, plus the menopause. She swung round, faced him.

'I'd put it up on a screen, if you had one. Some office this,' he said dismissively. 'Everyone expects slick presentations nowadays. I'm pleased with what I've done, in the time. I did learn something in London.' He smiled some more.

'OK,' she said, returning to her seat. 'Pull up that chair.' The visitors' chairs weren't so elaborate, even though they were from the same designer.

Ben propped the iPad on the glass desk, swiped away until the screen was filled with computer-generated images of a wind farm. Every angle, every blade was pictured, while the perfectly blue sea rippled with uniform ease. A support vessel then sailed into sight, moored up against one of the platforms. A couple of cartoon characters climbed onto the platform, disappeared inside the turbine. One of the men then reappeared on the top, gave a wave.

Always men in such jobs, Tatty thought, struggling to contain a yawn, as the supply ship sailed off, visited another platform. She needed more coffee. Ben was talking numbers, fast. 'So what's our cut?' she eventually said.

'None of this exists. Or rather we set up as a key financial partner, a bridge between state subsidies and private concerns, if you like. With equity options, of course. I can see how those might fly, especially if we push the tax advantages. Our USP is that we're on the ground, local, the only such financial services operation. We'd get leverage on the grants to start with, then we could create a whole chain of bogus suppliers and operators. We'll work on the fact that Yarmouth initially lost out to Lowestoft when it comes to wind farm support operations, by stressing the government's regional regeneration programme. This is all about renewables – sexy as hell.' He laughed. 'For God's sake, Mum, East Anglia One is worth two point five billion. If we can't make anything out of that, who can? We're the right players in the right place. Goodwin Financial Services, I thought we'd call it. There'll be returns, like no one's ever seen before in this part of the world.'

The financial manoeuvring around the £200 million super casino operation had become complicated enough. She was beginning to wonder if she was in the wrong game. However, she admired Ben's enthusiasm – the work, the thinking he appeared to have done in just days. The graphics, as well, if not all the characters. Smart boy. Though she couldn't help wondering about the fine details of the necessary financial instruments, even if they were to be fake. Appearances were vital. At some point paper would need to be presented, signed. 'How long can you keep up such a charade?'

'Think of it as a pyramid,' he said, still excited. 'We'll set up the Financial Services arm as a separate company, plant it offshore. That's the bit I like. Offshore feeding offshore. I don't see why this shouldn't keep going for years. You look out to sea, watch those turbines turning round and round, it's like impossible to count how many there are, who owns which bit of each one.'

'What's out there now, or on your screen?' Tatty said, not sure it made any difference. He was beaming back at her – a smile as broad and deathly as Breydon Water. His father's child all right. Being sacked from his London job could well be the making of him, she thought. If he didn't fly too high, too fast. She was quickly learning that ambition needed to be carefully managed, certainly in a place where there was so little of it. Jealousy was in far greater supply.

'What difference does it make?' Ben said.

'Will you still be able to keep an eye on the super casino deal?' That was in his job description, she thought, the key part. 'The first lot of money from the Americans is due by the end of the month. It'll need spreading around, quietly, and sharpish. They're expecting returns, as well. Off the scale, if you ask me.'

'Of course – I'm fully aware of that.'

'If the Europeans sense that the Americans are stalling, they're not going to be happy with what they've already coughed up.'

'Oh, I'm sure the Europeans are happy enough to have found someone willing to look after their cash – what with the new gambling laws that are coming in across the EU, and the Albanians ever on the march.'

'They want to see that casino being built, Ben – one day. There aren't even any foundations. It's still a patch of scrub, a toxic waste ground.'

'Trust me, Mum. I'm used to juggling numerous, highly complex deals at any one time.'

Ben was twenty-eight. He didn't look a day older. The suit wasn't helping. Tatty glanced beyond him, taking in the calm luxury of her vast office, exquisitely restored, twice as it happened, both times by Nathan Taylor. She knew that the business, her business – her and Frank's business – couldn't sit still. There were too many people who didn't want it to exist as it was.

'Who exactly are you meeting today?' she asked.

'The Regeneration Committee.'

'Crikey. Who's heading up that shower now?' The last chair, Graham Sands, had died in June – eight, nine, months ago.

'No one yet, from what I hear, which is why it's the perfect opportunity to get a project noticed, and supported.'

'Be wary.' Tatty leaned back in her seat. It was both extremely supportive yet flexible when you wanted it to be. The covering was some sort of black mesh – with a lifetime guarantee, whatever that meant. The control knobs were chrome-tipped. Everything about it was masculine – the language that continued to have undue currency in the business world. Definitely in her neck of the woods. 'Never trusted them an inch.'

'A bit of help is all we're asking for.'

'All *you're* asking for,' Tatty reminded him.

'They have purse strings. The thing is, you get the committee members on side before the next head takes charge.' That smile of his, of Rich's, came back. 'Hey – I've just had a thought. Genius, that I am.' He clicked the fingers of his right hand, before pointing straight at Tatty.

7

'Come on, Mum, *you* have to do it. For the good of the business, the good of Yarmouth, the family's name. You should have put your hat into the ring months ago.'

'What?'

'Yeah – you'd be perfect.'

'No. No way.'

'Dad did it.'

'Exactly.'

'Then Graham Sands got in there, didn't he? It's our turn again, before someone else spots the opportunity.'

'It doesn't appear that anyone's rushing to do it,' she said.

'Maybe that's got something to do with the fact that the last two heads were murdered,' Ben said quietly.

'Thanks for reminding me.' Tatty sighed. 'And you want me to put myself in that position?'

'It'd be quite different. You know how the land lies. Plus, you'll have the right people behind you – protecting you.'

He had changed so quickly. Or maybe he'd always been like this. She hadn't seen much of him over the last few years. His father had got him the job in London, had been friends with Ben's boss. She wasn't going to ask him why he'd really been sacked.

'Oh, for God's sake, Ben, it's a ridiculous suggestion. Besides, when would I have the time? I'm busy enough as it is.'

'A couple of meetings a month? And you know what those old codgers are like – they can be bought. Anyone can be bought in this town. That's the point.'

'How long have you been back here?'

'As Sam says, it doesn't feel like I ever left.'

8

'Well I missed you for long enough. Have you seen Frank this morning, by the way? Is he in?'

Ben shook his head. 'Nope, don't think so.'

'The lazy sod. That's what happens when you give someone too much money, and too much power.'

## 2

'Where are we?' Zach opened his eyes, saw a block of grey straight out of the window. Looked harder, caught some brightness in the distance, emanating from the low sky, and a sheen of frost out on the marshy fields. Was that a cow as well? A herd?

No, they were horses, still and skinny. 'Mate, where are we?' he said again, shaking his head, trying to clear the fug from his overworked body, his taxed brain. He kicked the back of the centre console. When he asked a question he expected a reply. He was paying, after all.

'Sorry, boss,' the driver, Abir, said, half-turning and hastily removing his earphones. 'Thought you were asleep.'

'I was asleep. I'd still be asleep if you drove more smoothly.'

'We're on the Acle Straight, start of.'

'I can see that now.'

'Why'd you ask then?'

'Don't be so fucking cheeky.'

'We'll be in Yarmouth in ten, fifteen minutes,' Abir said.

Zach checked his phone, the time. It was approaching noon. He couldn't remember the last time he'd been to bed. 'Take me straight to the caravan park, will you?'

'Sure, boss.'

Zach hunkered down once more in the nearside rear seat. He'd grown used to travelling in the back. It was where he did most of his business nowadays as well, even if the Sport wasn't big enough. He'd put in an order for a larger vehicle, the new Autobiography, with rear executive seating, tinted windows, the lot. That's what he needed, deserved, the amount of cash he was pulling in weekly, daily, and the miles he had to cover. So, it was going to cost £100K plus. He could afford it. The local Range Rover franchise needed to hurry the fuck up. They knew who he was, his connections.

His mum, like his dead old man, got her vehicles from the Merc dealer, always on time. So he'd been branching out, at Frank's suggestion. As it was, Frank had given up on Range Rovers and defected to Lexus. Zach didn't get that at all.

Alert now, he clocked the briefcase on the seat beside him. It was black, boxy, with brass-effect combination locks. It looked absurd, but it did the job. Inside it was compartmentalised. Supposedly it was what the Masons used, when they went for their meets, to exhibit their medals, regalia and other weird shit.

He should have got Abir to put it in the boot, under the spare tyre, which was where it normally lived when they were in transit. He was just the passenger, wasn't he? They couldn't breathalyse him, swab him for residue, despite the vehicle being in his name, even though Goodwin Enterprises paid the tax and insurance, the running costs. Which he supposed could prove to be a problem.

He'd change that for his next chariot, and get Ben to help him sort out his own holding company. He needed a new structure for the caravan park anyway – his plans for it. He didn't want his greedy family crawling all over it, once they realised the cash cow he'd created. Once they finally realised that the super casino was dead in the water – the cold North Sea, anyway. He almost laughed.

The outlay for his current venture was peanuts in comparison. He looked at his phone again. They were coming to see him at two p.m. He had plenty of time to do a bit of clearing up, if he got Abir to give him a hand. The lad had enough muscle on him. One of the key reasons he was employed.

Outside, more horses appeared to be motionless in the marshy fields. Remains of ancient windmills were dotted here and there – crumbling brick bases, fragments of wooden sails. The freezing mist was hanging around spookily. Somewhere beyond the horizon to his left was the sea. He couldn't discern any twenty-first-century wind turbines, which you normally could from here, because of the mist, the sheer weight of winter. To his right would be Halvergate Marshes. That was creepy as hell.

It was like they were suddenly driving through a ghost film. He shook his head again. Too much fug, too little sleep. Where was the executive seating?

A car was just ahead. Large vehicles were coming the other way, shaking the Sport as they passed. The road was dead straight. Abir was sticking to the speed limit. The Sport needed more heft. It should have been an Autobiography.

He tapped the briefcase. Who'd be a fucking Mason? Though he supposed it might have some advantages. Presumably they all swore allegiance to their particular lodge, a loyalty oath like no other. Not able to discuss anything outside the group. A real code of silence. He should reinforce that among his crew, but real Masons wore those stupid suits, with grey pinstripe trousers – he'd seen them in London, Holborn, when he was wandering over to Covent Garden – carrying briefcases just like his.

Except his was full of proper merchandise, worth a small fortune. And it should have been in the boot, under the spare tyre. But that space was stuffed to the brim with new supplies, he seemed to remember. This was why they were driving along the Acle Straight in the middle of the day – if you could call what was going on outside day. You didn't carry this gear around in the dead of night. In plain sight was the way to do it. Fresh supplies. Would last them no more than a week or two, the way business was picking up.

Who didn't need a lift, a bump, bumpety bump, this time of the year?

'Abir, you feeling fit?' Zach huffed.

'Yes, boss.'

'Can you lend me a hand when we get to the park?'

'Sure, boss.'

The man was a machine, kept going for days on end without stimulants. He was also well tapped in, knew geezers the length and breadth of the British Isles. Zach had been lucky to lure him to the dizzy heights of Yarmouth. Couldn't believe how cheap he was.

His phone pinged, taking him out of his reverie. A WhatsApp message. It was an order, from a punter he hadn't heard of before. Not a bad-sized order it had to be said – five Gs, of 92 per cent purity. At least that's what he was marketing it as.

However, everyone knew his operating hours. Who'd passed his details on, missing out that vital piece of information? Or was someone trying to take advantage? Take the piss, more like. Besides, the delivery location was in Lowestoft. He was not in the mood to drive to Lowestoft anytime soon. He didn't reply, despite knowing that one missed piece of business could mean ten. That was how it could escalate. So what the fuck?

'Activity ahead,' Abir said sharply, nervously.

'You what?' They were by the Vauxhall Holiday Park already, closing in on the New Road roundabout. Didn't seem to be too much traffic.

'Cop cars,' Abir whispered loudly. 'Looks like they're doing spot checks.'

'No way.' Zach tried to sink further into the rear seat. 'Who are the dorks? Recognise them?'

'They all look the same to me,' said Abir. 'White fuckers in uniform.'

'Cut the racism,' Zach said.

'ANPR checks, maybe,' Abir said. 'This thing all legal?'

'Don't go there,' said Zach.

'They could be doing checks for tax, or insurance. Can't see what else. It's not an obvious speeding zone.'

They were edging closer to the roundabout by the millisecond. Just when you wanted a jam there wasn't one.

'We've nothing to worry about, then,' Zach said. 'My paperwork's squeaky clean, unlike thousands of other fuckers around here.' He tried to laugh, though it came out as more of a spluttering snort. His nose was bunged. Yeah, he knew better than to mix business with pleasure. What Frank banged on about, relentlessly. But you take delivery of a new shipment – you have to check out the goods. Quality control. He had a reputation to maintain. Ninety two per cent etcetera, etcetera. Lies, damned lies – it was how business worked.

He also had pain, man, deep inside him. That needed controlling. See, he could admit it to himself, when he was feeling lonely, trapped, exposed. Life could be one mean motherfucker – there, he'd said it to himself. You only got one chance, and for some that didn't last long.

'Zach, they're pulling us over.'

'Why the fuck . . . ?' Zach sat up. Caught the cop cars, some cones, the white fuckers in uniform, through watery eyes. One of the dorks looked like he had a clipboard. No other cars appeared to have been pulled over at that moment. He ran his sleeve across his eyes. Fuck's sake, he was tougher than this. 'Did you notice a van back there?' he said. 'With a blacked-out window hiding one of those cameras? The ANPRs?' Frank was obsessed with them. 'Did you, Abir?'

'No, boss. What do you want me to do? Run it?'

'And keep going, for ever?' For a split second Zach thought that that would be a fucking good idea. He wanted them to head for somewhere warm and sunny. He should never have come back from Ibiza with fancy new ideas of how to get the place rocking. It was frozen solid here, the year round.

They knew how to distribute on the island, all right – from the back seat of a spanking-new Range Rover. There were fleets of them. Guys as cool as cucumbers dolling out the goodies from the rear executive seats, while the muscle sat behind the wheel, shooters in the glove compartments. They all had false plates, false documentation. Ghosts in ghost ships.

Perhaps that was Zach's problem right now. He'd played it too straight, with everything out in the open, in broad, frosty daylight. The briefcase was staring at him. He'd like to open the window, fling it into a dyke. No, better, Breydon Water. That was just over to their right. Let the tide take it out to sea, or the mud swallow it up for ever.

But there was still the gear in the boot – a big fucking mound of it. Thirty K's worth, wholesale, treble on the pavement. What were they meant to do about that? Drive the Sport off the bridge into the drink? That was how his dad had met his maker. There was too much water around here, too much mud. Even when you wanted it.

Abir had pulled the vehicle into the cops' clutches. Zach didn't remember saying he could do so. He was now opening the driver's window, under more orders, though not from his boss. Loyalty for you. Some oath. Freezing air spurted inside, slapped Zach on the cheeks.

'Afternoon, sir.' The cop addressed Abir.

Afternoon started early in Yarmouth. Crackers, smackers. Zach was shitting himself.

'What's the problem?' Abir said, though not rudely.

'Is this your vehicle?' the cop asked.

Zach didn't recognise him, though he wasn't looking too hard. He was trying to remain invisible in the back. The briefcase beside him was beginning to glow with a nuclear intensity.

'No,' Abir said. 'I'm just driving it.'

'Do you have your licence with you?'

'Sure. You want a look-see?'

'That is what I'm asking, sir.'

Abir undid his seatbelt, retrieved his wallet from the back pocket of his jeans. Handed over his licence.

'What are you doing in this neck of the woods?' the cop said. He was now staring past Abir, into the back of the car. Zach tried not to look his away.

'I live here.'

'Not what it says on your licence.'

'I'm living here temporarily. I've got a new job.'

'Yeah, what's that doing?' Before Abir had time to reply the cop had stuck his head further into the car, sniffed a couple of times, loudly, obviously. 'Hello,' he said, looking Zach straight in the eye, 'who are you?'

'I'm the passenger,' Zach said.

'You like it in the back, do you?'

'I've been getting some kip.'

'Officer,' Abir said, 'can you tell me why you've pulled us over?'

'What was it you said you do?' the cop said. 'Your new job?'

Zach was vaguely aware of traffic merrily going around the roundabout. But of no other vehicles being pulled over.

He wasn't sure where the second cop was now, though two rigs were still there, out in the shit for weather. He leaned forward. 'He works for me.'

'Yeah?' the cop said. 'And what do you do, young man?'

Zach didn't recognise him, which was troubling. 'Goodwin Enterprises,' Zach said, sitting back. 'I'm a director.' It wasn't strictly true at that moment in time, but he felt the weight of the family name might provide some protection, some leeway, anyway.

'Put your hazards on, will you?' the cop quickly said, looking away from Zach and addressing Abir, stern and officious as anything. 'I'm going to run some checks. Shouldn't be long.' He turned and walked away, with Abir's licence.

'Wanker,' said Zach. 'Fuck did he want?'

'He didn't say, did he?' Abir said, angry. 'Are we going to sit here and obey him?'

'You pulled over.'

'I asked you whether you wanted me to run it.'

'Did I say no?'

'You didn't say yes. We can make a dash now, ditch the gear. The vehicle. They can't tie us to anything.'

'No? How's your advanced driving skills?' Zach asked.

'I've been driving since I was twelve,' Abir said. 'No one can fucking catch me if I put my mind to it.'

Zach wasn't so sure. Besides, the Sport wasn't the throatiest beast on the block. It was a dead fucking weight with shit rear seats. Who'd he been pretending he was, commanding the perch? Well he knew, didn't he, but he was in the wrong vehicle, the wrong country, with the wrong gear. The choice those fleets carried out in Ibiza was staggering. There was call for it there, such variety – from a far richer, more sophisticated crowd.

'Too late,' Abir suddenly said.

'What?'

The cop was back already, his pale chops leering into the driver's window, the peak of his cap nudging the door-frame, Arctic air curling round him. 'Get your licence updated, with your correct address. I could haul you in for that. But I'm feeling generous today. The vehicle checks out. Goodwin Enterprises? Could have guessed. You're free to go – for now.'

He glanced at Zach in the back. Zach smiled.

'What did you pull me over for?' Abir said.

'Driving too close to the vehicle in front.'

'I was approaching a roundabout,' he said.

'Exactly,' said the cop, straightening. He then leaned back, stooping and catching Zach's eyes. 'We'll be watching you. Get used to it.'

With that he walked off, all high-vis jacket and low-rent provincial attitude. But with some knowledge, some agenda, Zach thought. 'Who the fuck was he?' he said, trying not to shake.

'Someone who ain't so keen on your family name, I'd guess,' said Abir.

'Fuck him, fuck them.' In Ibiza, Zach was thinking, cops appeared to be so indifferent to the drug trade, they simply weren't around, patrolling, trying to sniff people out. Though some had to be getting backhanders. He needed to up his contacts in this frigid white world. Frank had

19

contacts with the top brass. However, Frank wasn't so keen on his new venture, the way he was branching out. He didn't think he could exactly ask him for help, even if it was the twenty-first fucking century.

Abir had closed the window, cut the hazards and put the indicator on. He pulled slowly out.

'Don't get too close to the car ahead,' Zach smirked, catching the cop, standing by his rig, staring straight back at him.

'If you ask me they pulled me over because of the colour of my skin,' Abir said. 'Fucking racists. Told you.'

'If only,' Zach said. 'Either way, we'll get our own back, mate, I promise you.'

Abir took the New Road into town, the small stretch of dual carriageway before the next roundabout.

'Those guys weren't local,' Zach said. He couldn't let it go. 'They don't know who they're dealing with. How dare they fucking pull us over? Because you're brown? Boy, do I wish I had some colour. Wasn't part of my fucking family.'

'No you don't. Not in this country.'

'It's dismal this time of year, I'll give you that.' They were at the next roundabout already. Zach tried to concentrate on the caravan park, thinking about how to make the office look presentable. Perhaps he'd have a crafty toot to aid his handiwork. His muscles weren't what they used to be. He should go back to the gym, get toned up before the summer.

Frank stared at his mobile. It was the only device on his desk, sitting stupidly in the middle of all the gleaming space. There was no PC, no in-tray, no folders, no pens, no ornaments or fancily framed photographs. Nothing that could specifically tie him to the office, or incriminate him, so he believed. He led by example. There was a landline, however – a solid chunk of Bang & Olufsen. The designer's idea. Except this, like the mobile, was refusing to ring.

Celine, his and Tatty's joint PA, receptionist, dogsbody, whatever, was two floors below, doing he had no idea what. Tatty was meeting Nathan Taylor at the Refuge to discuss another renovation – and have a shag as well, probably. Ben was heading for his meeting at the council.

Yet despite the lack of clutter, Frank felt hemmed in. The office was too hot, even for its vast size.

The room was almost a mirror of Tatty's, which was at the other end of the building. As much as Frank enjoyed his elevated position in the organisation, or thought he did, he was not good at sitting still. Not today, anyway. Waiting was not how it worked. Wasn't it how you handled a crisis that showed your real mettle? Leadership through adversity and all that bollocks? Not sitting around waiting for the phone to ring.

It wasn't a crisis quite yet, however, and maybe it wouldn't become one, but the silence was killing him.

He picked up his phone, rang the number again. Got straight through to an anonymous voicemail message. He ended the call before it was time for him to speak. He pushed his chair back, stood, walked over to the nearest window. The cloud had thickened, and darkened. The days were meant to be getting longer already, though it didn't feel like it. The near rooftops were dotted with gulls. There were few crumbs for them.

It was even warmer by the window. A discreet radiator directly below was pumping out hot air like there was no tomorrow. Something of a chill then swept around him – a draft like a ghostly blanket.

'Frank?' came an all-too-familiar voice.

He turned. 'Oh, it's you.'

'Sorry, should have knocked. Your door was ajar.' Tatty had stepped into his office, continued towards him.

He remained by the window. 'I thought you were meeting Nathan Taylor at the Refuge.'

'I postponed it. Head's not in the right place.'

'That makes the two of us, then.'

'Do you want to sit down?' It still felt odd having the boss walk into his grand office, offering her a seat. She looked the part, as always – suede suited her. But she wasn't his boss any more, was she? Not that she'd been his boss for very long anyway. They were partners – for the time being. Maybe he'd start wearing suits. Ben wore suits. He still hadn't got used to having Tatty's eldest around, but then it had only been a few days.

'What have you heard?' she said, hovering.

Frank glanced at his desk, the swanky B&O landline. Not that he'd used that to call the assistant chief constable, on her burner and then her official number – nothing so traceable. He looked back at Tatty, who was frowning. How old was she, really? 'Nothing,' he said, 'from the person who might be able to tell me something. The police are everywhere, though. Cops I haven't seen before. It's like there's a new line of command, or something.'

'Is that surprising? Do you reckon they've found more than one body?'

'Who knows?'

'What were you thinking?' Her tone had changed.

'They can't tie any of this to me, us.'

'So you say.' Tatty swerved round Frank, headed to another window.

His office had a huge stretch of glass, reinforced by steel. Industrial chic, was the phrase he'd heard – far too often. Seemed an odd concept. Mixing things that should never be mixed.

'You've got a better view than me,' she said.

'Yeah? Of what?'

'Possibility. Look at all those buildings. Most of them are redundant. There's meant to be a chronic housing shortage in this country. Why can't they convert these brownfield sites into residential blocks? Live work spaces for SMEs, start-ups, at the very least.'

'Because who'd want to come and live here? There're no jobs, no opportunities. It's a hole, a dead end. That's why we love it, isn't it?'

'People have to show some initiative, don't they?'

He was still to be convinced by the new Goodwin Enterprises HQ, all Tatty's window dressing. Rich would be turning in his grave.

'Put the effort in, some seed money, make things work for themselves,' Tatty continued. 'Besides, that's where we come in, isn't it? The knock-on from the super casino. Think of the jobs, and not just in construction.'

'Look how long it's taking already,' said Frank. 'There're no quick solutions round here, whether you do it above or below board. The infrastructure's shit, besides.'

'The new bridge,' she said, 'that'll help, won't it?'

He exhaled, long and hard. He hadn't been thinking about that. He supposed he'd had in mind all the other services, and amenities – like roads that weren't potholed, shops that sold goods that weren't second-hand, streets that were lit at night. 'That bridge's going to help us a right fucking treat.' He looked away from Tatty, out of the window.

The view from this part of town had been much the same for years, decades. Nothing was going to change anytime soon. He doubted the super casino would ever be built. There'd never be a glass ballroom, for the slots, suspended between two piers. At best, they'd be able to look after someone else's cash for a while, maybe pump some of it into the renovation of the old casino, the caravan park, the boatyard. Do something with the racecourse.

Skim bits here and there. There were always limits. 'There's so much other shit they need to get in place before they build that bridge.'

Whoever went to a casino nowadays, anyway? He was depressed, he realised. No, daunted. No, scared.

'You're just down on it because it's unearthed a problem,' Tatty laughed. 'Come on, Frank, where's your sense of humour?'

'Do you know how many bodies are buried there?' he whispered. He was not proud. Or maybe he was. Did she have no idea how easily her late husband had made enemies? He'd made a few himself, as well. The cleaning up he'd had to do.

'I don't want to know, Frank. The past is the past.'

'Until it rears its head again. There's no escaping it, you know that. Where's Simon, do you think?' Tatty's brother-in-law, and the murderer of one of those bodies buried in Breydon Water, had kept complete silence since last June, following his aborted attempt to screw them and the then head of the Regeneration Committee, Graham Sands. It was an audacious plot, though Frank and Tatty weren't fooled for long. Long enough, nevertheless, for Simon to scarper once more.

'Dead?' said Tatty, after giving it ten seconds' thought.

'Doubt it somehow,' Frank said. He'd failed to put a bullet in Simon's head back then, letting Tatty and the business down. She'd still made him partner, but he didn't sleep too well on it, not believing he really deserved this big office, the Lexus. Good things didn't come to him easily – or ever. 'People like Simon are born survivors, not that he'd ever be so stupid as to show his head around here again. But if he dares, no second chances.' Frank made his right hand into the shape of a gun, pointed it at Tatty. 'Bang.'

'Third chance, isn't it?' she said. 'Don't point that thing at me.'

'You know what I mean.' He dropped his hand, feeling foolish.

Tatty was looking out of the window again. 'I'm getting impatient.'

'Nothing new there, then,' Frank muttered. Would she ever relax?

'I'm sick of this weather as well.'

'It's not raining. Wish it was.' He was thinking of Breydon Water, the excavations, the properties of mud, clayey mud that stuck to you like shit. Wondered how it might dissolve evidence, DNA. He had an idea that salt water had an effect. Though this water was brackish, maybe not quite enough salt. But he was no scientist. He had no qualifications whatsoever.

'I've decided I want to buy the Pier View Hotel,' Tatty said. 'As well as Gorleston Pavilion and the Ocean Rooms. Smarten that corner up. I do live in Gorleston. Why can't I walk down there on a summer's evening? Enjoy a glass of Sauvignon on a terrace.'

'Global warming's got a way to go.' He was also looking out of the window now. It was hard not to in this office. 'I thought it'd already been smartened up.'

'You call that smartening up? Not by us, in any case. We don't benefit one iota. We need to control that corner. The street deals that we know go on. It's outrageous. In my backyard.'

'We did a deal,' Frank said, 'unless you have forgotten.' He paused. 'You sure you don't want to sit down?'

'With those wankers? You call that a deal? No, I don't want to sit down.'

This was so like Rich, Frank couldn't help thinking. He'd do a deal, or rather make Frank sort out an arrangement, and then a couple of months later he'd change his mind. Get Frank to renegotiate. It was true, the Hummer gang had proved to be a walkover. They weren't Albanians, Eastern Europeans – well, one was Latvian. They were mostly old lags from Essex, a big geezer called Gary Winslow in charge. Except they'd saved Zach that time, and all they wanted, so they said, was a patch to sell their gear and women, claim protection dues, for which they'd leave Yarmouth alone.

Frank and Tatty let them have Gorleston basin readily enough a year or so ago. In fact it was under a year ago. He didn't care how obvious they'd be down there. It wasn't Goodwin Enterprises' lookout. Presumed they'd be closed down by the real authorities sooner rather than later. Openly enforcing from a shiny white Hummer – honestly.

'Do we have the assets, the manpower?' Frank said, distracted.

'People power, Frank,' Tatty said, cross. 'Sure we do. As for the cash, the first tranche from the Netherlands is in the bag, and the Americans are due to deliver by the end of this month, remember? We're going to be swimming in it.'

'You want to divert that from the super casino, getting proper foundations in place?'

'Why not? We could get Sam to help us with the legals,' Tatty continued, 'if she's feeling up to it.'

'Otherwise, what? We'll have to stick with that Norwich shower Rich was so keen on?'

'We'll find a way,' Tatty said.

Frank nodded. 'Nevertheless, our backers expect certain results. There are conditions.' He was already sick of trying to keep the balance between the legal and illegal operations, he realised. It was fine when he was on the street – where everything was wrong. But occupying an office, putting on that sort of a front, was seriously doing his head in.

'They want returns. You think they care where they come from? Ben's got some ideas as well.'

'They understand gambling, casinos.'

'Plus the rest of it,' said Tatty. 'It's in their blood. Same the world over.'

'They still see a market for physical gambling,' he said. 'The laundering possibilities that will always come with cash. That's what they want us to provide.'

'We'll be able to clean their money just as well with an interim development or two,' Tatty said. 'Be silly not to use something we've already got our hands on.'

'Limited possibilities,' Frank said. 'They're not going to be happy.'

'I want the Pier View,' she said, 'and then I want my guests to be able to look out onto something that's attractive, that works. No one's ever made enough of the Pavilion

– it's a beautiful building, historic. Or the Ocean Rooms, for that matter.'

'Rich always made sure to keep his business on the other side of the Yare, well away from home.'

'The family's grown up now,' Tatty said. 'Time to spread our wings.'

'Hardly,' said Frank. 'Plus the basin's right on your doorstep. Couldn't be closer.' Tatty seemed unable to stand still, and was clicking the fingers of her right hand. 'Ben's got you fired up, hasn't he?' Frank continued.

'His scheme sounds ambitious enough. He's told you? Deposits flying from one umbrella to another, with the portfolio growing on a premise – or is that a promise? If I've understood him half correctly.'

'Not sure you're meant to understand it all.'

'I still like to see some of what I'm getting for my money. Buildings and the like,' Tatty said. 'Call me old-fashioned.'

'Well I did think you were more modern than that,' Frank said. 'It's a virtual world now, however you look at it, isn't it?'

'I'm trying to keep up.' She smiled.

'You should take Ben's advice, then.'

'About what?'

'The Regeneration Committee. You'd be just the person to shake up those old farts – give them something to think about at night.'

'Cheers.'

'I'll also give you some of my own advice, if you like – business advice.'

'Yeah, from you? Business advice?'

'From me,' Frank said.

'I'm all ears.'

'You'd be surprised what you can get around here without paying.' It was his turn to laugh now. 'Don't be too liberal with our cash reserves. Plus, to get Gorleston, we'd have to move on a nasty bunch of thugs. They're not going to like it. From what I hear they're already advancing in the wrong direction.'

'All the more reason. We should never have let them take the patch.'

'It wasn't our patch, was it? Besides, they did us a favour.' Frank was thinking of Zach again. How the Hummer gang had played Zach – and his young associates, Liam and Sian, and a stupid MDMA business – to a T. Zach was lucky to survive, and even more lucky not to have been fingered in the forensic aftermath. They had Britt Hayes to thank for some of that. And now he was having to call on the assistant chief constable once more.

'The tide moves fast around here,' Tatty said.

'Meaning?'

'It's a metaphor, Frank.'

'Don't get fancy with me.'

'Your phone's ringing, by the way. Are you not going to answer it?' She was looking behind him, to his desk.

She was right. His phone – his mobile – was ringing. Maybe he was going deaf in his old age. He stepped over, aware of his bulk, his sweaty armpits and back, in the ludicrously smart space. Too much luxury was not a good thing, even if you were trying to make a statement, he reckoned. You were either born with class or you weren't. He hadn't been, even if Tatty had. Rich certainly hadn't. There were moments when Frank missed him crushingly, he realised, grabbing the device, glancing at the screen. *No Caller ID* – what he was expecting, finally.

'I need to take this,' he said to Tatty, showing her the door with his left hand.

'New lover?' she said, looking quizzical and not hurrying out of the room.

He rolled his eyes, tilted his head back. 'Yeah,' he said, 'and he's hot as hell.' Then, watching Tatty's back take an age to disappear, Frank said, 'Hello,' into his phone.

'You're in trouble, Frank,' came the assistant chief constable's not-so-calm voice.

'Tell me something I don't know, Britt,' Frank said. First-name terms today.

'They've found three bodies so far. The public only know of one, but I'm not sure how long we can keep this development out of the news. How many more are buried there?'

'Not you as well,' he muttered, looking up at the door Tatty had slowly departed through, not shutting it after her, either. Bloody born in a barn. The draft was back, trickling in from the vast interior of the Smokehouse. There was only so much modernising a building like this could take. He dreaded to think what its carbon footprint would be.

Or his. He needed to go back on a diet. It was so much harder in winter. You needed that layer of fat to keep warm, when you were out in the garden. Or trudging through Breydon Water mud.

'How many, Frank?'

'Why are you asking me?'

Britt Hayes sighed long and hard on the other end of cyberspace. 'I also have a job to do. I don't like surprises.'

'Neither do I.'

'The more I know, the better I can direct this investigation, and direct it away from you and that bloody family you love so much.'

'Are you sure you are directing this investigation?'

'What's that supposed to mean?'

'I don't know – seems to be odd cop activity. Something doesn't smell right. I've got a nose for such trouble.'

'This is a big deal, Frank – what do you expect? We don't find bodies every day. Why don't you help me identify who we've dug up? The more I know, the more I can direct operations elsewhere.'

'Yeah?'

'Frank, you're lucky this has come straight to my desk.'

'Sounds like it.'

'We need to meet.'

'I'm not liking your tone, either.'

'Don't turn your back on me now.'

Frank ended the call, confused. Britt was panicking. This was definitely not normal. He narrowly avoided flinging his phone across the room. Norfolk Constabulary, and their mates in the NCA – Britt's mates? – certainly needed to be diverted from an utterly pointless investigation. This was public money going to waste, yet more of it. It made his blood boil.

Though he wasn't sure giving Britt Hayes any more information would help him, or Goodwin Enterprises

– which was effectively the same thing. She obviously knew less than he feared she might, plus he couldn't see how she could help him this time anyway. He felt a little bit of himself fall away, leaving him unbalanced, on shaky ground. He shouldn't have rung her. That association had gone on for way too long. The balance of power had always been wrong.

Tatty, however, might just have provided him with a neat idea.

## 4

'Lovely job, Abir. Cheers. Beats sitting behind a wheel, doesn't it, mate?' Zach looked around the reception area. In the time it'd taken him to pop to the bog – never a good idea to use in front of your staff – all the rubbish had been cleared away. Even the floor had been swept.

'You've got to be joking,' Abir said, wiping his brow. 'This was some shithole.'

'I think I might take that map down.' Zach was looking at a large map of the local area on a wall behind the old counter. The sea had faded to the palest of blues, while the land had only the slightest hint of green. No, it was more a puke yellow. The town, Yarmouth, was a smudge of grey. The piers were represented by the faintest of dark lines.

He supposed they'd be better off taking the whole lodge down – getting a steamroller to flatten it. He could almost hear the crackle and crunch. Then he'd get the steamroller to trundle around the park, squashing the statics as it went. He looked out of the smeary windows, across a curve of drive, towards the first row of caravans. They were all empty – officially, anyway. The park had closed for good last autumn, a couple of months after the owner, Rolly Andrews, died in suspicious circumstances. There was the small matter of an on-site fire as well, a caravan torched. Nothing so unusual about that, except this one contained two bodies.

Zach shook his buzzing head. Ninety-two per cent pure? Yeah, it had to be something like that. Some batch.

It was only logical that he, Goodwin Enterprises, took control of the park. However, his plans didn't yet extend to flattening it and starting again. He was sticking, for now, with what was there, and going kitsch. He'd seen this place in Ibiza, in the north-east of the island, where someone had turned an old crazy golf course into an upmarket B & B. You could sleep in a gypsy caravan, a miniature castle, a bus. At night stars played the decks in the giant plastic hamburger. It was so cool. The North Denes Caravan Park was not cool – yet. It was only a matter of a paint job, and playing up the tack, surely.

Golf carts. Genius! That's what was needed – a fleet of golf carts for everyone to shift around in. He could just see them taking the drive out front at speed. Almost by magic, as he was watching, imagining, a vehicle did appear at speed. Not a golf cart but a big black thing, which came to a halt inches from the reception window.

He couldn't believe what he was seeing – a brand new Range Rover Autobiography, long wheelbase too. The plates weren't personalised. No self-respecting crook would drive around with personalised plates, advertising your wares like a cock in a hen house. But this dude was not a crook, as far as Zach knew. He was a DJ, a DJ entrepreneur – from Peckham, originally, Norwich more recently. And he had an Autobiography. Zach was mad with envy.

'They're here,' he shouted, knowing he needed to calm down. He looked behind him. 'Abir? Where the fuck are you?' His driver was nowhere to be seen, just when he needed a show of strength and diversity. Abir wore his rags well.

Paul Zee and his little brother Pete, Zach presumed, were out of their chariot, marching up to the front entrance of the lodge. They were in matching black hooded puffas, tight trackie bottoms, shin-short, and trainers like ocean liners in the night. Zach waved through the glass of the main door, then realised it was bolted and locked. He didn't have a key to this door. He'd only ever used the side entrance. He waved again, with his left hand, indicating that they needed to go round the side of the building. He felt his face reddening. These were important people. They didn't seem to be getting the gist of his directions.

He ran through to the back room and out the side entrance and round to the front, as if he were a bolting donkey. He didn't know why he thought of himself as a donkey. Because he wasn't being cool. How could he be? His chest was bursting. His blood felt like lava, his skin crawling. Still no Abir. The guy had vanished into thin air. He hadn't driven off, at least, as Zach's rig was outside, looking a lot less impressive than the Zee brothers' vehicle. What a monster that was.

Weirdly, and despite the puffas, Paul and Pete were short and slight. A couple of titches. Zach had met Paul once before, briefly – hadn't clocked quite how diminutive he was. 'Yo,' he said, squaring up to them in front of the building. 'Good of you to come to the throbbing heart of the east coast. Dig the sea air.'

'Zach Goodwin,' said Paul, 'you're not much of a stand-up, are you? Can't see a damn thing either. It's like the cloud's stuck to the ground. Freezing fog – whatever you call it. Is it always like this?'

'You've been to these parts before?' said Zach, aware that he was skipping on the spot, the imaginary rope being twirled faster and faster. He was looking at Pete, wondering whether it really was Pete, Paul's legendary brother, or just a guy who looked a lot like his boss. That's what happened in this runaround. Your crew start to dress like you, walk down the street like you. Cough the same words of wisdom, until they are a mirror image. Not that Abir seemed to be aping his master. Abir was too damn cool – too damn cool to show his bloody face.

'You what?' Zach said. Paul had muttered something, Zach realised, but he had no idea what. 'Didn't catch your drift,' he added. He needed Paul, and Pete, if it was Pete. No one introduced anyone to anyone, he'd been realising for a while. You needed to know who was who without asking. He felt the cloud weighing on the caravan park, the freezing fog, like a glacier, full of rocks and stuff – terminal moraine. That was it, a flash from school, a lesson he'd actually attended. This deal had to work.

'Never been to these parts in winter,' Paul said.

'Yeah, well the plan is to open in May,' said Zach. 'The first of, thereabouts. That bank holiday weekend.' He couldn't remember what the exact dates were. He was struggling to remember anything right now. 'You want to come inside?' Zach looked behind him, down the dim, dank side passageway, covered by a shitty lean-to. Despite the door being wide open, it didn't look so inviting.

'What'll this building be?' Paul said, indicating the reception lodge.

'Meet and greet,' Zach said. Paul looked bemused. 'You know, reception, I guess.'

'What about security?' Paul was rubbing his hands. Pete remained silent.

'Let's discuss that inside, shall we?' Zach took another step towards the side entrance. 'Take shelter.'

'What happens when there's a storm?' Pete said. He was also now rubbing his hands.

So he did have a voice, Zach thought. He sounded just like his brother. 'Pete, yeah?' Zach said.

The guy nodded. 'It'd be washed away, wouldn't it?'

'No,' said Zach. 'Not even a surge would do that. I mean storm surges happen – but like the flooding comes up by the river, the docks. Round the back. Not this way.' He pointed casually in the direction of the sea. 'The sea would never get all the way over the dunes.'

'Obviously,' Paul said, 'we don't want to pump a load of cash and expertise into a project that's in danger of being swept away.'

'It's not, believe me. We haven't talked cash yet, either,' Zach said quickly. Having been boiling, he was now freezing, as if his blood had stopped circulating and was forming ice crystals. He needed another hit. He was prepared to break out a little powder, for his guests. They'd be impressed with the quality, the zing, anyone would be.

But he had a suspicion that these dudes stayed clean. So many of the DJs, the promoters, the entrepreneurs did nowadays. It was how they kept their edge. But boring as hell, man.

Zach struggled to remember where he was in the conversation. 'It's your expertise, your name we want to bring to the project,' he said. 'We can talk money, upfront development costs if you want. Though we'd probably need my accountant and legal team to do that.' He was thinking of Ben and Sam. 'I'm just the blue-sky thinking. It's all up here.' He tapped his nut. 'Plus, I'm the dude on the ground – with the assets,' he added. 'Come on guys, let's huddle, in the bubble.' What the fuck was he talking about?

He headed the rest of the way towards the side entrance, not looking back. 'What are you doing lurking inside?' There was Abir suddenly, finally, by the doorway.

'It's cold out,' Abir said. 'Are they coming in?'

'That's how it generally works,' Zach whispered furiously. 'You ask a couple of geezers to a meeting. Seems only polite to ask them in.'

'Didn't realise it was them,' Abir said, peering round Zach's shoulder. 'You could have told me.'

'I did, didn't I?'

Abir shook his head, stepped aside. Paul and Pete then followed Zach into the hastily tidied lodge. Zach watched Abir make for the furthest, darkest corner, and realised, as if he hadn't always known, that this was not a place for a meeting. There was no table worth the name. No proper chairs. What there was an old single bed shoved against a far corner, where Abir was now lurking. A rug had been thrown over it, but there was no mistaking the shape.

What had he been thinking? But he'd needed to show the guys the assets – such as they were. 'We can put the security in here, sure,' he said, brightly. The place stank of damp, a truly dismal past.

'This is some dump,' Paul said. 'How long have you owned this park?'

'I only recently got the keys. Just beginning to spruce it up.'

'This place needs keys? What's he do?' Paul said, looking at Abir.

'He's my driver.'

'Yeah? He looks familiar.' Paul then returned his condescending gaze towards Zach. Sighed. 'This is not what I had in mind.'

'Let me show you around. It's a large site,' Zach said. 'Lots of scope. We can put up temporary structures, a big top. Fairground stuff. Get rid of some of the older caravans. Paint others. Bring in some colour. Cosmetic stuff, really. Cheap as chips.' He glanced over at Abir. Or where Abir had been. His driver had disappeared again. 'Play up the kitsch.' That was his best line.

'You think you can attract, what, a thousand kids a time?' Paul said.

'Minimum,' Zach said. 'Two, two and half, would be my target. Friday and Saturday, all-nighters both. We'd get going at like six p.m. Friday night, push through to six p.m. Sunday.'

'What about the bars, catering?'

'Food wouldn't be top of my list. However, we'd be able to call in some pop-ups. Same with the bars. Lot of SMEs round here looking for this sort of opportunity.'

'Yeah?' scoffed Pete.

'DJs? How many are you thinking?' said Paul.

'A dozen a weekend, I reckon. Something like that. That's where you come in, with your contacts. I know some guys, here and on the island. But there's always room for more. The up-and-coming dudes. Names of the future. I'd like you to shape it, Paul Zee. Be the musical director.'

Paul looked at Pete. Shook his head. Exhaled. 'What about licences, the authorities? This would attract some attention.'

'That's the idea,' said Zach, feeling himself smiling like a dork. 'I want this to be international – big as it gets. Holland's just across the way. Belgium, Germany, Denmark are close, man. I want our European friends and partners to enjoy the fun.'

'No one else does around here, I bet,' Paul said, sniffing. 'Security, protection, what are your plans? How are you going to keep the riff-raff out?'

'A partner in my family's firm – he'll be able to take care of all that. No need to worry there. He's a monster of a man.'

Paul was still shaking his head. 'The licences, the author-ities?'

'Yeah – all covered. My family's well connected. No one touches us around here.'

'Daddy's boy, are you?'

'No, he's dead.'

'Mummy's boy?' Pete said, smirking.

'You don't want to get on the wrong side of her, believe me. Do you want me to show you around the park?' Zach said.

'Step out into that shit they call weather?' Paul said.

'To save us any more time and effort,' Paul said, 'I'm not interested.' He shook his head. 'Coming here, on day like this – it's been a mistake. This is like the end of the fucking world. Besides, there're cop cars all over the shop. Bet you can't move without them breathing down your neck. There're no licences, are there? You're going to need more than good connections. Nothing's in place except a few shitty caravans, and your driver who owes me ten grand. Where's he hiding now? I want a word with him.'

'We can sort this out, Paul,' Zach said, pleading. 'Some misunderstanding, I'm sure.' What the fuck had Abir got himself into? Paul and Pete were both now shaking their heads, backing away towards the door. 'You want a toot? Either of you? I've got some great gear, just in.'

'Call yourself an operator? An entrepreneur?' Paul said, looking at Zach as if he were a smear of dog shit.

'Sure,' said Pete, suddenly animated. 'Anything to perk this day up.'

'Come rain or shine – coming right up,' Zach said, heading for the bathroom, at the back, pleased that Pete at least appreciated the finer things in life. Fucking Abir, though. 'I've got some ninety-two per cent pure,' he shouted over his shoulder. He wondered whether it was more like ninety fucking nine. Hey, that's what he'd market this batch as. He could add a flake of crack for free.

He removed the panel on the side of the filthy bath with a simple toe punt. Crouched down, reached under the stinky tub, got hold of the case, mindful not to dislodge the other packets. Not the most secure or secretive of hiding places, he knew. However, following last summer's fire, and the hefty police investigation, this place had sunk back into obscurity – for the time being.

Not bothering to replace the panel, Zach stood, cradling his black, faux leather-clad case, hard as nuts. The brass combination locks, glinting under the old neon tube, were the killer. When he sprung them, flipped the lid, to reveal the twenty compartments of pre-packaged goodies, the Zees would change their minds about the park, and his genius plans for a summer of love meets saucy British seaside fun and games. Bingo, he was going to call it. Plain and simple. If the titches agreed. They would – oh, they fucking would, following a couple of ninety-nines.

He stepped back into the main room, holding the briefcase in both arms, like he was presenting it to them. 'OK, guys, if you'd like to take a pew, I'll show you my wares. There's plenty of choice, but if I could be so bold, I'd recommend a ninety-nine. New in town, as of a couple of hours ago.' While he'd been talking part of his mind was taking in the somewhat changed positions and postures of his guests.

His mouth dried up as he quickly glanced over his shoulder, urging Abir to come barging into the room, fully loaded. He didn't. Zach returned his attention to the Zee brothers. It was little Pete who had the shooter, and the biggest smirk on his face.

'Open the case for me, will you?' Paul said. 'Let's see whether this'll cover your debts.'

'Hey,' said Zach, 'my debts?'

'The ten K,' Paul said.

'They're not my debts.' Zach felt like bursting into tears. 'You think I'd have asked you here if I had any idea that this was in the air? I can smooth it over. A simple misunderstanding, I'm sure. We can still be partners. Don't dismiss the opportunity. This is a gold mine in the waiting. Bingo all the way.'

'Open the case,' said Pete, waving the pistol in the direction of Zach's head.

'OK, OK.' He thought Paul Zee was a DJ, a DJ entrepreneur, not a fucking C-list crook, shadowed by a juvenile with anger-management issues. He'd also thought that Abir was a driver with long experience for a man of such a young age, and impeccable skills. Zach's intel was coming up very short.

'Hurry up, twat,' Pete said, all mouth now.

With some difficulty, because he was standing, and his hands were beginning to shake – and he was desperately trying to hide the fact – Zach did eventually get the case open. The sight sort of took his breath away. What an achievement. Yeah, he was proud. The gear was so neatly laid out. What else was he meant to have done on the long drive back to base, except rearrange the packets? This was Ibiza cool. 'My box of magic tricks,' he said. 'We could have any number of these going round the park. Door-to-static-door. A heap of backup supplies on site.'

Paul was taking a close interest now, as was Pete. 'What do you reckon?' Paul said.

'This lot? Skimpy,' said Pete. 'Three Ks worth, tops.'

'Where's the rest?' Paul said. 'Your current heap?' He was smiling, a smile that used to adorn websites and posters, proclaiming impeccable Euro House credentials.

'Come on, guys,' said Zach, 'we can work this out.'

'Yes, we can,' said Paul, his benign expression unchanged.

## 5

Tatty was in her usual corner seat in the bar, looking out at the night that had just rolled in from the east like a marauding army. Blinds, curtains, would be a good idea, she thought. At this time of the year, anyway. Or maybe the lighting needed a tweak, some candles perhaps, to detract from the yawning nothingness on the other side of the glass.

Except there wasn't quite nothing out there. The longer she looked the more she could see of Gorleston pier, the weak light on the Coastwatch station. She didn't think she'd been on the pier since the night she shot Sam's boyfriend, Michael Hansen – at least that was what he'd called himself. He'd deserved it, and she'd got away with it. Though she had promised herself that if she did remain a free woman, she'd never kill anyone else, ever. Or was it shoot anyone else? She'd spend the rest of her days doing all she could to protect her children. She supposed she'd always been good at making promises she couldn't keep.

She couldn't see any lights from ships out to sea, only a smattering of red dots beyond the blackened industrial rooftops to her left, which marked the nearest wind turbines. She looked away from the window, at the nearly empty bar. Checked her watch. He was late. He was always late. Youth for you.

Tatty took a sip of Prosecco, glanced outside again, thinking that when she owned the joint they'd serve champagne by the glass. Prosecco was no substitute. She'd never had a sweet tooth.

Just down the cliff, at the foot of the pier, was the Ocean Rooms, lit only by the nearest street lamps, and not all of them were working. A few more street lamps were vaguely illuminating the long concrete rain shelter, a relic from the 1950s. No one was ducking out of the weather, and making use of it now. There seemed to be no one out and about at all. A handful of cars were dotted face on to the sea. Some people might have been sitting in them, doling out wraps, blowjobs. It was the Hummer gang's patch, after all. They'd done nothing worthwhile with it, of course. It was still a desperate eyesore. Though not for much longer.

She was going to tear the rain shelter down first of all, and create a deck area leading from the Ocean Rooms to the beach. Then she'd build a pergola, and illuminate it all with beautiful fairy lights. The Pavilion, sitting back from the curving front, needed some proper exterior lighting as well, while the interior would have to be completely renovated. She wasn't sure how best it could then be used, what the most appropriate entertainment to keep the locals happy would be, while attracting a more fashionable, younger crowd, with proper money to spend. Maybe she should talk to Zach about it. Give him another chance. The caravan park was only ever a stopgap. A place to keep him out of trouble.

Her eyes drifted down and along the pier once more, trying to penetrate the darkness. They'd never found Michael Jansen's body. The tide must have been going out. Maybe he'd been swept closer to the land of his birth, across the North Sea. Unless his body had got snagged on some under-water cables. Or perhaps he'd been carried inland, and was stuck on a remote mud bank, in the wilds of Breydon Water. They weren't about to find his body too, were they?

'Tatty, sorry I'm late.'

She turned her head. 'Hey,' she said.

'Are you OK? You look like you've seen a ghost.'

'I'm fine, love,' she said. 'You're late.'

Shane bent down to kiss her, on the lips, hard and wet, which was no surprise given that he was a fireman. It still made her tingle. Not that she was in the mood right now.

'Traffic's a nightmare, backed up for miles,' he said. 'Only one lane on the Haven is working. Police are doing checks. I recognised one of the patrolmen, luckily. He waved me through. Over by North Quay and New Road it's totally solid. I know they're investigating, but it's like they've forgotten people do live here, work here.'

'Some,' muttered Tatty.

'There was a TV van, on the quay by the Historic Quarter. Not sure what they're hoping to film from there. But it's a nice view, I guess.'

He'd sat down opposite her, which was a nice view for her, that was for sure. A very nice view. He hadn't removed his coat, because he wasn't wearing one. Out of work, uniform, he never seemed to wear anything remotely warm, protective, just shirts, tight fitting, and snug jeans. It

48

would be hard to cram those thighs and muscly calves into anything looser without losing a sartorial edge. She supposed his jeans were what Zach'd call skinny. They were what all the men, of a certain youthful age and gainful employment, seemed to be wearing. Zach and his mates were more into street gear. When they could be bothered – designer trackies, trainers and the like. Drug-dealer gear as Rich would have called it. He was also a drug dealer, of course, yet he wore suits.

Tatty preferred denim on a man, or, yes, a suit, she supposed, but then she thought of Ben, and how you could get it so wrong. However, Ben's mind was always elsewhere, which wasn't such a bad thing at all. His dad's mind had been elsewhere too, though that invariably wasn't a good thing – the wrong business deals, the wrong women. She was trying to take a leaf out of his book – though she was beginning to doubt she was any good at it.

She smiled at Shane, hoping it appeared genuine. She hadn't been out with him too many times in public. His body was what she'd gone for. Didn't see too much point in straying far from the bedroom. Yet she was aware that her feelings were changing. She was comfortable in his presence. He respected her, desired her. That she had feelings at all, she supposed, was part of the problem. Rich had never cared about anyone. 'Sorry about the traffic,' she said.

'Not your fault.'

She smiled again. Had his eyes suggested something else?

'I'm here now,' he added quickly, before looking around the room, then out of the window. 'I haven't been in this

49

bar for a while. Good spot though, isn't it? Better in the summer, I guess. Have they got a terrace?'

'It caters for the older crowd,' Tatty said, sweeping some hair from her forehead, tilting her head. She didn't need to flirt with him. She was too old and proud to flirt with anyone, or so she thought.

'What are you doing in here, then?' he said.

'Compliments will get you everywhere, young man. What are you having?'

'Come on, let me buy you a drink for once. I do have a job.'

She looked at her glass. The Prosecco was still sitting there, going warm and flat. 'OK. Gin and tonic, please. I can't get on with that stuff.' She indicated her drink, in the silly flute.

Shane started to get up.

'They'll come over.' She waved at the skinny girl behind the bar. She knew who she was – the late owner's daughter. Tatty was surprised she was still working here, and also alarmed to see that she appeared even skinnier than the last time she'd seen her.

The waitress walked over in nothing other than a fragile way. A gust of wind would have lifted her off the ground and blown her away. She was trying to smile, to look pleasant and welcoming, but it wasn't working very well.

The bar of the Pier View Hotel was hardly the centre of the universe. Couldn't have been much fun working here. Though this was going to change, Tatty was thinking. She also thought the waitress should have been tucked up in a hospital bed, on a drip. Tatty suddenly felt an overwhelming sense of concern, sadness and shame. At least Sam hadn't suffered from anorexia.

The girl's expression froze and she stopped dead, not looking at Tatty, nor Shane, but at the floor.

'Hiya,' said Shane, warmly, too warmly. 'Lianne, right? How are you?'

The girl nodded, kept looking at the floor, at her feet, which were in dismal, flat black pumps. The girl's tights were too loose for her ankles, her lower legs. Glancing up, Tatty wondered if Shane's cheeks were colouring. Maybe she couldn't take him anywhere, be seen out with him. She felt her own cheeks flaring and a wave of heat rise from the pit of her stomach.

She had to stand, and as she did so the heat rose to her head in something like a mini explosion. She put her hand on Shane's shoulder for support, waited for the dizziness to subside. 'Excuse me,' she said, pushing herself off Shane, 'I need the Ladies. You know what I want to drink.'

She hurried out of the thickly carpeted room into the corridor, which was also beige, and padded with dense carpet. The oppressively low ceiling was studded with boiling halogens. There were some prints on the wall, hunting scenes – twits in red jackets on horseback galloping across fields chasing foxes. She was with the foxes.

As soon as she took ownership of the hotel these would be the first things chucked into the skip.

The ladies' toilet was another hot, claustrophobic, interior-decorating disaster. Tatty supposed she owed Nathan Taylor some credit for educating her in such things, lending her a sense of taste and style. And his body when she'd needed it – though he'd become needy as well. What was it with men, except Rich? What was it with herself? Why couldn't she be so cold and calculating?

Taking a close look at herself in the large mirror was a shock. Was it ever necessary to light a toilet in such a way? When the hotel was hers the Ladies would be a place of refuge, of calm, flattering tones, with perhaps some scented candles. She could smell bad plumbing, or someone's rich bowel movement.

Her cheeks were flushed scarlet, her eyes bloodshot. Her forehead was not as smooth as it should have been. Crow's feet stretched from her eyes like ugly spiders' webs. She didn't want to think about how old she was, or what the hell she was doing with Shane, taking him out for an evening. She was old enough to be his mother. But she did know what she was doing – trying to act like Rich. What the hell was Shane doing with *her*? That was the bigger question.

He seemed so young and innocent when you spoke to him. Like he'd never come across the harsher truths of growing up in Yarmouth. He must have known who she really was, what she represented. Perhaps she hadn't seen him enough to know what he really thought, believed in. She barely knew him. She wasn't sure that people that age, that generation, believed in much any more.

She pushed a tap, leaned over the sink, cupped some water, bathed her face. Her doctor had suggested that she should give HRT a go. He suggested a private doctor in Harley Street, who was very liberal with the dosages. Maybe she should go and see him.

However, she'd remained resolute about not taking any pills since she'd given up the antidepressants. Oestrogen was not addictive, was it? Even in huge quantities. Maybe it was time she accepted her age – and acted it. Yet she'd been under someone else's thumb for so long she wasn't sure she'd ever been able to act her age. It was her time to have some fun, behave however she wanted – that's what she'd been trying to think. Her kids were grown up, even if they still weren't always very responsible.

Having splashed some more water on her face, she leaned closer into the mirror, frowned, smiled, caught the tiny drops running down her nose, her cheeks. She'd have to reapply her make-up. Men, of any age, had it so easy. Shane would have to wait.

As she went to open her Birkin, which she'd put onto the ledge by the sink, it practically went for her, making her jump. Her phone, deep inside its luxurious folds, had started up. The ringtone, though muffled, was shattering the muzak, which had been doing so little to enhance the exhausted décor. She shook her hands dryer, reached in and retrieved the device, though not before voicemail kicked in.

The screen said it'd been Sam. It looked like she'd called a couple of times earlier that evening as well. Frank had also called. She glanced at her watch. It was not remotely late. Frank could wait. She was having an evening off work, even if all hell seemed to be breaking loose in the town around her. Sam couldn't wait though, she was her child. She returned the call.

Sam picked up before the second ring. 'Mum?'

'Hi, darling. What's up?'

'Where are you?'

'Out.'

'Where?' Sam sounded anxious – though no more anxious than normal.

'I'm just having a drink, with a work contact.'

'Who?'

'No one you know. Are you at home?'

'Yes. When are you coming back?'

'Is Ben there? Zach?'

'Ben was here earlier. I don't know where he's gone now. I haven't seen Zach all day. Didn't see him yesterday, either. When did you last see him? He won't answer my calls or texts.'

'He might be using a new number. Have you had tea?'

'Mum, some people came to the house. I shouldn't have answered the door, I suppose, but they were knocking and knocking, and wouldn't give up. I thought they were going to bust the door down.'

'You answered the door when you were at home alone?'

'I am twenty-five. Nearly twenty-six.'

'We've been through this. You can never be sure. You mustn't open the door to strangers, ever. Ring Frank if anyone turns up. That's what we're meant to do. He'll send someone straight over.' Tatty looked at herself as if for reassurance, in the large mirror, under the awful lighting. Her make-up needed quite some repairing; her hair wasn't in the best shape either. She wondered whether Shane was still chatting to Lianne.

'They weren't exactly strangers,' said Sam.

'What do you mean? Who were they?' Tatty's mind began to leap through terrible possibilities.

The toilet door opened. Tatty half expected to see Shane's stupidly blue eyes appear, followed by some dumb question, like, 'Is everything all right, love?' But even he wouldn't barge into the Ladies, concerned for her, would he?

It wasn't him, though. It was a badly dressed older woman. She must have come from the restaurant because Tatty didn't remember seeing her in the bar – she would have remembered, because she knew her. It was the woman from the lingerie shop, Knickers and Twist, on the high street.

To Tatty's great embarrassment she smiled a hello. Tatty wished it wasn't the case, but she'd been into the boutique only the other day, in search of something that she thought Shane, in all his youth and vigour, might appreciate. She hadn't found anything. It had been a shocking waste of time. She was now signalling to the woman that she was on the phone, in mid conversation, as if that wasn't obvious. 'Sam? You still there?'

'Did you hear what I said?'

'Sorry. I'm actually in the loo.'

'It was the police, Mum. That's why I opened the door. Two of them. They were in uniform.'

'It doesn't matter who it is,' Tatty said firmly. 'We never open the door unless we are expecting someone. You know that.' The woman still hadn't gone into a cubicle and was standing there staring at her. Tatty held the phone to her side. 'Do you mind?' she said. She remembered the tackiness of the boutique's lingerie, the shoddiness of her own thinking. She'd been in a rush, she supposed, to get laid. The woman finally backed hurriedly into a cubicle, shutting the door behind her and locking it determinedly, or fearfully.

'I thought something might have happened,' Sam was saying, her voice wobbling. 'To you.'

'To me? Don't be silly, darling. You mustn't worry about me. What did they want?' She was struggling to speak quietly, though she knew that uniformed coppers were usually a better bet than higher-ranked plain-clothed.

'Zach,' Sam said.

'What? They wanted Zach? What for?'

'They didn't say.'

# 6

Frank knew he hadn't put enough thought into this as he headed on foot up England's Lane. But he felt time accelerating, knew how things could quickly develop. Freezing fog smelling of fish and diesel had slumped onto the corner of Pier Road Walk and Beach Road, like a block of something poisonous, fatal.

He slowed, pulled the collar of his dark, baggy anorak up. Felt the weight in the inside left pocket. Looked at his shoes, a pair of fine derbys, knowing at least that well-worn leather soles, smooth and polished and hard as nails, were about the most untraceable of footwear. The kids today in their ridiculous trainers might as well lope around leaving autographs.

What Frank really wasn't sure about was his new Glock. It was a 17, smaller and lighter than his previous 19. It hadn't been easy to get hold of, and he hadn't yet tested it. Wasn't convinced by the quality or the provenance of the bullets, either. There were too many bad imitations on the market. The weapon couldn't fail. He wasn't out to issue a warning. He knew there'd be two of them and that he'd have no chance with a knife. Besides, a shooter always made more of statement.

He shouldn't have been trudging up Beach Road, at this hour, in such weather, in any case. He should be paying people to do these sorts of jobs. But there weren't many of the right people around any more. He'd seen to that. For a job like this they needed to be brought in from Manchester, or Glasgow, or Tirana – and sent swiftly back to their dismal lives, never to set foot in this neck of the woods again.

Reaching the patch of grass, where more freezing February fog was heaped, and the last side street before Beach Road opened up to the short stretch of promenade, the old concrete rain shelter and all the sand and the sea you ever could wish for, Frank realised he was missing Howie. He was missing his wisdom, his strength and cunning.

He'd been the one person Frank could call on. Except his last communication with Britt Hayes had unnerved, and then Howie had informed him he was out of town – not that Frank had spelled out the mission, of course. He'd got the feeling, from the sound of Howie's voice, that he was being brushed off – that's what it felt like now, for sure.

There were fewer cars than he was expecting, lined up, facing the wintry night. The council had done a good job of not maintaining the street lamps. The Hummer wasn't there, not that he was expecting it to be. There was no one on the street who wasn't at least in a car. He wasn't sure there was anyone in a car, either, waiting for a trade. It wasn't the weekend – though addicts, those that this gang catered to, didn't care too much about what day of the week it was.

He crossed the road quickly, aiming for the rear of the Ocean Rooms, which were shut up tight for the night, the winter, though the old pub and hotel at the beginning of the pier was lit, open.

Frank didn't know why Tatty was so focused on buying the Pier View, at the top of the cliffs. He'd always thought that this was a better location, a property with more potential, views north across the Yare to Yarmouth and south straight out over the vast beach. Something was holding her back. He wondered whether it was an episode from her distant past. He dreaded to think of everything she must have put up with.

Nothing was holding him back right then, however. A surge of adrenalin was coursing through him. He was young again. Not an overweight, overpaid business executive.

He was at the beginning of the shelter, on the far side, nothing between him and the beach. He could have sat down, listened to the sea gently crashing onto the shore a hundred metres or so away, and considered retirement. No, he couldn't. He was never going to sit still, take it easy. Besides, if he didn't move now, he might not have the choice. He was too old to be banged up for the rest of his life, however long that'd be. He'd go out fighting. He'd grown up on the street. A Lexus RX was not going to take the street out of him, tame him.

He made his way along the shelter, keeping the structure between him and the parked cars. Reaching the end he gazed towards the esplanade, where everything also appeared shuttered, except the steak joint. He couldn't see a soul inside from where he was. It was hardly late. Not if you needed a steak – or a wrap of crack.

He was looking for a Ford Mondeo, ten years old, navy. The Hummer was for the day, and the brass; this was for the night and the foot soldiers. He knew their practices – straight out of the rule book. Such easy prey.

As expected the Mondeo was slotted in, one from the end. Frank thought that the last parked car on the row, a knackered Saab, was theirs as well. In this it paid to work in pairs, as a team.

He scanned the area again. The immediate vicinity was clear of people out in the open. No one was rushing to buy any gear just then. The Lower Esplanade in February was about as attractive and comforting as a kick in the chest, even to a junkie. He and Tatty should have left the Hummer gang to it. But Tatty had other plans now, and a shedload of police trouble was heading his way. History for you.

In the distance, half a mile south along the promenade, there might have been a couple of figures, and a dog. Perhaps an adult and a child. He realised that the air on the front was clear. The fog must have been hanging around in the backstreets only tonight, like a bad rash. Frank couldn't tell which way the people were walking. They seemed to have paused, the dog having run off. In any case they were still far enough away.

Whether the old Saab was part of the set-up or not, there was no one in it right now. Perhaps that was because there were two figures in the Mondeo. Its engine was chugging away warmly. In the shadowy dark it looked like the occupants were napping. Frank couldn't blame them.

Something about them – maybe it was their posture, the fact that they were napping – told him that they weren't too young. This cheered him. These geezers would have had a generation of wasted opportunities, crime and violence behind them.

Frank didn't know whether he believed in rehabilitation. He'd have thought Zach would have learned his lesson by now. He didn't know how to get the kid to see sense. His spell in Ibiza had only made him worse, coming back with a business plan that was entirely inappropriate for the temperate world.

The North Sea was on Frank's back, he felt, like a hard, cold boulder. He unzipped his jacket, reached into the left-hand inside pocket, put his fingers round the handle and slowly removed the semi-automatic. He wasn't proud, or particularly impressed with himself. He was a survivor, that was it, plain and simple. Which was why he appreciated gardening so much, how plants had this canny way of taking root, adapting, growing, despite the odds. They'd smother the world in a shot, without human intervention. Human beings fucked everything up. Most people weren't very nice.

He strode out from behind the shelter, took a couple of steps and was at the driver's window. Holding the gun down by his side he gently tapped on the glass. He doubted he looked much like a punter, or a plain-clothed. They probably knew who he was, anyway, which might have been why they didn't seem so bothered. There weren't stirring at all, in fact.

This was going to be easy, as easy as pop, pop. Raising his gun, he noticed that the driver's window was open a good way, noticed too that the man in the driver's seat was not leaning back so much as slumped, his head at an unnatural angle. His companion didn't look like he was sleeping comfortably either. Dark stuff had spilled all over his neck and chest. Blood. Blood that'd had a few moments to settle and congeal.

Frank moved his head closer, trying to see through the gap. The man in the driver's seat had a neat hole in the side of his head, temple area, barely a hint of blood. He presumed the other side of his head wasn't so neat. The exit wound may have been contributing to the mess all over his companion's chest.

It wasn't clear where the passenger had been shot. In the neck? Frank could see how it would have happened. The shooter walks up, taps on the driver's window. The driver lowers the glass, gets a bullet in the head for his efforts. The shooter then aims for his companion as he's beginning to realise what's happening, but too late. He gets it in the neck, maybe.

This had been Frank's plan. He'd have been pleased with such a result. He couldn't fucking believe that someone else had got there first. He wasn't going to hang around, look for more evidence, try to work out who it might have been. Wasn't that a job for Serious and Organised?

He backed away from the car, suddenly conscious of potential witnesses, CCTV, even though it was so dark and he had his hood up. He was also conscious that he shouldn't retrace his steps through the foggy, dismal backstreets, where he didn't now know who might have been waiting for him. The only person who might have had an inkling about his plans this evening was Howie. But Frank had only asked him for a meet. He couldn't have joined that many dots. He'd have had to have been listening in on all Frank's conversations that day, and still made some impressive guesses.

Frank dropped down onto the beach, planning to take a longer, sandier route to avoid the Lower Esplanade. He couldn't afford to get too close to the dog walkers now, even if he'd have liked to know who exactly they were. But a child as cover? Or just a very small person. Maybe his eyesight wasn't what it used to be. Fuck's sake, could he trust no one?

Heading straight towards the shoreline he knew his footsteps would be masked in seconds on the soft, damp sand, even if the soles of his derbys were making heavy weather of it. Once he was close enough he considered flinging the Glock as far as he could into the salty drink. The last thing he needed now was to be stopped in possession, for a crime he hadn't committed – there were enough police crawling around town.

He couldn't believe he'd gone to all the effort to come down here, ready to divert attention from some of his earlier work, only to find someone else had already done it for him. He should have plumped for a TV dinner and an early night.

As he trudged along the beach, a storm raging inside his head, he knew he wasn't going to give up his weapon just yet. It appeared that someone else wanted this patch as well as Tatty – unless it was some kind of a set-up, but he hadn't been nabbed. The sea was strangely quiet and still, until he realised that all he could hear was the shortness of his breath and his aged heart pounding away.

## 7

'Where have you been?' Shane said, looking up, the skin on his smooth, young forehead failing to frown.

Oh, those stupidly blue eyes. Why did they make her melt? Because Rich's had been a dark, dirty brown, reflecting nothing but his own depraved, duplicitous thoughts. That wasn't quite right. There'd been moments of clarity, insight, determination. Love? Protection, anyway. She shouldn't forget so easily what he was responsible for, and where she came from. Frank had reminded her of that only the other day. 'I had a call, from home,' she said, sitting and brushing some hair from her own lined forehead, hoping she'd done a good enough repair job with her make-up.

Her new drink was in front of her, the gin and tonic. The ice appeared to have melted. Some other people had come into the bar, three Chinese-looking guys. They were sitting at a round table in the far corner and were half-heartedly studying the menus. One of them kept glancing around the bar, at her and Shane.

Shane was still smiling at her expectantly. She had a sudden feeling that it could get very tiresome hanging out with him for too long. She'd always struggled to relate to people of a younger generation, her own children included.

'It was Sam,' she said, 'my daughter. She wanted to know whether I was coming home for dinner. Whether she should make me anything.'

'That's nice of her.'

'How do you know Lianne?'

'The waitress?' he said quickly, before leaning forward and sipping his drink – lager, a new pint. He had to wipe his mouth afterwards. 'My sister went to school with her. They were best friends for a bit. She seems OK, given what she's been through.' Shane took another hasty sip of his lager, making less mess.

'Some people have it rougher than others,' Tatty said, thinking not of Lianne particularly, or Lianne's late father, but her old PA, Sian – shot dead at the age of nineteen, and in front of Zach. 'What do you make of this hotel?' she added, desperate to brighten up her thoughts.

She was also trying to work out what the three visitors at the far end of the bar were doing here. She decided they were talking Chinese – Mandarin. They were in suits. In town for business? What business? This was the smartest hotel in the immediate area. It would be where international business people stayed, if they had to.

'Nice place for a quiet drink,' Shane said, looking over his shoulder, focusing on Lianne, who was behind the small bar now, seemingly trying to shrink further out of sight. 'It was her old man's, wasn't it – this hotel?'

'Yeah,' said Tatty. 'It's for sale.'

It wasn't, not as far as she knew. She didn't normally talk business with Shane, and she couldn't stop other dark, troubling thoughts from surfacing. Where was Zach right now, and why did the police wanted him? She should try to locate him, or at least get Frank onto it. But there'd been enough drama and anxiety for one day. She was having a night off, she had to remind herself, with her boyfriend. It was her time to have some fun, relax – not that she'd ever been any good at that sort of thing. Zach was old enough to look after himself. But she knew he wasn't, that was the trouble.

Tatty stood. She couldn't sit here, sit still. 'Let's go,' she said. This, her evening out, was all wrong. Besides, she'd only wanted company, or was it cover, while she scoped out the Pier View.

'Right, OK,' said Shane. 'Where to?'

He seemed to be paying more attention to his drink than her. Gratitude for you. She fucked his brains out, not the other way round. Or so she liked to think, but she was not Rich. She glanced out of the window, down at the Pavilion, the Ocean Rooms, all that would soon be hers. She was better than Rich, smarter, tougher, more ruthless.

Some people were by one of the cars, parked up along the front. It was quite a crowd. She hadn't noticed them before. They seemed animated. Something was going on. Something was wrong. Her mind flicked from Zach to Frank. The look on his face when she'd left his office earlier today – the scheming bastard. Surely he hadn't moved so fast?

Whatever was happening down in the basin had not escaped the businessmen's attention. One of them had left his chair for the window. A flashing blue light was coming from somewhere. Two, three emergency vehicles. Sirens could be heard. She strode out of the room.

Shane took his time to catch up with her out in the corridor, meaning she was stuck contemplating the hunting prints again, the foxes not doing such a good job of getting away. The odds were always stacked against the hunted in such silly pictures, such stupid sports.

'Looks like trouble down by the pier, the Ocean Rooms,' Shane said, a touch breathlessly. 'I should go down, see if I can help.'

'No,' said Tatty, taking his hand. 'You're not on duty. Let's go to your place. Come on.' She tugged a little harder. 'Life's short enough, isn't it?'

'My place?'

'You do have a home, don't you?' She'd never been there. He'd been to hers when the kids had been out, away. They'd been to Dunstan Hall, as well, though they'd avoided the spa. She wasn't entirely sure she wanted him ogling her body in a brightly lit treatment room.

'It wouldn't be the sort of home you'd be used to,' Shane said. 'I've got a flatmate as well – Malc. He's a fireman, too, when he's not doing door work. We all have to moonlight to make ends meet.'

She knew this, Frank had kept her informed. She couldn't take him to her place, however, despite it being so close. Sam was there and Ben should have been, and she supposed, hoped, that Zach would turn up sooner rather than later. He always came home in the end, crashing into the hall, trudging straight up to his room, not having taken his shoes off. Unless he'd been nabbed by the police elsewhere.

Except the police must have other, more immediate things on their hands now. Her mind quickly shifted to

Gorleston basin, and then the mouth of the River Yare just the other side of the pier. How fast the waters moved.

Shane was talking to her. 'He might be in – Malc that is,' he was saying. 'I don't know what his schedule is. To be honest, he's bit of a slob at home.'

'What are you saying? You don't want to fuck me?' She let go of his hand.

He looked at her, by the entrance to the Pier View Hotel, with the eyes of a little lost puppy. He put his arms on her shoulders, pulled her to him, kissed her on the lips with purpose.

She hadn't been kissed in such a way, in public, for she didn't know how long. She didn't reciprocate, but she did close her eyes for a second or two.

'Maybe we should get a room here,' he said, breaking off, removing his hands from her shoulders.

'With whatever's going on down by the pier?' she said. 'I don't think so. Besides, I don't know who else is staying here. I'd worry about the thinness of the walls. Do you want to come to my office, fuck me on my desk?'

That's what Rich had done, in his day, hadn't he? Taken his tarts to the old Goodwin Enterprises HQ. Her turn now. Except the new offices were a damn sight smarter, and cleaner, and furnished with designer goods that were neither cheap nor fake.

# 8

'Hey, Sis,' said Ben, as he stepped into the kitchen.

'Christ,' Sam replied, dropping a cup into the sink and turning her head, 'you made me jump.' She stood back, frowned. 'I thought it was Zach. You sound just like him.'

'No I don't,' Ben said, walking over to the coffee machine. He flipped the frothing arm out, flung it back in, tried to get one of the coffee compressors off. Couldn't make it budge this morning. Banged the arm harder, to no avail. He hated this damn machine. What was wrong with a cafetière? Or a Starbucks around the corner?

He could murder a flat white. Avani had started drinking the turmeric latte, the latest in a long line of whatever that corporation came up with next. It was absurd. They needed to stick to what they were good at – flat white. He was all for businesses diversifying, expanding, keeping themselves young and fit – but turmeric in a coffee? Before that it had been coconut, almond, oats, endless variations of Frappuccinos. That's why he had dumped her. She didn't know what she liked.

Actually, it wasn't why he'd dumped her. He hadn't. She'd dumped him. She didn't know what she liked, that was true – even in a boyfriend, so it seemed. Could he blame her? He was a boring City boy, who wore shitty suits to work. His mum was right to have said something. He looked down at his trousers – his suit trousers, which he'd been planning to wear for work today. He was also wearing a white shirt, not totally clean. He hadn't put on his tie yet, a silky blue thing from he didn't know where, but he'd been intending to. Black lace-ups as well. But Frank wore those, didn't he? And he was a real gangster.

With another huge wrench he managed to loosen the coffee compressor thingy. There must have been a proper name for it. He got it off the machine and slammed it onto the marble counter.

'Steady,' said Sam, over her shoulder, as she walked across to the kitchen table. She was in her pyjamas, with a sweater on top. 'You'll break it treating it like that.'

'Good.' He tipped the old coffee into the sink. Had to think for a minute where the fresh ground was kept. He went to a cupboard, struck lucky first time. It should have been kept in the fridge, but at least his mum had fresh ground nowadays. Growing up there'd only been instant, and no stupid, hulking machine of course. Pros and cons, as ever.

He looked at his trousers again. It was what you did in the office, at your desk that counted, wasn't it? Trying to spoon fresh coffee into the device, he managed to scatter grinds all over the granite top. It now looked like the kitchen had some abysmal infestation of termites – like what happened in their kitchen in Ibiza, not that he'd been there for a while. He'd been working too hard, in the City, and chasing Avani.

There was nothing wrong with turmeric in coffee. You could put whatever you wanted into coffee. Starbucks had more than proved it knew what it was doing – you just had to look at the figures. He missed Avani like mad. He swiped the spilt coffee towards the sink with the side of his hand. Most went on the floor.

Avoiding looking over in Sam's direction, he set about cranking the machine up and then hunting down a mug and milk. He hadn't got used to living back at home. It was ridiculous at his age. Though he loved Sam; it was good that she was back home as well.

'What's up with you?' Sam called over. 'Got out of bed the wrong side?'

'Nothing,' he said. 'Late for work, that's all.'

'You think they care? It doesn't operate like that, nine to five.'

He looked her way now, caught the dull daylight that was falling on the garden the other side of the long stretch of floor to ceiling windows. Couldn't tell what sort of day it was, except damp and cold. When he'd been a kid the kitchen hadn't been anything like as large, or as full of expensive surfaces and useless gadgets. Then his mum went and met some architect designer guy called Nathan Taylor. God only knew what she'd paid him. Everyone used to rip them off. Or what she'd paid that same guy to do the Smokehouse – her pet project that'd gone on for years. Sam said their mum had been fucking him all along. He couldn't believe that. Their mother would never have dared have an affair when his old man was alive. He'd have killed her had he found out.

'You're not going in today, then?' he said.

'What makes you think that?'

'Because you haven't been in all week.'

'Are you aware of this body they've found in Breydon Water? It's been in the news all week,' Sam said.

'What's that got to do with the business?' Ben asked.

'Do you think Mum and Frank are behaving normally?'

He seemed to have got the coffee machine to work this time. His cup looked reasonably full. Getting the milk to froth was another matter. 'I'm not sure what that'd look like – them behaving normally.' Thinking about it he supposed they might have seemed more on edge than normal, particularly Frank. How the hell had that guy got himself into the position of running the company with his mum? What did he know about business? He was barely educated. He'd never worked, as far as Ben knew, outside Yarmouth – work being an interesting term in the context. 'Are you saying they're something to do with that?'

'Do you remember when Mum came home with mud all over her trousers, her mac? That was around the time when Simon's wife Jess disappeared? She was our aunt, Ben. Dad was shagging her, you know.'

'Is this what happens when you spend too much time here? So much shit seeps into your mind you start to lose all sense of the truth.'

'The truth, round here, can be bloody lethal,' Sam said. 'The police came to the house yesterday evening, you know, looking for Zach. Where did you disappear to last night, by the way? And where's Zach now?'

73

'Zach? He's mixed up in this as well? Don't tell me, please. Sam, are you still on medication?' He looked back at the mess he'd made with the ground coffee. He didn't want to get into the habit of leaving a dirty trail behind him.

'Fuck off and die,' she said, but sweetly.

He shouldn't have asked her whether she was on medication. That was cruel of him. Given what she'd been through, she could take whatever was necessary, and for as long as necessary too. 'Sorry, but what did the police want with Zach?'

'They didn't say.'

'I guess if they didn't say, it can't be that serious.'

'They're not going to tell me, are they?' She sighed, looking small and pale and timid. She used to be so much tougher and more professional, even for her age. He was always really proud of her. Daughters needed strong fathers, as well as mothers, didn't they? His dad was no role model. Sam had always had terrible relationships. He believed it was connected.

'Nothing seems right again,' she said. 'I don't like it. Where was Mum all night?' She was looking straight out of the window.

Ben watched her head waver, framed by the fat chunk of slowly freezing air the other side of the glass. 'She didn't come home last night either?' he asked. He'd presumed his mum was tucked up in bed, fast asleep, when he arrived back after his drive, before hopping straight in the shower.

'She came home, though not until like three in the morning. A couple of hours after you.'

'Was she out clubbing again?'

'That's not even funny.'

'She goes clubbing in Ibiza.'

'Once, maybe, years ago. This is not Ibiza, in case it's escaped your attention.'

'Maybe she's got a boyfriend.' He walked over to the table with his coffee, realising he hadn't even asked Sam whether she wanted one. 'You want one?' he said, placing his on the table.

'I'm not drinking caffeine at the moment. Mum said she was meeting a work contact when I called her, at like eight, just after the police were here.'

'Work contact? What does that mean?'

Sam looked at him now and smiled, before grimacing. 'Exactly.'

'We can ask her when she gets up.'

'She's normally up by now,' Sam said. 'Do you think she's OK? Should I check?'

'Sam, I know things have been really, really hard for you, but you must try to stop worrying about everything. Of course Mum's fine.'

'Zach?'

Ben took a sip of his coffee. Drained the cup. It was barely warm. He'd managed to get some sort of froth going, though the temperature was not right. 'Why not get your head around some work, the business? That'll distract you from worrying unnecessarily.'

'Goodwin Enterprises – you honestly think that'll help?'

'We're moving it into a new chapter – me and Mum.'

'Yeah? How so?'

'What I've got in mind is highly complex, involving a series of offshore holding companies. Private and state investors.'

'A pyramid scheme?' Sam said.

'That would be a crass way of looking at it.'

'A pyramid scheme, then. What's Frank say about that?'

'It'd be way beyond his brain power. Though I'm going to need some legal help, setting up the holding companies and so on. I'd like to do as much of this in house. I'm not sure Mum gets it all, not that she needs to. I was hoping you could help me, though.'

Ben looked over at the tiresome coffee machine. He wasn't sure he could be bothered to crank it up once more. Whose idea had it been? That interior designer-stroke-architect fellow? He didn't think his mother would have thought of it. His father certainly wouldn't have. Ben was surprised he'd even allowed it in the house. However, the last few months, years probably, of his life, he hadn't been himself. He'd taken his eye off the ball.

'I had a meeting with the council yesterday,' he continued. 'Low level pen-pushers like that are for the taking.' He shook his head, thinking that's what you get in the provinces. He'd done his apprenticeship in the City, so he knew how it rolled – until he was sacked. Avani once called him an aloof, arrogant fucker. He had nothing to be arrogant about now. He needed to watch what he said, blend in. 'Though they can't all be hopeless, incapable,' he added stiffly.

He stood up, embarrassed with himself again, and walked back to the marble island, not sure what he was after, or what he'd find in this kitchen to sustain him. 'The thing is I'm trying to persuade Mum to take up a place on the Regeneration Committee. A person in her position – she should chair it. Dad did.'

'Dad was a bloke. You've met them. Not sure it would be Mum's scene.'

'She has to do it – for the business, for us. It'd be easy to persuade the powers that be. Come on, Sam, think about it. They wouldn't be able to keep their eyes off her – as long as she wears the right gear. You know, one of her short suede skirts.'

'You're talking about our mother – in the twenty-first century. I don't want to think too hard about what you've just said.'

'Give me a break, Sis. I'm just being realistic.'

'See, you sounded just like Zach again. What were you doing at the council anyway?'

'I was outlining my investment project.'

'The pyramid scheme?'

'I didn't use that phrase, obviously.'

'You guarantee them contracts, with very healthy margins – backhanders, if you want to use another word – as long as they invest up front, that's how it works,' came a voice from close behind him. 'While the exposure, your exposure, skyrockets.'

He turned. 'Hi, Mum.' She'd remained by the doorway. 'We were just talking about the council, the Regeneration Committee. You know, what I mentioned yesterday.'

'I heard.'

'Were you like, wigging in?' He tried to make that sound light and jokey, not defensive.

77

'She never misses a thing,' Sam said from the other side of the room.

His mother stepped into the kitchen, went over to the island. Looked at the mess he'd made. She was dressed for work. Not in one of her little suede skirts – he shouldn't have said that either – but what seemed to be a new pair of skinny designer jeans, and a fluffy, roll-neck sweater. It was the creamiest of off-whites. She looked tired.

'That's not true. For a start, I'm missing Zach right now,' she said. 'He's not in his room. I can't reach him on his phone. You haven't seen him since when, Sam?'

'Days ago,' Sam said, dismissively. 'You know what he's like.'

'Did you recognise the cops who were here?' Tatty asked.

'No,' Sam replied.

'What do you reckon they wanted exactly? This has been troubling me all night.'

'I told you, I have no idea. Why does everyone think they're going to broadcast their intentions all over the place? They didn't say what they wanted with him.'

'All we need,' Tatty sighed. 'Ben, can you make me a coffee please?'

'On that thing?' he said. She was giving him one of her stares. 'OK.' She shouldn't have been looking at him like that – he was not Zach. He was the responsible eldest son. In a different era he'd have been in charge. Though that sort of thinking was exactly what Avani would not have been impressed by. His father's son – that should have been something to be proud of. Now that he was back here, tail between his legs, he was doubting it more and more.

He shifted over to the coffee machine. His father would have shoved the bloody thing off the top, sent it crashing onto the stone floor, had he had his wits about him.

'Has anyone tried the caravan park?' said Sam.

'I can't believe he'd be dossing there in this weather,' Tatty said.

'Well, you know the plans he's got for it,' said Sam. 'It'd certainly be time consuming getting that off the ground.'

Ben watched his mother sigh again. She was becoming more and more expressive in her old age. Maybe the lack of tranquilisers had something to do with it.

Tatty laughed. 'A super club, in that rundown old caravan park? Yeah, I am aware of that idea.' Her voice became serious. 'Who do you think's backing it? Me and Frank. Give Zach a chance, we thought.'

'Another chance,' said Ben.

'You've got a scheme going,' Tatty said, looking at him. 'I'm not going to start dissing that already.'

'Nevertheless, Mum,' said Sam, 'there are schemes and schemes. Zach wants to attract two, three thousand people a weekend. Where're they going to come from?'

'You don't think we haven't asked the same question about the super casino?' Tatty said. 'We want more people than that a weekend. All these ventures require a certain amount of ambition – blue-sky thinking.'

'Mum,' said Ben, 'what the fuck does that mean, round here?' He couldn't believe she'd come up with that old cliché. Even his smug associates in London didn't use such terms any more, if they ever had.

'We have to be ambitious. Pave the way,' Tatty said, making Ben shrug some more. 'Change this town for good.'

'Mum,' he said, 'you and I know that the super casino plans, and our cut more importantly, don't hinge on us actually building the thing.'

'I'll need to show the Regeneration Committee something,' she said, winking, 'if they are to believe in me.'

'You're going to go for it?' Ben said.

'We'll see. Where's my coffee?'

'At least Zach is serious,' said Sam, standing, and walking over to the counter. 'Oh, I'll make the bloody coffee. It's not that difficult.'

The space she had left by the window allowed Ben a better view of what was going on outside in the back garden. It had started sleeting. 'I don't think Zach's serious about anything' Ben said. It had always irked him how much Sam adored Zach. Zach was not very nice to his sister, or his elder brother. Whereas Ben at least always looked out for Sam. He liked to think he'd done the same for Zach, but knew he probably hadn't. The fact that his mother had always so clearly preferred Zach hadn't helped matters.

'He knows the club world,' said Sam. 'If anyone can make it work, he will.'

'Don't count on it,' said Ben.

'He was meant to be meeting some big-name DJ there this week,' said Sam.

'I hope he showed up,' Ben said, shaking his head in dismay. 'I can't believe the police came knocking on our door, looking for him.' He shook his head. 'I need to get to work, proper work.'

'That's what you do, is it?' said Sam, effortlessly preparing the coffee machine.

'Don't you start,' Tatty said, giving Sam one of her looks, before retrieving her phone from the back pocket of her tight new jeans. She began tapping the screen furiously.

'Where were you until three in the morning, then?' Sam asked her.

'I need to get hold of Frank,' she said.

'Sod this for a breakfast,' said Ben. 'I'll pick something up on the way to work.' He also wanted to get up to his room, change. He wasn't sure he'd find anything better to wear, but he'd have a look. Leaving the kitchen, he thought he might raid Zach's room. As kids it was always the other way round, with Zach going for his equipment, gadgets and any cash that happened to be lying around, if not clothes. Time to get his own back. Not that he held out much hope he'd find anything remotely suitable, or clean. Maybe that was the point.

## 9

'OK, I'm on it,' he said, ending Tatty's call with a tap on the steering wheel. Yes sir, right away sir, three bags full sir, the conversation continued in his head. He drew a deep breath. If he wasn't hearing voices he was talking to himself. Doddery old fool.

Trying to shut out any untoward voices Frank stared back at the weather, the traffic. Despite the new destination, the new orders, he didn't need to turn around and change bridges to cross the Yare.

It had been dry when he'd left home, even if the sky was white with menace. The rain had begun before he'd edged out of Bradwell. Sleet soon followed, which, combined with the growing traffic, had forced him to spend far too long scrutinising the Gapton Hall Retail Park. He'd never understood the appeal of out-of-town shopping centres, not for consumers. Gapton Hall housed a Halfords, Poundland, Carphone Warehouse, the twenty-four-hour McDonalds and Pizza Hut. Shopping had always baffled him, even if fast food hadn't.

He understood the retail and business park attraction for some developers, however – the cheap rates, other financial incentives. The spaces behind the units where all manner of trade could flourish neatly out of sight. His mind wandered. Goodwin Enterprises had had no part in Gapton Hall, nevertheless. There were plenty of other businesses they should have kept their noses out of as well.

By the time he joined the A12, with the sleet turning to snow, Frank was thinking not of expansion but contraction – how he and Tatty should concentrate on their core activities, what had always worked for them so well in the past. Not that that had all been plain sailing. Maybe he was still tired. His body ached from having walked so far in the freezing cold last night. Four, five miles, and a good chunk of it on soft sand – for nothing. He hadn't done a thing wrong. For once he was totally fucking innocent.

Except he hadn't got any closer to the dog walkers, which was still troubling him, along with the fact that it had clearly been a professional hit. He didn't believe Tatty could have been involved. He knew she was with Shane last night – she was not good at keeping such secrets. He didn't blame her. She had to be proud to have pulled a man half her age. Frank had failed countless times to hook up with a man his own age, or even someone a decade or two older.

A riptide of loneliness tore through him, more piercing and violent than any 9-millimetre bullet. For the first time he could remember, Frank suddenly had a desire to live in another part of the world – somewhere warm and open, where there'd be no problem meeting like-minded men. Last night had been a wake-up call. He needed to move faster, be more aware, have better intelligence if he were to continue serving Goodwin Enterprises, the Goodwin family.

He stared ahead again, at the vehicle in front, an aged Transit, and realised that he really was thinking about packing up and moving on. A retirement of sorts. He was also thinking once more about Howie, his oldest friend, his only friend. *Friend?*

Frank's phone blared through the car's eight-speaker sound system. He took another deep breath before looking down at the screen on the dash, where he was informed that Tatty was calling him back already. The ringtone filled the warm, plush interior as the wipers continued to deal automatically with the wet snow that was slapping onto the windscreen, while the Transit pulled slowly ahead.

Exhaling he pressed the answer button, trying to get comfortable in the extraordinary seat, as he crawled on towards the Breydon Bridge. He was no executive. He wasn't sure he was much of a minder, let alone a professional murderer. You know what, Frank, he said to himself, as his eyes followed the wipers, the back of the van, you've started to think too much. 'Yes?' he said aloud.

'Are you there yet?' she said. 'Where is he? What's he doing? I'm worried sick.'

'No, I'm not there yet. We only spoke a few minutes ago.'

'However long does it take?'

'The traffic's bad,' he said. 'Wrong choice of bridge.'

'You don't know what the traffic does every morning, at this time? How long have you lived here?'

'Too fucking long,' he said, meaning it.

'That new car of yours, does it not have a decent satnav, with live traffic updates?'

'I don't need satnav, Tatty, to get around Yarmouth.' He couldn't believe she ever used such a thing. 'I need a fucking break — all right?'

'Hey, calm down, Frank. What's up with you this morning?'

'You're the one who's hassling me.'

'What do you expect? More bodies are turning up. Two dead in Gorleston last night, by the Ocean Rooms.'

'They've found more than one in Breydon Water as well,' he said calmly. Right then he didn't care who else might have been listening in. 'The cops are just not telling everyone yet, unless I've missed something on the news this morning.'

'Fuck's sake, Frank. I'm not going to ask you where you get your information from, nor what you know about what went on in Gorleston last night. Not on the blower.'

'Get off the phone, then.'

'We need a proper chat. You can't go running around causing chaos without my say so.'

'Me, running around without your permission? Who said I was doing anything of the sort? Where did you get to last night, I might well ask?' But he knew, of course. Where she was earlier, anyway. He couldn't believe she'd taken Shane to the Pier View Hotel. Hardly a place for youngsters.

'That's none of your business.'

'I thought we were a partnership now, Tatty. I didn't think you were my boss. I didn't think I needed to ask your permission to do anything.'

'Think again. You need to tell me what's going on, where this is all heading.'

'There's a time and a place for everything. If we're to continue as partners, then yes, I'm up for some transparency. But that goes both ways. If you want to play the boss, as I've always said, you're better off on a need-to-know basis only. That's the point of people like me, what we're for – we protect, we shield. We do the dirty work for people like you.'

'We're partners, Frank. How many times?'

'Behave like one then, and stop ordering me around. I'll see you in the office in an hour or so, once I've swung by the caravan park, as planned,' he said. The traffic was starting to shift. He knew they'd said too much on the phone. Did he care? As for what she'd said – *partners*? He wasn't sure he'd ever feel her equal. Or ever tell her the whole truth. The snow was not settling, nor was his mind, his heart.

'That kid better be there,' said Tatty.

'He's your son,' Frank muttered, ending the call.

As he reached the bridge, he tried to glance over the sides at the mud banks of Breydon Water, being dusted by snow, which almost as quickly as it landed disappeared. Without pulling over and getting out he knew he wouldn't be able to see what the cops might have been up to this morning. Whether they were still there, digging. Or whether they'd been hastily relocated. Couldn't have been a popular assignment, in any weather.

As it was there was no sign of police activity on the far side of the bridge, or by the New Road roundabout, just past the giant twenty-four-hour Tesco superstore. Did people honestly buy groceries at four in the morning?

It was the same story at the North Quay roundabout, though with more snow, just beginning to make a mark. He turned left and followed the River Bure for a short while until it was hidden by sparse greenery and a large care home, with the car dealerships on the other side of the road going on for ever. He wondered what the old codgers thought, entrapped by age and infirmity, when they looked out at the acres of new and used cars. The suggestion of mobility, freedom, transport to warmer, friendlier climes. If they could have afforded them. This was Yarmouth, after all, where money was scarce for the many, though not for the brutal few.

'Doddery old fool,' he said, aloud this time, putting his foot down.

The road swept into suburbia and dribbled on and on, before the lights by Salisbury Road. He took them at amber, pushing fifty miles an hour. There was rarely any traffic to talk about in this part of town, except on race days.

Frank made it to Jellicoe Road defying his usual driving caution. He knew there'd be no coppers this end of town that morning. He had someone to thank for that, he supposed. But fucking who?

Frank pulled up next to Zach's Sport, livid with the kid for not keeping in contact. It was against all the rules. What was wrong with him? He had everything he wanted, chucked at his feet. He'd come back from Ibiza worse than he'd left. He'd only ever been good at doing one thing, as far as Frank was aware, and that was computer hacking. Yet he could no longer be bothered to get his hands dirty on a keyboard. How much effort did that require? You barely had to get out of bed. You *didn't* have to get out of bed.

Zach had become so jumped up he'd even taken to being chauffeured around town, the countryside. When Frank was Zach's age he was living rough, in Peterborough, recently out of Young Offenders, shortly to be taken back under the wing of HM Prison Service.

Climbing out of his car, sniffing the freezing air, clocking a thunderous block of grey cloud hovering over the nearest wind turbines, Frank knew exactly what Zach was up to, with all the attitude. He'd gone independent again. Drug dealing from the back of a Range Rover Sport? Fuck's sake.

Revamping the caravan park should have been enough to have kept him occupied, out of trouble, so he and Tatty had thought. But no, Zach had bigger ideas. Seemed to run in the family.

Walking round to the side entrance of the lodge, Frank couldn't believe he was being ordered to come over here and check up on Zach. It was Tatty's job. She was his mother, whether they were partners or not. Banging on the door he also realised what was getting to him – above and beyond the wind and sleet as harsh as sandpaper. This place gave him the creeps. Big time.

'Zach?' Frank shouted. 'Open up.' There was still no reply, as the lethal sea air tightened around Frank's neck. He needed to get himself a scarf and a bobble hat. Howie was into beanies, like all the kids. The only garb Frank had ever cared about was shoes. A good pair of well-made shoes kept you on your feet, your toes. Like fuck. At least he'd never tried to be anything other than what he was, dressing this way or that. Except in the last few months, he supposed. Some big-shot executive, with a Lexus.

He put his shoulder against the door and nothing budged. He then tried the handle. Zach hadn't even locked the fucking thing. The rotten door, in its rotten frame, creaked open easily enough. Just a stone's throw from the surging, grey North Sea, Frank couldn't help thinking that some people had funny ideas about entertainment.

'Zach?' he called again, his eyes growing accustomed to the dimness, and hating even more forcefully everything they were taking in.

The place stank of damp and bad drains, and something chemical, though not cordite at least. But puke too – yeah, that was it. The smell of vomit grew as he ventured further into the dump. It was little warmer inside than out. No heating seemed to be on, if there was such a thing in the lodge.

'Zach, where the fuck are you?'

Someone had made an effort to tidy the room up. This was a surprise. 'Zach?' Frank checked his watch. It had gone nine in the morning. Tatty would be ringing him again any second. The kid had to be conked somewhere. Was he using a nearby caravan for his shut-eye? He had his pick. Would have been a good security measure as well, presuming the twerp was using the park as his distribution hub. Frank didn't fancy having to go outside to check every bloody static, door to door. It would take hours.

He didn't have to, he suddenly saw, edging into the bathroom at the very back of the lodge. 'Zach?' He'd seen the lad's feet and legs first, tidy trainers for him, and a pair of skinny slacks that weren't ripped and frayed. Then he saw the rest of him. He was lying on the floor, half curled, next to the tub, with his head at the foot of the toilet.

By the colour of his face, his lips, Frank knew he wasn't quite dead. He could see no blood, no obvious injuries. Believing he could also see the slight rise and fall of Zach's chest, Frank edged further in. It was a small, decrepit bathroom. This was no place for Zach to have passed out in. There was puke all over the toilet. Frank began to gag with the smell of it.

Crouching, he found himself having to reach across Zach to the side of the bath to stop himself from falling into the slosh. 'What the hell would your mother have to say if she saw you like this?' he muttered.

Gently he began shaking Zach's shoulder, seeing as he did so more of Zach's face and the puke drying around his mouth. Surely he hadn't OD'd, the idiot? Though that's what it looked like. How many times had Frank told him not to mix business with pleasure? If this was what kids today thought pleasure was.

Frank brushed Zach's cheek, wanting to warm him, warn him, love him. Yeah, Zach drove him nuts, but he was Rich's and Tatty's youngest, and like all youngest sons he was reckless and wild and wanting to live on the edge of things. Maybe he and Tatty expected too much. For the briefest of moments Frank wondered whether he'd become too aloof, too distant, too like Rich, now he was an executive, and not just the guy who served and protected.

A good chunk of the side panel of the bath had been kicked in. It looked as if Zach had been trying to reach further under the bath before passing out.

'Hey, Zach, wake up, damn you.' Frank was shaking him harder. Frank stumbled, found he had to get on his knees, sod the puke. He could feel the blood racing a tad quicker around his massive old frame. He put his ear to Zach's mouth, tried to hear whether he was breathing and check it wasn't just the light in the tiny cubicle doing something weird with the colour of Zach's skin.

He was certain he could pick out faint puffs of air coming from Zach's mouth against the background silence of a caravan park in the depths of the winter. Unless it was the sea he was hearing, relentlessly washing onto the shore on the other side of the dunes.

'Zach,' he said yet again, shaking him more vigorously and turning him onto his back. Frank could now see bruising on his left cheek, his temple, on that side of his head. There was no sign of any powder, spent wraps or drug paraphernalia, but there was whitish froth around Zach's mouth, with the flecks of puke. His breath smelt like the Yare after a storm.

Frank slapped the boy's right cheek gently, thinking that if he didn't come to soon he'd have to call for medical assistance. He was wracking his brain. There were names, contacts, friendly doctors he'd used before, though not for a good while.

He decided he needed to get Zach out of the bathroom, get him into what stood for a lounge, where he must have been dossing on and off. Hooking his hands under Zach's armpits, he half lifted him, half dragged him, managing to get him into the main room more easily than he'd imagined. There was nothing to him. He'd become rag and bone. The boy needed feeding up.

In the lounge, Frank dropped him on what appeared to be a single bed, shoved into a corner and covered in old rugs and a jacket or two. As he did so his phone started up and Zach's eyelids fluttered open, then as quickly shut.

'Hey,' Frank said. 'Anyone home?'

Ignoring his phone, he attempted to open Zach's eyes with his fingers. He wasn't used to saving people, he realised, but shutting out their lights for good. That was so much easier. This was bloody hard. On what stood for a bed in the shocking room, Frank had a better view of Zach's face. He'd been swiped – with something other than a hand. A pistol?

'OK, buddy,' Frank said, still trying to prise open Zach's eyes, having waited for his phone to shut up, 'who hit you?'

Frank slapped Zach's better cheek with some force, and anger – anger at himself as much as with the boy. He'd let Tatty down. They both had.

'Why'd you do that?' Zach muttered, his eyes suddenly wide open. 'Frank?'

'Zach? You in there?'

'What the fuck?'

Frank brushed back the hair from Zach's forehead. 'I found you passed out in the bog. How long had you been in there?'

Zach started shivering. 'Man, it's fucking freezing. Get me a blanket, will you?'

'You're lying on them.' Frank reached over, found a jacket of some description, chucked it onto Zach, his skinny body. 'Your mother's been worried sick – we all have.'

'I've been here.' Zach tried to sit up. Quickly he seemed to think better of it and lay back down. 'Where am I?'

'The caravan park, in the lodge,' Frank said, dismissively. 'Where'd you think?'

'Where is everyone? Abir?' Though curled on top of the bed, Zach was managing to shake his head, while his body began to tremble.

'Your driver?'

'Yeah.' Zach's voice was strengthening. 'A couple of other guys were here as well.'

'Who hit you, Zach? That's some bruise you've got developing.'

Zach closed his eyes, feigned sleep for a few seconds. Gave up pretending. 'There was a difference of vision,' he said. 'Fucking Abir – fucked everything up. He hasn't taken my car, has he?'

'No, your car's out the front.'

'Where's he gone, then?' He was trying to sit up again. 'He owes me. Man, my head's killing me.'

Zach needed sorting out, that was for sure, though Frank didn't think he needed medical attention. 'Where's your phone?' he asked.

'Why?'

'Because I want to see what the fuck you've been up to.'

'That's my business, Frank.'

'Technically, Zach, this park is Goodwin Enterprises' business, which makes it my business. You're only here because you begged your mum and me. So we leave you to it and look what happens? Where'd you keep the drugs?'

'There're no drugs here. Not now.'

'Abir's run off with them, has he?'

'If only, mate.'

'I'm going to ring your mum,' said Frank, 'tell her you're safe and sound, then I'm going to beat the shit out of you until you tell me everything that's been going on in your stinking life – ever since you came back from Ibiza.' Frank stood. 'You take a fucking mile, don't you? The police came looking for you yesterday as well, by the way. Knocked on your front door. Sam had to deal with them. Any idea what that might have been about?'

Zach shook his head dumbly, as Frank only expected. He then marched across the room, went out of the side door, not wanting Zach to hear the conversation, not sure what he was going tell Tatty anyway. He should have been meeting her in person about now.

Outside, standing under the carport in Arctic air that wasn't remotely invigorating, Frank glanced across the sweeping entranceway that led up to the lodge. The nearest statics were over to his right. Peering round the corner of one was a face, a head, set against the dirty white corrugated structure.

Frank put his phone away, relieved of the distraction. He wasn't one for difficult conversations. Actions suited him better. He began walking towards the figure, was soon trotting as the person ducked out of sight. Frank had a good idea who it was – Abir – and a stupid idea that he was as young and fit and fast.

No, he wasn't. 'Doddery old fool,' he gasped, increasing his pace.

Sam parked on Fenner Road, having slotted in next to her mum's car, which was bang outside the entrance to the Smokehouse, nose first. A few other cars were lined up a short distance away – Ben's and a couple she didn't recognise. There was no sign of Frank's car, thank God. She wasn't feeling in the mood for him today.

She got out of her car gingerly, her legs feeling unusually stiff. It was absolutely freezing, with wind funnelling down the cobbled street like a demon. At least it had stopped snowing. Stepping onto the kerb she tried to shake some blood into her limbs, her fingers. It had taken for ever to get here this morning, this week. First, she couldn't decide whether she would actually go in, then she couldn't face the idea of being stuck at home again, all day, worrying that the police might show up at any time asking for Zach, probably with a warrant this time.

Or for Ben to bang on at her about doing nothing. She was every bit as useful to the organisation as he was, she believed. He was just out to prove himself as quickly as possible, given that he'd been sacked, and dumped, and had had to come running home begging for help.

Getting dressed for the office was another ordeal. In London, in her old world – which she wasn't sacked from, but had left voluntarily – it had been easy, there was a uniform of sorts. In Yarmouth it was pick and mix. Nobody got it right, which, she was beginning to think, served as some sort of analogy for the whole town. It had an identity crisis.

Finally, once out of the house this morning, she'd been stuck in the most horrendous traffic. Gorleston was snarled up from the high street all the way to Southtown Road. Because it was a Friday? The police were everywhere. Bodies were being found everywhere too, according to the news. Two more in Gorleston last night, only a short stroll from Marine Parade. They'd been shot dead in their car, on a quiet Thursday evening – suspected drug dealers, so they were saying. She couldn't believe it, and only hoped that Zach wasn't caught up in anything like that again. Whatever he was he was not a murderer. She wasn't so sure about Frank.

She should have left town after her miscarriage, after Michael had disappeared, and gone back to London. Or fled the country altogether. There were certain things she couldn't think too hard about in Gorleston, in Yarmouth, in her world here, otherwise her very existence, she had the feeling, would start to crumble. It was like she was in limbo, just hanging on, incapable of making the next move. All she had was her family – and look at them.

With more force than was necessary she pushed opened the fancy inner glass doors, etched with the building's name, not the firm's – another identity crisis in the making she reckoned, not that her mother would admit to it – and crossed into the sparse ground-floor lobby. It was a large space for just one reception desk and four Eames Barcelona chairs. The walls were bare brick, while everything else was glass, chrome, more leather and wood. A couple of minimalist standard lamps were trying hard to add a warm glow.

Celine was sitting behind the desk, staring at her.

'Hi,' Sam said casually, walking straight towards the lifts. 'Everything OK?' By the lifts, Sam looked over her shoulder. Of course everything wasn't OK. It didn't take a genius to work that one out. Celine was no genius. She was still staring at Sam, now opened mouthed. 'I'm Sam,' said Sam, pressing the up button. 'I do work here.' Sam couldn't remember the last time she'd actually been in, though the last time she was certain that Celine had been sitting in the exact same spot. 'Sam Goodwin,' she added robustly, before the lift door opened and she stepped inside, taking a second to remember what floor her office was on. Two, that was it, the floor below the executive suites, as her mum had dared to call her and Frank's offices.

It was absurd that Frank had all that space up there. She couldn't imagine what he did in there except pick his nose and polish his shoes.

Stepping out onto the second floor she had to think for a moment which way to go. Ben's office was somewhere on this floor, as well as space for Zach, plus auxiliary office staff, for when they needed them. For when the super casino was up and running. As if. Goodwin Enterprises was a particularly lean operation, her mother liked to say. Best kept to the family.

Venturing further from the lift, the only sound Sam could now hear, she decided, was the calm before the storm. No one knew she was in the building except Celine. She pushed open a door; it was to an empty store cupboard. She closed it quickly and carried on trying not to think about such empty, confined spaces and all the uses and misuses for them. She was becoming spooked with the unfamiliarity. Zach had told her that Frank had once smashed someone's kneecap with a bowling ball. He'd also, apparently, pulled someone's eyeball out with a corkscrew.

The windows running along one side of the hallway looked onto the backs of a row of old industrial buildings, one of which was now a brewery. It didn't look as if anything was brewing right now – except trouble, a voice in her head reminded her. She couldn't decide whose voice it was – one of the dead they'd found?

A heavy white sky was sinking onto the nearby roofs and spilling down between the buildings, the yawning cracks. It looked as if it might snow again. Now she was safely here, inside such a strong old building, Sam wanted it to snow, and for the snow to settle and make everything pristine and beautiful.

She couldn't remember the last time it had really snowed. Perhaps a couple of times when she was a child. There was a vague memory of snow even settling on the beach. How weird it was watching the waves tumble onto a white shoreline. There were hills on Gorleston Golf Course, where her friends had gone sledging with their parents. No parent had ever taken her or her siblings sledging. They'd had to fend for themselves.

Another door led to a large space, ready for desks and chairs. The third door opened into Ben's office, must have been. His laptop was on the desk, though what looked like one of Zach's hoodies was on the back of the chair. The room smelt of Zach as well – a sticky sweet and sour smell, like an opened packed of Twizzlers that had gone off, combined with the reek of ripe weed. Surely Ben hadn't started smoking weed?

She'd braved the weather and endured all the traffic, and where was Ben to recognise the fact? She got out her phone, rang him. At some point it went to answerphone. 'Ben, I'm here, in the office, your office – all set for a hard day's work. Where are you?'

Only after she'd finished leaving her message did she notice that his phone was in fact on his desk – obviously on silent. She walked round the desk, another glass-topped minimalist thing, and sat, feeling the seat sink expensively. She'd made a terrible mistake. She didn't want to be here. She shouldn't have come in.

His screen showed her missed call. It showed a couple of other missed calls, as well, from names she didn't recognise. She couldn't scroll down further because she was locked out.

There was no paperwork on the desk, except a copy of the *Great Yarmouth and Gorleston Mercury*. It was a week out of date. There was no mention of course of any bodies being found.

'Sis?'

She looked up to see Ben walk into his office.

'You do still have your own space, don't you?' he said, cross. 'Your own desk?'

'Fuck, you sounded like Zach again. This is doing my head in. And what are you wearing? Are you trying to look like him as well?'

Ben was no longer wearing his suit, but a pair of unflattering jeans and old trainers, and a T-shirt that Sam was certain was Zach's. The other stuff was probably his too. She hadn't seen him leave the house earlier. He must have run upstairs to get changed. What was he playing at? Trying to be something he wasn't – like all of them?

'Mum's in her office,' he said, ignoring her question. 'I'd steer clear. I tried to firm up some details to do with the wind-farm business, getting the brokerage terms straight, following my meeting with the council yesterday.'

'Straight?' said Sam. 'If we're offering these packages, where does brokerage even come in to it?'

'Goodwin Financial Services will be an expansive operation. Not that Mum gives a monkey's right now. She's still beside herself about Zach. Is he all she ever cares about?'

'Yeah,' said Sam. 'You know that. Why not try me?' She stayed sitting at the desk. 'I am a lawyer. That is why I'm here. We're all working for the family business now, aren't we?'

'All of us? When you turn up, Sis.' Ben's laugh was more like a dirty snigger. 'Anyway, you're sitting at my desk. Do you mind moving your arse?'

'Is that the way to talk to a female colleague? I could make an official complaint. Get HR onto you.' She smiled. Ben had slipped into his new role in days, she reckoned. However, she'd always thought of him as the most like their dad. Zach had traits, though he was too wild, careless, vain. She supposed she was just timid. Did what anyone expected of her.

Sighing, she stood, walked round the desk, found another chair, stiff and hard and unused to visitors. It had been a while, she had to admit to herself, since she'd sat down ready to be briefed.

Ben had barely got comfortable before he was standing up again, looking over Sam's shoulder, looking livid. 'Celine, it's usual to knock before coming into someone's office,' he said.

'Not round here,' said Sam, catching Ben's eye, then turning to see Celine by the door. Something was up.

'What is it?' he said.

'There're two men down in reception,' Celine said, breathlessly, 'who want to see Mrs Goodwin.'

'And?' said Ben.

'She's not here,' Celine said. 'She's not answering either her office line, or her mobile. I've just been up. Her office is empty.'

'She was here only a few minutes ago,' said Ben. 'I was with her in her office.'

'She's not in the building now,' said Celine, adamant. She was shaking her head in an odd way, as if trying to communicate some other message.

'That's impossible,' said Ben.

'Mr Adams – Frank – he's not in either.'

'Who are they?' said Sam. 'The men in reception. Police?'

Celine was shaking her head in an even more disturbing way. She had shoulder-length, mousy-coloured hair, and a normally pale, vacant face, which was beginning to come alive. 'They don't look like police to me.'

Sam wasn't sure the coppers who'd come to the door yesterday evening had looked much like police either – they were too young, boyish.

Celine stayed by the entrance to Ben's office, as if she were afraid to go back down to the reception. Ben stepped round his desk, walked towards her, saying, 'Who do they look like?'

Celine shrugged. Sam felt for her. She was not a match for her mum's last PA. Sian had had a certain style, and guts – the poor thing.

Ben stepped over to the nearest window. His office looked down onto the street, as did all the office space on this floor, with the corridor running along the back of the building. Sam watched him clock something, then pull his head back sharply.

'There's a massive white jeep thing parked up,' he said, leaning closer to the window again. 'A Hummer. Can't see whether there's anyone inside.' He moved along the window. 'Yes, there is, driver's seat. Big bloke.'

'There're two other big blokes downstairs,' said Celine faintly. 'I don't think they want to be kept waiting.'

Ben had reached for his phone, was tapping away.

'Who are you calling?' Sam asked.

'Mum,' he said.

'I have tried ringing her,' Celine said. 'She's not answering. She's not here, I'm telling you. I've checked everywhere.'

Sam didn't think she could have had time to check the whole building.

'Even though her car's here,' Celine said. 'I don't get it.'

'It's a big building,' said Ben. He was looking back outside, holding his phone to his ear. 'Actually, her car's not here now,' he said. 'Not out the front where it was earlier.'

'It was there when I looked,' said Celine. 'I promise. She couldn't have left the building without me noticing, and just driven off. I do sit by the entrance.'

'Perhaps she doesn't want to face those guys,' Sam said, believing that there were at least two other exits at street level. It would have been easy enough to have slipped out. However, something much more troubling had started niggling away at the back of her head.

'Was she aware these men were here?' Ben said. 'Must have been, I guess. What do they want?'

'That's not obvious?' said Sam, the niggling turning into a concrete thought – as solid as a paving slab. She couldn't believe it. Her mum had scarpered, leaving her children behind.

Except her mum wouldn't have known she was there. Sam perked up a little at that idea, only to realise that of course her mum would have known – she'd have seen her car, when she was making her escape. This wasn't like her at all. Sam didn't understand what was going on.

She didn't think that Ben did either. He looked flustered, a bit panicked. It had all to be so new to him.

'Well, I'm going down to see what they want,' he said, marching out of the room.

Sam looked at Celine, who had begun to shake with fear. She knew what had happened to her predecessor, of course – a young woman who'd had the misfortune to get involved with a Goodwin. Sam doubted she was any less scared herself. But she mustered some energy, and anger, from somewhere, and turned on her heels in disgust at herself, her family. They were always abandoning each other. 'Ben,' she shouted, heading for the door, having thought that he was at least the one reliable sibling she had, 'wait for me.'

Out in the corridor, with no Ben in sight, she had to think for a second which way to go. This building really was a maze – no modern finishes or expensive revamps could disguise the fact. It was worse than a maze. Despite the rows of windows and the solid brick and concrete walls and floors it suddenly felt like a deathtrap.

She didn't have to think which way to go for too long because raised voices were coming from her right, along the corridor, just around the corner. She stepped that way, only to pull up before she could be seen. She didn't like what she was hearing one terrifying bit.

## 12

Tatty was set on shooting the next set of lights, defying the traffic, the one-way system, the weather, while her heart was back in the Smokehouse. Why the hell had Sam decided to come to work today, of all days? She put her foot down, then as quickly braked.

What had Frank said was the best course of action, when all else was lost? He'd either used the word distraction, or deviation. She wasn't sure of the difference. Her father had spoken Polish for much of her childhood – when he'd been around. She couldn't remember a word of it now. Didn't want to.

She'd got as far as the model village on the front, all the while urging the Hummer to appear behind her. Or suddenly in front of her to block her off. She didn't care which, as long as it was there, and not back at the Smokehouse, where her children were. She'd practically waved at the driver before she'd got into her Merc and sped off. The dunce appeared not to have taken the bait.

South Beach was devoid of traffic doing anything other than killing time. A handful of pedestrians were out braving the freezing air – people waiting to die from natural causes, being hurried on by their pets.

Tatty's phone was on the passenger seat, remaining silent. Frank was still not answering. He should have been in the office ages ago, once he'd swung by the caravan park, having sought Zach out. Now she had Frank's mess to deal with, all on her own. Except it wasn't on her own. She'd just put her children in terrible jeopardy. She practically burst into tears.

OK, she might have told Frank that she wanted the Ocean Rooms, the Pier View, that part of Gorleston under her control, but there had to be a more diplomatic way of doing things, didn't there, than shooting two young men dead while they were sitting in their car?

Presuming Frank was responsible. He was meant to be her partner, wasn't he? Couldn't they have discussed this first, exactly what he was planning to do? Why'd he have to move so fast? Frank would say that the less she knew the less likely he was to incriminate her. That wasn't the point. This was strategic. Besides, she was nobody's accessory, never had been, never would be. Nor was she anybody's business partner.

She yanked down hard on the steering wheel, making a U-turn in front of Wellington Pier. As she accelerated south back towards the Smokehouse, her phone filled the sense of emptiness. She reached over, grabbed the device, not slowing, not seeing the screen, who was calling her, remembering vaguely that the Bluetooth hook-up only worked if the radio was on. She hated this new world of technology as much as the old world of thuggery.

'Yes?' she said.

'Mum?'

'Zach?'

'Who'd you think it is?' he said.

'You OK? Where've you been? We've been worried sick. Is Frank with you?' The Pleasure Beach, on her left, went by in a flash of long-forgotten fun.

'Yes,' he said, 'Frank's here.'

That was something, she supposed. 'Where? Where are you?' She was now passing the land for the super casino. It was as empty and undeveloped as ever – a patch of scrub, once used as an overspill car park, and some tufts of a few half-baked dunes. The frozen North Sea swallowed the horizon beyond.

'I'm at the caravan park, in the lodge. It's freezing. Frank's fallen over, done his hip in or something. He's in a lot of pain.'

'I need him right now,' she said. Salmon Road was fast approaching. 'At the Smokehouse.'

'He can barely move, Mum. It's his fault. Thought he was younger than he is. And those stupid shoes he wears? Man, they've no grip.' Was Zach daring to laugh?

'I don't believe this,' said Tatty. 'What about you? Where've you been? The police came looking for you yesterday evening.' The sleet seemed to have somehow flooded her thinking. Everything was a blizzard, a white-out.

'Is that right? No idea what that'd be about.'

'Nothing to do with what went on by the Ocean Rooms last night – you better bloody promise me.' Despite knowing that the timing didn't work, her frantic mind couldn't stop making links, connections. Drawing the worst. She didn't know anything any more. Not least who to trust. She wanted to be far away. For the first time in months she wanted a pill. She needed a pill.

'What are you talking about?' said Zach.

'Two men getting shot – dead. In Gorleston. It's all over the news.'

'Really? In Gorleston? First I've heard of it. Haven't checked the media this morning though. I haven't been feeling great, to tell the truth. Frank's said nothing about it.'

Well he wouldn't, would he, Tatty thought. She needed to give Zach more credit, of course she did, and to stop being so bloody suspicious of her youngest son. But as that stupid saying went, old habits die hard. There was still a swirl of sleet inside her head. 'I hope you're telling the truth – I am your bloody mother.'

'Cheers. Who'd you take me for? I saw my girlfriend being shot in the chest, at like point blank range. Blood spraying everywhere. You think I'd ever go near a gun on purpose, let alone use one? I know what damage they can do. Get it?' He sounded close to tears.

'Sorry,' she whispered.

'I've been at the lodge since yesterday lunchtime. Not that there haven't been a few problems over here, but that's another story, Jackanory. Frank's in a bad way, though, Mum, honest. He said I should call you.'

'Put him on – I need to speak to him. NOW.' She was turning into Fenner Road, not knowing how she was going to handle the men who'd got out of the Hummer. But she had to do something, whatever it took. Not for her sake – she didn't care about that of course – but her for kids.

Charm, feminine charm, maybe she could she use that. Play to the old rules. It had been extraordinary how weak at the knees she'd been able to make men, some men – at least until they'd got what they'd wanted. Then they weren't weak. However, she wanted Frank here, like twenty minutes ago.

What the hell? The Hummer wasn't there. It hadn't followed her as she'd raced away, and now it wasn't sitting brashly on the street, bang outside her offices, like some ugly joke, either. The only vehicles parked nearby were Sam and Ben's modest vehicles. Celine got the bus to work. Her stomach flipped, while the storm in her head took on a new intensity. 'Frank?'

'Tatty?' came a feeble voice.

She stopped the car. Took a breath, knowing she should never have left the building. Not for the first time in the last year and a half she felt completely out of her depth. Felt tears of frustration and fear well once more as she watched the view out of the window blur. 'Your mates who drive a Hummer paid the office a visit,' she said. 'When you should have been here.'

'Shit.'

'Yes – shit.' She got out of the car, clutching the phone to her face for dear life. 'Any idea what they might have wanted?'

'You spoke to them?'

'No. I didn't think they'd come over for a cosy chat. I saw them arrive from my office window and decided that the best way to get them away from here would be to drive off, thinking they'd chase me. I didn't want to put Ben, or

Celine, in any danger. Or Sam. I didn't know she'd come into the office until I'd left the building and saw her car sitting there. I was even more determined to get them out of there, and after me. Seeing as you weren't in situ to protect us.'

'But they didn't follow you, did they?'

'How do you know?'

'Because they're violent bastards, who've been around the block a few times.'

'Meaning?'

'Where are you now?'

'They've gone, Frank. The Hummer's gone. I'm back at the Smokehouse, having driven halfway across town. They're nowhere in sight.'

'Panic over then.'

'Just get here now,' she shouted, not having it in her to explain to him that she was still out on the pavement, with a ferocious winter crashing from the sky, and that her mother's intuition was telling her that while the men might have gone everything was not at all right.

'I can't drive,' Frank said. 'It feels like I've broken my hip.'

'Get Zach to drive you.'

'He's not well also,' Frank said.

'You got us into this mess, Frank.'

'Not sure what you mean by that,' he said.

'Get here.'

'There's someone one else kicking around who might be able to help us out, though,' he said.

'Why am I even talking to you?' She ended the call,

pocketed her phone and pushed open the glass doors to the Smokehouse. Celine was not at her desk, though the doors had been left unlocked. She was not meant to leave her post without securing the entrance first. That girl was so bloody dim.

## 13

Not wanting to wait for the lift, Tatty took the stairs two at time, aware that she wasn't armed. She'd promised herself that she'd never use a gun again in anger – that was the pact she'd made all those months ago, for her children being safe. However, this was different. She needed a gun to keep them safe, alive. You only got so far using your intelligence, your charm – your sex. Force could only be met with force. Frank's way.

The first floor was vacant, as far as she knew, and she carried on up the next flights of stairs. It was floor two she cared about, where Ben and Sam's offices were, and the computer room for Zach.

By the time she'd reached that floor, she'd convinced herself that this was not a business for Ben, Sam or Zach. For anyone under the age of – she didn't know what – fifty? Which would include her on a good day.

She should never have got them involved. She should have sold the bloody business, whatever it really amounted to, straight after Rich had died. They could have kept the villa in Ibiza, not that that property seemed to have done Zach any good. Perhaps it was because she hadn't been there last summer to look after him, guide him.

Natural white light was flooding the second-floor corridor, pounding through the long row of renovated windows, and as she rushed along, shouting breathlessly, 'Ben, Sam?', she had the eeriest of feelings that she was in some sort of channel, or tunnel, the whiteness getting brighter as she progressed. It was like she was heading towards the gates to heaven – or hell. It would have to be hell. There was no way anyone sitting up there on a cloud would be looking down on her too kindly.

She passed the door to an empty store cupboard, which Nathan had once joked could be turned into a panic room. 'I could make it bomb proof,' he'd said, 'with a hotline to the local cop shop. Or maybe that wouldn't be appropriate,' he'd added. 'A heavy of your choice?' Too late, she thought as she reached the door to Ben's office. It was open. Wide open. 'Ben, Sam?' she said again, sharply. 'Celine?'

More of the white light was tumbling into the office, piling across the polished bare wood floor, until it hit the glass desk. No one was sitting at the desk. The room was empty.

Tatty felt her eyes widen, as her feet were glued to the floor. She couldn't move. There were signs of Ben's things on his desk: a mobile, an old newspaper. The air smelt overpoweringly male as well, like a sports-club changing room, she couldn't help thinking. Urgently, she scanned every centimetre of the room, finding she could at least move her head.

There was no sign of a struggle, or any blood. There

were no bodies. She gulped some air. Instinctively, she felt her jacket pocket for a weapon, uselessly weighed her Hermès in the crook of her left arm. It was far too light.

Turning to leave the room something in the far corner caught her eye. It was a drab, light brownish-coloured shape, in the dimmest part of the room, half camouflaged by the bare brickwork. A jacket? Ben always used to fling his clothes on the floor of his bedroom. They all did, except Sam. She'd always been careful with her clothes, her possessions.

Tatty took a step that way, finding her feet weren't stuck. Then she practically sprung forward. The jacket appeared to be shielding a crouched body, trying to fit into the tightest of corners.

'Celine?' Tatty spotted hair, Celine's mousy, straight, shoulder-length hair. 'Celine?' she repeated, bending down and gently grabbing the girl's shoulder. Slowly Celine turned her head.

'Mrs Goodwin?' Her voice wavered, her eyes wide with shock and disbelief.

'Celine?' Tatty leaned closer. 'Are you all right? What're you doing here?'

'Have they gone?' she said.

Tatty shook her head, but knowing. 'Who?'

'Those men.'

'Where's Sam, Ben?'

'I don't know.'

'Are you hurt?'

Celine shook her head now. 'No.'

'You can get up,' Tatty said, standing back. Slowly Celine got to her feet, faced Tatty. Her hands, her arms were shaking. Her face was as pale as the weather outside. Inside the building, however, it couldn't have been hotter. Tatty had ensured that Nathan put in the best possible heating system. She hated being cold. But she didn't know what temperature she felt now. She was numb. 'Where are they, my children?'

Tatty was on the verge of slapping Celine when she finally opened her mouth. 'I thought they were going to come in here and shoot me,' she said. 'Like, you know . . .'

'They had guns?'

Celine shrugged her underdeveloped shoulders. Rich used to say the locals were either malnourished or over-weight – he was technically obese. At that moment Tatty hated everything about Yarmouth, Gorleston, her life – her past, more than anything.

'They were shouting, out in the corridor.'

'Who? These men? Sam? Ben?'

The girl nodded.

'Where are they now – my kids, Celine?'

'I don't know.' Celine began to cry, the stream of tears immediately playing havoc with her thick eyeliner and heavy foundation.

'You let them in,' Tatty said, suddenly wanting to accuse her, punish her, blame someone else, anyone. But it wasn't Celine's fault of course. None of this.

'There were two of them,' she said, with a little more conviction. 'They were huge. What could I do?'

'Nothing.' Tatty sighed. 'You saw them leave, these men?' Tatty needed to search the rest of the building. She needed Frank to hurry up. Shane's name came to her like a message from God. He rescued people for a living, didn't he? She searched her mac pockets for her phone.

'I was trying to hide,' Celine said. 'I didn't want them to find me.'

'What about Sam, Ben? For God's sake,' Tatty said, scrolling through her contacts. 'The police,' she said, 'why didn't you ring them?'

'I didn't want to be heard,' Celine said. 'We're not meant to call the police, anyway, are we?'

Tatty paused, finger brushing the screen. It was true – Rich had always made it abundantly clear that whatever the problem a Goodwin Enterprises employee was never allowed to call the police. They had to go to the boss first. The police, like HMRC, all the authorities, were the enemy. She'd effectively continued the rule. She'd castigated Sam only yesterday for opening the door to a couple of coppers. She wished she hadn't. The police had more resources than she did. 'This is a fucking crisis,' she said. 'All rules go out of the book.'

Firemen weren't police, anyway. She'd been in the Smokehouse only hours ago with Shane. He'd come running in an instant. She lifted her finger as a chill wind swept through the office. It felt as though the weather had broken through the old brick walls, the triple-glazed windows. Nothing could keep Great Yarmouth at bay for long. Tatty looked over her shoulder. Couldn't believe what she was seeing. 'Sam?'

'They've taken Ben,' Sam said, stumbling towards her.

'What?' Tatty looked from Sam to Celine, then scanned every spare corner of Ben's office once more, glanced back at her screen, stabbed at the red icon. At least Sam was here, standing in front of her, alive. Her precious, fragile daughter, who'd already met enough tragedy in her short life. She reached for her.

'I had to hide in a cupboard,' Sam was saying in her arms. 'I thought they'd find me. I've never been so sacred. Ben went to talk to them, and they started having an argument in the corridor – Ben and these two thugs. They were pushing him, and saying he had to go with them, and I should have said something, done something, Mum. They dragged him away and I just hid in this cupboard. I didn't even have my phone on me, and then I heard you walk up the stairs and call our names and I didn't know whether they'd all gone, whether they might take you too. I should never have hidden. I should have helped Ben more.' She burst into tears.

Tatty couldn't stand it when anyone cried, let alone one of her children. 'It wasn't your fault,' she said, hugging Sam more tightly. 'I'd have done the same.' However, she didn't think she would. She would have intervened, put her body in the way. She wouldn't have cared whether she got shot, as long as her children survived.

Sam was a fraction taller, and not quite as slight, and Tatty wasn't sure she was providing much comfort. It was the same when she tried to hug either of her sons. They were so much bigger and stronger than she was, and Ben in particular had his father's build. But did he have his father's fight in him, his ruthlessness, his strength? She hoped so, her poor boy. He was going to need it.

'Did you hear anything else they said to him?' she asked, frantic now. 'Do you know why they were taking him?' Tatty had a mouthful of Sam's hair. She could feel her daughter shake her head.

'He's not in the building, is he?' Sam wailed, pulling away. 'Dead somewhere? Has their car gone?'

'Yes,' Tatty muttered.

'They must have taken him. Better that, I suppose, than killing him here.'

'We need to try to remain calm,' said Tatty, 'until we know what's what.' She'd never taken enough care of Ben, never showered him with enough love. It wasn't easy. He'd always been so awkward and stand-offish – reserved. Like her, she supposed. They were both cold fish.

'I saw them,' Celine's pitiful voice quietly declared.

Tatty removed herself from Sam and looked her shaking PA straight in the eye. 'What?'

'From the window, from here.' She pointed vaguely at the row of windows in Ben's office. 'I saw them push him into this big white car. Then I thought they were going to come back for me, so I hid.'

Breathing was meant to come naturally to people, wasn't it? Tatty thought. But she was struggling to take in enough air. Fear, rage and a catastrophic sense of failure were hammering on her chest.

'What are we going to do?' Sam said.

She needed Frank, Zach, all the advice and support in the world. Frank's special contacts, as always. She couldn't do this on her own, that was abundantly clear. Where the fuck were they? She'd never been able to do anything on her own. She was pleased she hadn't called Shane, because his sort of sparkly-eyed support was exactly what she didn't need right now. Besides, she didn't want him involved in her mess, for him to see her like this. She'd made enough trouble for the people she really loved.

She turned her back on Celine and Sam, and walked slowly, unsteadily towards the door, knowing time was critical, and that it had to be running out. She used to think that, compared with her late husband, she was the patient one. Perhaps she was beginning to understand that there was no such thing as patience in this world.

'Where are you going?' Sam called after her.

'My office,' she said, fixing her eyes straight ahead. It wasn't just about trying to remain calm, but seemingly in charge also. She was the boss.

Her phone started up as soon as she was in the corridor. Angling the screen away from the glare of a dull winter's day, she saw a withheld number appear, clear and defined. *Unknown.* Who wasn't, around here, really?

'Yes,' she said, answering.

'Tatiana Goodwin?' It was a woman's voice. Clipped, official sounding.

'Yes? Who is this?'

'My name's Britt Hayes. I'm the assistant chief constable, Norfolk Constabulary.'

'I know who you are,' Tatty said. 'You're Frank's mate.'

'We need to talk – privately, in person. As soon as possible.'

'Now's not a good time,' Tatty said, heading for the stairs, not the lift.

'I can help you.'

'Really?'

## 14

Something hard was jabbing him in the side, the kidneys. It had been there ever since he'd been shoved into the back of the car, and the stinking heavy had lumbered in next to him. Ben didn't need to look down to see what it was, and he didn't need the constant reminder that the guy next to him had serious personal hygiene issues.

The man hadn't said a word yet, just grunted. He was white, middle-aged, huge, but not in shape. Ben had a feeling he was also Eastern European. Had he said as much to Avani, she'd have accused him of being racist. She used the word when what she meant was xenophobic. Neither were great accusations to have chucked at you by your girl-friend, nevertheless.

Except Avani was no longer his girlfriend, and he came from Great Yarmouth, which wasn't the most politically liberal of British seaside towns. Plus, he was white, and it wasn't his fault that the thug driving the Hummer had a thick Eastern European voice, and an even thicker neck, which was sporting plenty of dark hairs, and a few chilling tattoos.

Ben would have liked him not to be here, anywhere near here. Though he wasn't sure it would have been fair to any country, any homeland, however corrupt and lawless, to have him sent back there either. The man should have been heading for a shallow grave, or the bottom of the North Sea – both places, Ben realised with a jolt, that he could end up in shortly.

'Where're we going?' he tried to say as calmly, yet firmly, as possible. He must have sounded like a private school kid whose voice had yet to break. Most of his education had been private, for what good that had done him in the end, unlike Zach who'd been turfed out of every school he'd attended. Zach wouldn't have got himself in such a situation. Ben should never have started arguing with them in the Smokehouse.

They seemed confused when he said his name was Ben, not Zach. Ben Goodwin. He was now wondering whether they might have let him go had he said he was Zach. He should have run a mile in any case when he first saw them – as his mother had. 'I said, where're we going?'

The man in the front passenger seat slowly turned his head, which was also on a monstrously thick neck, though this one was without tattoos, or so much dark hair. Ben was reminded of Frank. 'You're lucky you're still alive, the way your family treats mine,' he said. He wasn't Eastern European. His accent suggested he was from Essex, had smoked most of his life and was doubly proud of both facts.

'I've no idea what the hell you're talking about,' Ben said, wondering for a moment what Avani would have to say if she could see him now. Or his few remaining friends in the City. They'd be pissing themselves with laughter. He was about to piss himself with fear. Hard to believe that the man in the front had a family. Ben had turned his face back to the road ahead, while the stubby barrel of the gun was being jabbed harder into his side. Ben had no idea what kind of weapon it could be. He'd never seen a pistol in real life.

They'd been driving for some time, having headed out of Yarmouth on the Lowestoft Road. The windows were heavily tinted, and small for the heft of the vehicle, while the men next to him and up front were so large Ben was finding it hard to see where they were. It was dark and cramped in the back, like he was in one of those armoured vehicles – which he supposed it was meant to be – with steel plating and a platoon of troops in the back, as it trundled into a war zone. The seats were nothing to write home about, either.

He guessed they were at Hopton. The vehicle appeared to be passing the Holiday Village, continuing to Lowestoft. Pleasurewood Hills would be the next sight. Bundled up for winter, he supposed. It had never been much of an attraction for him in the summer.

He hadn't brought Avani to Yarmouth. She'd have hated it. But she'd have hated Lowestoft more. There were fewer immigrants, and it always felt even more right-wing. They were all populists here, except the place was about as unpopular as you could imagine. 'Where're we going?' he tried again.

'You'll see,' the chap from Essex proclaimed, without turning round this time.

'What do you want with me? What have I done? This is kidnap.' Ben was feeling increasingly angry. He wasn't going to be driven anywhere quietly. It wasn't like it was a fucking Uber. 'What's this got to do with me? I've only been working in Yarmouth for a few days. What's my family supposedly done to yours? What's your fucking name anyway?'

The next jab in his side was the worst yet. It made him groan loudly. 'Fuck's sake,' he wheezed, trying to shoulder some distance between the mute, stinking brute and himself.

'When people have such a callous disregard for human life they're always going to pay a heavy price,' said the man in the passenger seat. 'I'm not talking about the poor fuckers who lose their lives; I'm talking about the cunts who are still breathing. They're the ones we're after.' He glanced over his shoulder, smirking. 'Oh, not you, Zach – you won't be breathing for long. It's your mum we want to punish. She's the one who's going to have to live with her actions for the rest of her shallow life. You see, it's simple really, you take away from them what they hold most dear, then watch them suffer.'

'I'm not Zach,' Ben practically yelped. 'He's my brother. I told your friends.'

'Same mother.'

'What's she supposed to have done wrong?'

'You know.'

'No, I don't.'

'You want me to spell it out?' The guy didn't bother looking over his shoulder this time.

'Yes,' Ben said, 'you're going to have to.'

'You think this gives me pleasure?'

'Beats me.' Ben watched him slowly nod his head, on that monstrous neck. For a moment he half wondered whether he was related to Frank. Could he have been part of the family he'd been referring to? But his mum hadn't done anything to Frank, except promote him.

'She executed two of my men,' the man said.

'Executed?'

'Bullets in their heads, last night, in Gorleston basin, in case you've just flown in from Mars.' His voice had grown angrier and angrier.

'That was nothing to do with my mum,' Ben said hurriedly. 'She's a businesswoman. She's going to be the new head of the Regeneration Committee,' he added stupidly.

Gruff laughter came from more than one of the men up front.

'Who are you?' Ben asked, pleaded. 'There's been a big mistake.'

'You can say that again – the things we've done for your family.'

The vehicle was now taking a number of sharp corners. Mini-roundabouts? A convoluted way to a dark backstreet where no doubt a lock-up would be waiting, or a quay and boat to take him out to sea to be dumped.

The jabs in the side kept coming as well as the swerves. Ben didn't have his seatbelt on. Neither did the man next to him. The two in the front did though. It seemed an extraordinarily futile gesture.

'I'm sure we can work something out,' said Ben, trying to calm himself. But he couldn't be certain his mum, or

Frank, had nothing to do with the murders in Gorleston last night. Surely not?

'We'll get what we want,' the man said, 'you can count on that.' He turned his head Ben's way once more.

'Which is what, exactly?'

'Like I said. Oh, and some more territory, if you are asking. Only what we deserve. You want to suddenly take our land back, with no negotiation – after we had a deal? That's not how you do business. We'll show you how it works.'

Ben was struggling to comprehend, and he was meant to have the business brain, the mind for figures. This man's eyes were set too close together, and far too deep within his face – like shiny pinpricks of hate. They were oddly light blue. Ben didn't think he'd forget them in a hurry. 'How are you going to do that?' he asked, sick of being flung around in the back of an armoured SUV, sick of being prodded in the side. Sick rotten of this part of the world already. He should never have come back. He searched for the door handle, having a good idea what the man's answer would be. He urged the vehicle to slow down, with all his willpower. He was going to try to escape, that was what he was going to do. Had to do.

In his dreams.

'Message in a bottle,' the man said, brightly. 'Where you come in.' He laughed again. As did the driver.

You couldn't make them up, Ben thought. How the hell had he got into this fucking nightmare? If only he hadn't been sacked. He shouldn't have been sacked. He hadn't messed up – he was stitched up. He could see all too clearly his nasty new colleague going behind his back, informing the compliance officer of a couple of irregular trades. They were all at it. It was that sort of firm. Everyone had turned against him.

'My mum's done nothing wrong,' he said, knowing it was futile. 'She had nothing to do with whatever you think went on in Gorleston yesterday. Our business is in Yarmouth.'

'I don't think, matey, I know. You think you're the only operation with police contacts? Fuck you.'

Now it was getting even more confusing, and alarming, plus his mum had done something wrong, Ben reckoned. She'd carried on from where his father had left off, and he'd happily joined her only this week, knowing that there was no such thing as a compliance officer at Goodwin Enterprises. Just Frank. *Frank!*

'What contacts?' Ben said, remembering a conversation earlier today, in the kitchen, Sam telling him that his mum hadn't got home until the early hours, way after him. Though when she did turn up in the kitchen, breakfast time, she wasn't acting as if she'd just popped two guys.

The vehicle came to sudden halt. As far as Ben could see outside, his worst nightmares were coming true, one by one. They were in a backstreet, semi-industrial, largely deserted.

'Now what?' he said. A bullet in the back of the head was one thing, but he really didn't fancy being tortured. Exactly what sort of message did they have in mind? How would he fit in a bottle? He could guess.

'This is where the fun begins, chum,' the man said, and the driver joined him in another throaty chuckle.

The front doors were opened, freezing air rushed in, and Ben knew that he'd missed any chance to escape. 'What about Frank?' he said, as his door was opened from the outside. The driver was standing there, reaching in to grab his arm, while the man next to him shoved him out with the tip of his gun and the full weight of his shoulder. Ben felt sore all over and beaten up already. He struggled to stand, was pulled upright by one of the men.

The boss was squaring up to him now, out on a dismal piece of concrete. Ben realised he was an inch or two taller than this man. Not that it made any difference. He'd never felt so weak and powerless. A gull was squawking loudly nearby. Those nasty little blue eyes shifted from staring at Ben, and were concentrating on something behind him. Ben didn't want to know what.

'We haven't met properly,' Ben said, holding out his hand, thinking that his only option was to try to talk himself to safety. 'Ben Goodwin,' he added brightly. His hand remained hanging in the winter chill, until he dropped it by his side. 'Can you at least tell me who you are?'

The man was still focusing on something behind him. 'My friends call me Gary,' he said slowly. 'You can call me sir.' Another smoker's chuckle.

Ben heard what sounded like a garage door being opened. Heard a flap of wings as well. The gull wasn't the only living thing that wanted to be out of there. He saw it from the corner of his eye rise into the white sky, like a peace offering.

'Freeze your bollocks off out here.' Gary said. 'Let's go inside.'

Ben looked at his feet, more of the oily concrete. Looked back up at the man. 'Gary who?' he asked.

'Gary Winslow,' he said, smiling. 'Come on, let's get warm, shall we? My boys have got some new tools that they want testing.'

'What about Frank?' Ben said, not moving from his spot on the soiled concrete. Dirty machinery might once have sat there. 'Why didn't you pick him up? If anyone's got anything to do with what went on last night, it'll be him. He has contacts.'

'I don't think Frank'd be too happy to hear that – you snitching him up. You're not so loyal, you lot, are you? Not a tight crew at all. Tut, tut.' Gary smiled again, and pushed Ben hard in the chest. 'Are we going to have to drag you inside?'

Ben looked up and across the street at some low-rise semi-industrial buildings and a short strip of knackered terraced houses. He had no idea where in Lowestoft they were, or why it was quite so devoid of other people at this time of the day on a Friday – it might even still have been morning. He was going to kill Zach, if he ever got out of this. And Frank.

Gary didn't appear to have a gun on him. He was too large, in all the wrong places, to be in anything other than in a shocking state of fitness. He was wearing city shoes, black lace-ups, like Frank wore. Little grip on frozen, oily concrete. Was this some sort of gangster uniform when you got to the top?

Ben finally looked over his shoulder, knowing he'd never borrow Zach's clothes again, though pleased at least that he was wearing trainers.

A double garage door to one of the lock-ups was open. He couldn't see anything inside, only blackness seeping out. The other two men were must have slipped into it, and were preparing their tools. He looked back at Winslow, who couldn't have travelled far in his life – fifty, sixty miles or so from Essex. His attitudes couldn't have changed much over the decades, either. He'd only got older, fatter and meaner.

Ben could feel his heart thumping. Winslow had pulled his right arm back, looked like he was readying himself to belt Ben harder. What he wasn't ready for was for Ben to spring up onto his toes and snap his own head forward, catching Winslow smack on the bridge of his wide nose.

Standing back, getting his balance, Ben then kicked the stunned and crumpling oaf of a man as hard as could between the legs. Next, he swerved, tore across the forecourt and ran onto the road, not looking back. He'd never headbutted anyone in his life. It hadn't hurt as much as he might have expected. He'd never kicked anyone like that, either.

The road quickly came to an end. To his left there appeared to be more industrial estate in terminal decline. To his right it looked more promising, with what seemed to be a bigger junction a hundred metres or so on. A main road, perhaps, running laterally. There were more forecourts this way, some with cars parked on them. The busy end of the industrial estate, then.

However, a noise growing in volume and menace behind him told him that neither way would be much of an option. Directly ahead was a two-metre-high chain-link fence. Scrub was on the other side, and what appeared to be a low wall. No, it wasn't a wall, it was the quay edge of a narrow waterway. So they were near the sea, or the harbour. Not that this helped.

Fortunately the fence was knackered and, two posts along, the cross-hatched wire was curling away from the ground. With the noise of the Hummer becoming deafening, Ben charged for the gap, dived through it, scraping his stomach and tearing a chunk out of the back of the hoodie. He heard the vehicle screech to a halt and the doors open. He wasn't going to look round to see who was chasing him, whether Gary Winslow was in the land of the living and raging.

The ground was wildly uneven. Building rubble was interspersed with clumps of weeds and dark pools of oily water. The icy wind had picked up, coming straight off the sea – not that the air smelt too fresh. He couldn't hear footsteps behind him, but he could hear hard breathing, and not just his own.

Quickly he was on a quay edge. There was a considerable drop to the water, a couple of metres or so. The distance to the other side was not great, but there was nowhere he could see that he'd be able to clamber out. No steps, no ladders.

Looking over his shoulder, two things struck him. He hadn't been shot in the back already, even though one of the thugs had a pistol in his hand. Plus he didn't have a choice, except to dive in, if he didn't want to be recaptured.

It didn't seem like they wanted to kill him immediately. He had to be worth more alive than dead, didn't he? He looked at the water again knowing he had no more than a split second to make his decision. Death either way.

## 15

Tatty caught Sam's eye. Sam had remained standing, leaning against the far wall, ashen-faced and silent. 'There must be something we can do,' Tatty said. She looked at her desk phone, the empty glass top. She needed a manual, a crib sheet to be lying there pointing the direction. 'Come on, Frank, think.'

'These people are not stupid,' he said. His refrain of the day. He was sitting in one of the office chairs, though clearly not comfortably. Served him right.

'Really?' she said. 'They seem stupid enough to me, to have attempted this.'

'They'll get in touch with us. They've got currency.'

'Ben? Currency, is he?'

'It's how it is. I'm sorry.'

'What do they want?' This was what she couldn't quite get. 'Money?'

'To punish us – you. And then a better deal, probably.'

Tatty didn't want to ask him why, not in front of Sam. She didn't need to. 'How's this going to benefit their business?'

'These people are always looking to expand. It's how it works. Anyway, let's wait to see what exactly their demands are first.' He rubbed his forehead and shifted awkwardly in the chair. 'I need to get to a doctor, Tatty. I've done something really bad to my hip. I'm no use like this.'

'You can say that again.' Tatty pushed her desk chair back, stood. She had her own rendezvous, not that she was going to tell the others, least of all Frank. She needed to be so much better informed. Had no idea who she could trust. 'You need to keep this strictly between you and me,' the woman, the cop, had said on the phone. Tatty didn't know why she should believe her but, looking at Frank now, listening to him whine away like a great fat baby, knowing it was his fucking fault that Ben had been taken, she knew she had no option.

'Where're you going?' Frank said. He looked generally perplexed – his brow a recently ploughed field, ready for a new crop of sugar beet.

'I need to get out of here,' Tatty said. 'I need some air, space to think.'

'You do realise that these people aren't only interested in money, profit?' Frank said. 'They can be mean, violent, for the sake of it. It's how they operate. Force first, negotiation after. They want to show you they mean business – how tough they can be.'

'It's how you operate, isn't it,' Tatty mumbled, avoiding looking anywhere near Sam.

'They've all got something missing up here.' He tapped his head.

'Like you,' Tatty said, meaning it.

Frank sighed. 'Don't go running after them. They could be anywhere. We've already lost sight of Zach, and his driver – again. That boy, Tatty, never takes anything seriously. Not even the fact that his brother's been nabbed. I'm going to spare you the details of how I found him this morning. He should have learned his lesson by now. I give up.'

'You give up?' she said. 'Yes, you do, far too easily. You should never have let him out of your sight. Yesterday, the day before. And just now, too. Not just Zach but his brother and sister as well. Where were you when Ben was taken? Your job's to protect us. That's what you were employed to do.'

'Until you put me on the board, made me partner.' He shook his great head. 'You were here, Tatty. You have eyes.'

He had a point. Though what was also getting to her was the fact that Zach and his mate had only been in the Smokehouse for little more than five minutes before they scarpered – and in such circumstances. She thought Frank had Zach under control, that Zach listened to him. She should have known better, and locked Zach in. He'd always been one to run off the moment she raised her voice. However, this time his brother had been taken and this was a fullblown crisis. Zach could have at least hung around and offered to help. He had connections, had to have.

Not that he'd been the most loyal and loving sibling to Ben. And her youngest had looked dreadful this morning, paler than Sam, with a dirty bruise on the side of his head. He had something to hide from her, as always. However, she wasn't going to quiz Frank any further, or castigate him over Zach. That could come later. Ben was her priority, the son she'd never paid enough attention to. 'Zach'll have to look after himself,' she said.

'He's got his driver,' Frank said. '*He's* capable.'

'Because we know Zach isn't,' Tatty sighed.

'Look, it's no bad thing that Zach's out of the way – he's enough of a liability as it is. We don't want him stumbling across the gang, or vice versa, the mood they're in.'

'So how do we approach them?' Tatty said, nearing the door. 'Arrange to meet for a coffee?'

'Right now we're a little short of intel and effective backup,' Frank said.

'That's your department, isn't it?'

'Not so much any more,' said Frank, sounding like he was in real pain. 'My attention's been elsewhere, in the boardroom – strategising.'

'Fuck's sake.'

'We're not a street operation any more, that's how you wanted it. It's hard to keep track of what goes on unless you're out there, day to day.'

'You've made a mistake,' she said, remaining by the door, 'and got beyond yourself. I know what you've been doing.' She couldn't let him get away with this. The pomposity, the arrogance. He needed to be reminded of his station. The debt he owed the Goodwins.

He'd changed in the last few months. She should never have promoted him. Was he armed right now? She wanted his weapon – if he thought his new position confined him to the office. Meetings with the accountants, lawyers, stakeholders. Hardly. He didn't even look the part, in his tired windbreaker and flannel trousers and ridiculous shoes. His great flabby body and big bald head. He looked like a thug, not a businessman. Always had. He was not fit for the office. She wasn't sure he was fit for the street any more, either.

She shook her head again, realising too late that that wasn't the way to clear her thinking. It just messed everything up in there again. She turned her back on Frank, started to walk away.

'Mum,' shouted Sam urgently, 'where're you going? Don't leave me here.'

Tatty stopped, returned to the room to see that Sam had ventured from the safety of the far wall – such a pale, shaken, fragile thing. For a second Tatty was reminded of Lianne, Graham Sands's skeletal daughter. However, Sam was sturdier, more robust – surely. She was a Goodwin. Besides, she'd got out of Gorleston, Yarmouth, for a time. Had gone to uni and begun a career as a lawyer. Her daughter shouldn't have been back here. As far as Tatty knew, she'd never done anything unlawful in her life, except get caught up with the wrong people and been taken advantage of – because she was open and honest and loving. Too loving.

'I won't be long,' Tatty said to her. She couldn't take Sam with her to the meeting. No one could know about that. She couldn't send Sam home on her own, either. 'Frank,' she said, 'if there's one last thing I'm ever going to ask you to do for me, it's to stay here and look after Sam.' She watched with alarm as Sam's face began to collapse.

'You don't need to ask,' Frank said. His tone had softened, like the old bear that he used to be. 'I've dedicated the best part of my life to your family. I'd never let you down.'

'You have already,' Tatty said, leaving the room and avoiding looking at Sam.

'Mum?' she heard Sam say, question, plead, behind her. 'Mum?'

'You'll be all right with me, Sam,' came Frank's pained but stern reply.

Tatty paused again, out in the corridor, not in sight.

'How are you going to protect me, then?' Sam said, surly.

Tatty didn't know if any of her children had ever appreciated Frank, let alone liked him. Zach might, she supposed, given all that Frank had done for him, having effectively fathered him for the last year or so. Zach had reason to appreciate Frank, that was for sure – not that it'd been so obvious. She was beginning to wonder whether Zach appreciated anyone. How she could have reared someone so selfish and uncaring?

Sam had never said anything complimentary about Frank, while Ben had had the least to do with him. Ben also had the most to be annoyed about. Ben should be hating Frank's guts right now, if he knew who was to blame for what. Ben should be hating her as well – and that's what really hurt.

'We'll be all right here,' Frank was saying. 'They're not going to come back. They've got what they want for now.'

Tatty couldn't listen to any more. *They've got what they want for now.* He was talking about a human being, her eldest son. She'd heard enough for one day, for one lifetime. This woman Britt Hayes had better have something helpful to say, some answers.

Tatty wasn't going to wait for the lift – she never waited for this lift. She ran down the stairs, feeling unarmed, practically naked. The reception was empty, Celine having been sent home whimpering. There were only so many people Tatty could keep an eye on, be responsible for – not that she was doing a very good job in that department at the moment. In fact she was terrible at it, as she'd always been. She supposed she'd had no role models. No one had ever taken much care of her when she was younger, except perhaps her sister, who she'd lost touch with. A further slice of guilt was added to the fat chunk.

But she realised that that was no excuse, as she struggled to let herself out of the building. You couldn't go on blaming others, your upbringing – as Rich had – for ever.

Having got the blasted glass double doors open, and relocked them – another struggle – Tatty ran towards her car. Just before she reached the vehicle she was aware of movement out of the corner of her eye, someone lunging at her from the pavement, then she was being grabbed, held back. Pulled into a tight embrace. She was overwhelmed by the smell of someone having just showered, shaved. She didn't have to look up, or resist, and she let him hug her more tightly.

'Tatty,' Shane said, 'is everything OK? What's happened?'

She looked at him then, trying to disentangle herself from his tight embrace. She found she could only shake her head.

'You rang me, but didn't say anything,' he said. 'I tried to call you back a couple of times. You were either engaged or didn't answer.'

Tatty didn't think that could have been the case, although she wasn't going to check her phone right now. Safe in his arms, she wanted to burst into tears, finally. Tears didn't come, however.

'Things are going on,' she said instead.

'Has this got anything to do with last night?'

'Yes,' she said. 'It's complicated.'

'I thought we were good.' He stopped holding her so tightly. 'I'm really into you, Tatty.'

'Oh, not that.' Tatty felt herself blinking, then blushing, out in the freezing air. Shane had been referring to their relationship, the hurried, passionate sex they'd had in her office.

'What did you think I meant?'

She looked at her watch, looked up at the Smokehouse, half expecting to see Sam waving desperately out of a window, waving for help. The façade was still, blank, beaten back by the frigid weather. Small, wet snowflakes were beginning to fall from the sky; a prelude, she felt, for the whole lot to come crashing down on her head. 'Shane, I have to go to a meeting. I'm late.'

'Can I help? I sensed something wasn't right last night. Then this morning, when you called.'

'I didn't call you,' she said. 'I didn't mean to.'

'My mum always says I have a sixth sense, which is why I make such a good fireman. I know where the danger is, where and when I'm needed. Let me help, whatever it is.'

Tatty had an idea that Shane's mum would be about her age, maybe younger. She'd be a good-looking woman, no doubt, with beautiful eyes, a happy, caring nature. 'No,' she said, 'not now. You don't want to be involved. I don't want you involved. You need to leave me alone.'

'Why? I'm falling for you, really.'

'Don't be ridiculous. You barely know me.' She stepped towards her car.

'This is something to do with those murders in Gorleston last night, isn't it?'

'No, Shane. It's not – it's not that. It's something else, closer to home, much more personal.'

'It is me then, our relationship – us. Isn't it?'

'No – how many times? It's nothing to do with us.' They barely had a relationship.

He was shaking his beautiful head. 'I don't understand.'

'Good. I don't want you to,' she said, her mind flashing to her office, in the dead of night, Shane's strength, stamina. Her lack of breath, agency.

'I can protect you.'

'You need to leave me alone.'

'No.' He looked crestfallen, pathetic, before his expression changed, hardened, and he moved towards her, arms spreading. 'I love you.'

'For God's sake!' she shouted, reaching for the car door, pulling it open, diving inside. 'Who do you think you are?'

## 16

'Steady,' said Zach, gripping the sides of his seat. The fine black aniline leather had been cured by hand in Italy, if his memory was serving him correctly, which it probably wasn't. More wishful thinking. 'I have been through the spin cycle – the death cycle, man. No thanks to you.'

He was sitting up front, realising that the back seat of the Sport made him feel queasy enough when he was firing on all cylinders. He was going to sit up front from now on. Pay closer attention to where they were going, who they were dealing with, while keeping a keener eye on his fucking driver.

What'd he need a driver for anyway? Frank's words. Because he thought he was in the Balearics, which he most certainly wasn't. Smudgy-grey-shitting-freezing-fucking weather he was staring at. What he'd been staring at for weeks, months. Wow, was the cloud cover heavy in this part of the world.

He should have been driving through it, except, even if he hadn't been feeling wrecked, like death-barely-warmed-up, Abir was the expert – he'd give him that. Not that all was forgiven, or ever would be. 'Sorry, boss,' he'd said, after he'd helped Frank back into the lodge, 'Paul's OK, but Pete, he's dangerous.'

'Could have told me you'd had a run-in with them before,' Zach had said, trying to work out where Abir had been for the last few hours, if not the whole damn night.

'Could have told me these were the geezers you were meeting,' Abir had replied, looking dead sheepish. 'You never gave me their names up front.'

'What did you want, their CVs? You could have come to my aid,' Zach had said, still on the disgusting day bed, in the recovery position Frank had propped him into, 'instead of leaving me knocked out on the toilet floor all night.'

'I was running scared – happy to admit it,' Abir had replied, while Frank was throwing a look as harsh as sulphuric acid.

'You weren't aware of them driving off?'

'I was lying low, enjoying the luxury accommodation elsewhere on site. Must have crashed straight out. We'd been up for the last forty-eight hours or something, hadn't we?'

Was that meant to be an excuse? Zach had been too tired, too fucked, too shaken, to quiz his driver further. Yeah, there were many more angles to explore, man to man, over a fine line or two, but needs must. 'Hey, steady, I said.' There was a good chance he was going to puke.

'I thought we were in hurry,' Abir said. 'It's not my fault the roads around here can't stick to a straight line. I don't get it, it's bloody flat enough. What'd they have to put these obstacles in the way for?'

'They're like adding some variety,' Zach said. They'd entered the outskirts of Lowestoft, an endless series of mini-roundabouts serving little traffic at this time of the day. At any time of the day, he thought, backwater like this. Gorleston was one thing, Yarmouth another, then there was Lowestoft – at the bottom of the bottomless pit, as far as he was concerned. 'Be even more boring without them.' A town that relied on mini-roundabouts to add some spark. Said it all. But now they were here Zach wanted Abir to slow down in any case. He hadn't thought this far ahead. The image on his phone was patchy, and a fresh batch of sleet was beginning to pepper the windscreen. Zach tried to hold his phone steady. He was looking at Google Maps. 'We were in a hurry to escape the mother-lode, but now we're out of her orbit, we can sit back, take it easy.'

'I thought we had a meet and greet,' Abir said. 'A rendez-vous.' He added this in a ludicrous French accent.

'Yeah, but in our own good time. So what if we keep them waiting?'

'New tactics?'

'Look where the old ones got us.'

'That business model was fine,' Abir said. 'It's your expansion plans that dumped us in it. Let the music play elsewhere, if you ask me. Let those with beat keep it neat.'

'Fuck are you talking about?'

'Always the way with you guys.' Abir wouldn't let up. 'You rush in thinking you know best, that you own the fucking world. But you don't, man. There're always others who were there first. Those properly acclimatised – true natives.'

'I don't need an anthropology lesson, thanks,' Zach said. 'Besides, I am a native. What do you think we're doing right now anyway? Resuming business as usual.'

'In extraordinary circumstances, no? Your brother's been taken and your mum's beside herself, while your security man Frank is well and truly crocked. What an operation. No wonder people are taking advantage.'

'I don't need a business lesson from you, either. You're fucking lucky you're still employed.' This was something Zach realised he'd have to address, with clarity, purpose and finality. But it would have to wait for a sunnier day, and when some other options had presented themselves. For now he knew he couldn't do any of this on his own.

Not that his last business partner had proved too reliable either – though fortunately Liam had been taken care of by someone else. Zach felt a lump in his chest – heart-shaped and weighted – thud a little more prominently.

'Frank's not security any more, anyway,' he said. 'He's my mum's business partner.'

Abir laughed. 'Which leaves you – and your brother and sister – where? Defenceless? I mean, what happened? These guys just turn up and drag your brother out? What's his name again?'

'Ben.'

'Does he look like you?'

Zach had made it so they'd never met. Until today he'd kept Abir well out of his mum and Frank's orbit as well. The whole deals-on-wheels operation was none of their business. 'No, he's much uglier.'

Abir exhaled loudly. 'That would be some sight I wouldn't want to see.' It was as if Abir had woken up in someone else's caravan, with a new voice, a new sense of status, the cheeky sod. 'Let's hope you get to.' Zach said.

'You don't seem too bothered about his safety.'

'Man, I'm devastated, truly. He's my bro – come on. But the world keeps turning. He'll turn up, safe and sound, I'm sure. Those guys that took him – Frank had done a deal with them yonks ago. None of this is quite what it seems, is my guess. Frank plays his cards close to his chest. They'll probably be having a pint right now, working out a new arrangement. It could all be some sort of cover – who knows. Or maybe Ben's gone behind Mum and Frank's backs, now he's finally back here, and wants to strike a new deal, with him at the helm, as the true heir to my father's kingdom. Family businesses are the worst, if you ask me – full of infighting. Why'd you think I like to keep a distance, do my own thing?'

'So we carry on, as normal, for now? That's the plan, is it?'

'Have you got a better idea?'

Leaving the Smokehouse, thinking he'd had a flash of brilliance, not just resilience, Zach had pinged a WhatsApp message back to yesterday's request for five Gs. He needed a trade, to feel all was not lost. Quickly decided it would be good to get out of the immediate vicinity of Goodwin Enterprises for an hour or two also. The heat had become oppressive.

Nevertheless, Zach was surprised he'd got a reply to his WhatsApp message almost instantly, with a time and a specific address. They must have been desperate. Who could blame them? This was Lowestoft – LOL. Yet Zach's business did revolve around a simple USP – anytime any place. Yesterday Lowestoft was a no-no. Despite the USP there were limits. Today, however, it was a different picture. Needs must and all that.

Except, and here was the crucial thing beginning to bite, he'd arranged the rendezvous without having any gear to sell. Pulling away from the Smokehouse he'd rambled something to Abir about Paul and Pete having missed a packet, which had been lurking behind the waste bend. Abir seemed to be so enthralled with his new sense of himself that he'd barely bothered to enquire further – like where was the stuff cut and quartered? Were we talking the 99 per cent pure? Or the other rubbish?

Perhaps Abir was crushed with guilt and didn't want to mention the word gear, or the lack of it, to his boss. Zach looked over at him now, searching for an eye twitch, a tell-tale blush, a smattering of remorse. Nothing was giving.

They passed a park and then Oulton Broad North train station and dipped further into an industrial estate, much of it abandoned, derelict, brownfield, despite the virgin snow.

'I'm getting a bad vibe,' Abir said, breaking the silence. 'Some new punter wants five Gs, this time of the day, and they hang out in a wasteland? Is that water over there? The sea?'

'That's why they want the lift,' Zach said, 'preparing for the weekend. Who wouldn't, faced with this? It's Oulton Broad, isn't it? Part of.' There was another stretch of water next to the broad, he seemed to remember, with a funny name, which currently escaped him. Something in his stomach was beginning to splutter, misfire, back up. He urgently needed to excavate his guts, from both ends.

'I guess you haven't travelled the globe,' Abir said, eyes flickering between his app and the winding road. 'The length and breadth of our country alone would show you many far more miserable fucking sights. I've seen places not so far away that make this look like a des res.'

'A what?'

'A des res – short for posh fucking home. It's a term from the last century, when people still had aspirations.'

'They still do. I do. You do.'

'Of a fashion, my friend – of a fashion.'

Zach realised that Abir's new airs and graces were contributing greatly to his nausea. The driver should have been bowing and scraping to make amends. The man needed to show some respect, and humility, for the mess he'd got them into – and for abandoning him for the entire night. He could have frozen to death, choked on his vomit, had a seizure. Whereas he'd been about as forgiving and forgetting as was possible – for the time being. He slapped the glove compartment, wishing there was a loaded pistol in there, as Abir brought the chariot to a halt.

'According to the coordinates, it should be the next left,' Abir said.

They were on a wider road, lined with more low-rent industrial units, the odd car muscling the forecourts. On their right was a chain-link fence, rusted and busted, doing little to protect a hefty strip of brownfield. According to the map, his smudged memory of it, this was meant to be the Harbour Road Industrial Estate.

A glint or two beyond the brownfield promised something else, but Zach couldn't work out what it was. Sheet ice? The sleet couldn't decide whether it wanted to be snow, rain or give up altogether.

'Why have you stopped?' Zach said, another spasm hitting his intestines, his bowels. He wasn't at all sure he'd be able to keep it in, and wouldn't soil the handcrafted aniline leather seat. *Handcrafted?* By robots, at best.

'You don't have the gear, do you?' Abir said.

'What do mean?' Zach turned his head, faced his driver.

'The Zees cleaned you out, didn't they? You don't have five Gs. You don't have one G. What's the idea?'

Zach looked away and stared at the potholed road, the knackered asphalt, wet with recently laid sleet. He supposed once upon a time there were fishermen's cottages in the vicinity. There were traces of old red brick walls amid the newer structures of concrete, breeze block and corrugated iron. No one fished out of Lowestoft any more, though the town was about to become some important service hub for the wind farms, a giant new one in the planning. Frank had been moaning on about it. How unfair it was that Lowestoft got the contract, not Yarmouth. Way of the world, the haves and haves-not, nothing to cry about.

'We're not there yet, are we?' Zach said. 'Did I tell you to stop? It's the next left, isn't it?' He prodded his phone, wanting the map to reappear, while knowing full well that the Google Street View camera cars wouldn't have made it all the way down here. Which was perhaps why this location had been given.

'You want to rob this guy?' Abir asked. 'Of five hundred smackers? What if he's some big fucker? What if he's got a weapon? Friends? Hardly worth it, Zach, is it?'

'Money is money,' Zach said slowly. The Sport's motor purred on, pouring heat, if not comfort, into the thick, recycled air. Pressure was building not only inside Zach's guts. He glanced at his driver once more. Abir was no fool – which was why he'd employed him in the first place. And why he shouldn't still be employing him. The guy had his own connections, a past, which had robbed Zach of a new batch – ninety Ks, if cut right – and landed him with a hefty swipe to the head. That he'd found a couple of spare wraps in his pocket was his concern, and his solace, when he came to late last night. Powerful stuff all round.

'You don't know who this person is, Zach. We haven't done business in this town before. How'd he even get your number? What's he look like? I'm suspicious, with everything else that's been going on. Course I am.'

'How do we know it's a he?' Zach said. No names had been used. Just numbers, which was usual.

'You're too trusting,' Abir said.

That was true, Zach thought. He was too forgiving as well. 'Yeah – you can say that again.' He tried to whistle but the left side of his face began to hurt as he pursed his lips. Where had Abir really been for all those hours last night? Tucked up in some decrepit static, not a care in the world?

'Are you going to move this chariot on?' Zach said. 'Or are we going to sit here all day? There's some loot around the corner, and I need to make ends meet. You want your wages paid, don't you?'

'Don't be a fool,' said Abir. 'Look where we are. It's got to be a set-up. Time to cut and run.'

'No way,' said Zach. You didn't get anywhere in this world bottling it at the last minute. 'Maybe he doesn't want his wife, his family, to know he uses on a semi-industrial scale.'

'So it is a he,' Abir said quietly, not putting the motor into gear.

'Do we have any female customers?' A thought then came to Zach, like the sky had suddenly cleared of snow cloud and a weak winter sun was doing its best to cheer up the Harbour Road Industrial Estate. 'Seeing as I've been so damn nice to you Abir, forgiving and all, seeing as you've got itchy feet, I want you to get out of the car, swagger round the corner, and scout it out for me. All righty?'

Perhaps this had always been in his mind, why he wanted Abir with him and hadn't sent him packing straight back to the frozen north the moment Frank had hauled him into the lodge this morning. Actually, it was more like the other way round – Abir had helped Frank back inside, with Frank not being able to walk unaided.

'If you come back with the five hundred smackers, all the better,' Zach said. He was the boss. Abir was his minion, regardless of experience, muscle. Because of muscle, in fact – that was why he was in the position he was in. Abir was so much fitter than Zach was, which was useful, seeing as neither of them was armed with so much as a Swiss Army knife.

'You've got to be kidding, mate,' Abir said. 'You want me to stroll into a trap? You arranged this.' He revved the engine as if he were about to push the Range Rover into gear.

'No, mate.' Zach hated the word 'mate', he realised. He hated being called mate. People only used the term iron-ically. He only used it when he was hating someone's guts. He shifted his weight, felt himself grimacing as he tried to hold his insides inside him. 'You owe me, Abir – big time, as it is. How are you going to pay me back? You've got history here, haven't you? You owed Paul and Pete, what was it, ten grand?'

'They were lying. It was nothing like that.'

'Now you owe me ninety. Time to start paying up.' Life suddenly seemed so simple.

'You've got no idea, have you? How this works? You're way out of your depth.'

If there was one thing that Zach never wanted to hear again it was this. No, he was not out of his depth. He was barely paddling. 'Get out of the fucking car and do as I say.' Zach reached across, pulled the key fob from the dash. 'We're not going anywhere until you've done one simple thing for me.' Zach hadn't been in a fight for a while, hadn't hit anyone for years. Didn't fancy his chances against Abir. However, he was suddenly so enraged he wasn't sure what he'd be capable of.

Maybe Abir sensed as much. He shook his head as he undid his seatbelt, opened the door and climbed out.

Freezing air flooded the car and kept on flooding it because Abir didn't bother to shut the door, and kept walking away from the vehicle, down the street, which was meant to be Man's Way, though Zach wasn't sure because the map on his phone wasn't playing ball.

'The first left,' Zach shouted after him. It seemed correct, as there was no side road on the right, just the chain-link fence blocking a strip of wasteland, and what he now realised must have water beyond. 'Look out for a vehicle, a white one, in front of a lock-up.'

The contact had WhatsApped to say they'd be waiting in such a vehicle, in such a place, on Tideway. Zach had originally been intending to do what he always did – to have Abir drive slowly past, so they could check out the punter, then WhatsApp them, telling them to head for a black Range Rover on the corner, and to make for the nearside rear passenger door. If he and Abir didn't like the look of whoever was approaching they'd floor it.

New tactics now, all right. Zach opened his door, also got out, being careful to shut it. He pulled the hood of his hoodie over his head, tried to shield his body from the Arctic blast. Found the pain in his guts had eased now he was upright. He hurried round the bonnet, got into the driver's seat. Inserted the key fob. Ignited the V6. Settled himself behind the wheel.

He got bored waiting after only a couple of minutes. His stomach wasn't too happy again either. He rolled the Sport forward. Stopped when he heard a message ping into his phone. Checked the screen. It was a WhatsApp message, from the punter. *Where are you?*

Zach checked the time. They were only twenty minutes late. Who was this man? Where was Abir, more fucking like? He couldn't believe he'd dare to do another runner after he'd been given such a whopping great second chance. How hard could it be to spot a white vehicle in such a drab place?

A white vehicle? Cogs were suddenly whirring. *Fuck*.

## 17

'Not the weather for a stroll on the beach,' Tatty said, attempting to shrug further into her pockets. Not that there was any further her hands could go. She was not equipped for this. She rarely ventured out onto the sand in what they called summer in these parts – as for the middle of February. . . Her mac was no protection whatsoever; neither was the silk Hermès scarf trying to keep her hair in place. She was wearing stupid shoes as well.

Rising from the sea, just beyond the wind turbines, was an iron curtain of cloud. It seemed to be shifting ever nearer, as if they'd soon be imprisoned, all routes out of Yarmouth blocked, yet it was doing nothing to cut the wind chill. Tatty looked over her shoulder, at a disappearing Britannia Pier, then turned her head towards the woman striding along next to her, leading Tatty further from civilisation. *Civilisation?*

Tatty had been immediately struck by the healthy glow about this woman's face, how Britt Hayes seemed to be enjoying the great outdoors, the shocking air. She was far more suitably dressed, in a hooded, puffy parka, slim trousers, sturdy shoes. She appeared strikingly fit and toned, tough and steely. However, she was older than

Tatty had been expecting, with a smattering of lines on her forehead, and marked crow's feet creeping out from dark, clear eyes.

She must have had plenty to worry about, Tatty reckoned. 'Not sure how much further I can go,' she shouted, wanting a reply this time. It was hard to speak, hard to hear, against the elements. She wanted to be indoors, listen to what this woman had to tell her. 'I didn't realise we were going walk the full length of the coastal path.' They'd only just passed the Marina Leisure Centre. Wellington Pier was like a distant dream ahead, and still the iron curtain was steadily advancing. Tatty wasn't sure what it would bring – rain, sleet, snow, a blizzard? The end of existence?

'Shame I don't have my dog with me,' Hayes said. 'He loves this beach. But I came straight from work.'

'What's the dog called?' Tatty yelled. She didn't give a shit what the dog was called.

'Baz,' said Hayes, stepping in front of Tatty, blocking her path. 'He's called Baz and he's a black and tan boxer, and I love him as much as if he were a child, *my* child. I really do.'

'Where's he now?' Tatty couldn't believe what she was hearing. She'd trekked across a great stretch of beach, on the most inhospitable of days, when her eldest son's life was in very real danger – presuming he was still alive – to be told that a grown woman loved an animal as much as a child. Plus she was a police officer, the assistant chief constable of Norfolk Constabulary. Did she have any perspective about what it meant to be a human being? Just who she should have been protecting?

'He's with his dad,' Hayes said, smiling.

Maybe she was the one who'd lost perspective, Tatty suddenly thought, looking down at her inappropriate footwear. 'That's nice,' she said, trying to smile, wanting to feel normal, human. She then looked up, trying to see round Britt, but all that was there was the advancing wall of cloud, marching across the North Sea, come to imprison her here for ever. Or crush her to death. Was there any difference?

'I don't have children,' Hayes said. 'But I understand people who do.'

'Really?' said Tatty.

'You have three children, don't you?'

'Hopefully,' Tatty gulped. Unless one had just been taken away from her for good. Could this woman help her?

'I get that you want to do your best for them, make sure they are safe, give them opportunities that frankly most kids around here don't get anything like.'

'What are you trying to say?'

Hayes looked over her shoulder, at the dark wall of weather. Scanned the beach. They were the only people out on the sand.

Tatty shivered. The wind whipped around her with the ferocity of a jellyfish sting. Tendrils were slapping her face, her neck. She didn't have time for this. 'What are you trying to say?' she shouted again.

'If you want to keep your kids safe, you need to do something about Frank. It wouldn't do your own security any harm either.'

'Meaning?' Having started shivering, Tatty couldn't stop.

'He's overstepped the mark this time.'

'Yeah?' Tatty tried to pull the scarf tighter over her ears, but silk was not a winter material. It was what you wore in the Mediterranean, Ibiza, in July. 'Can we get out of the weather? Go inside somewhere, have a cup of tea?' A drink was what she needed.

'I can't be seen with you,' Hayes said. 'Not in public.'

'No, I expect not. Not sure it would do me any favours to be seen with you, either.'

'Yarmouth's crawling with cops.'

'You're in charge of them, aren't you?'

'It doesn't work like that.'

'No? How does it work then, for you? You're bent, right? Frank's mate. So who are you in charge of? Or is it the other way round? Who's in charge of you?' Tatty searched Britt Hayes's face for clues. 'Tell me.' Nothing was giving. 'Why go out on a limb?'

'I could ask you the same thing. Who are you doing all this for? The simple answer is that I work for myself, my partner and our dog. It's always been that way. You get involved in an institution, a set-up, thinking that's the way to earn money, survive. Maybe even do some good. But other people always have other ideas, so then you have to prioritise, work out what's really important to you. My partner and I, we protect each other. Everyone needs someone. However, once you've gone down a certain route, you can't backtrack totally. The forces are too great. You have to keep going. You understand what I'm saying?'

Tatty thought she did. Except she hadn't been going down any route, consciously, for very long. She thought of the moment she shot her daughter's boyfriend dead. But it hadn't begun then. It was when she discovered her sister-in-law's body, and decided that she wouldn't go to the police, fearing the end of Goodwin Enterprises, her and her children's livelihoods. There was no going back from that.

Though there were other things she'd seen and known about, had been party to for years before then. She'd never been completely blind to what Rich had been up to, despite the endless prescriptions, the pharmaceuticals. He'd got her to sign enough documents, putting her name to this and that. She'd enjoyed the money, the lifestyle his way of doing things brought her and the children. She'd been complicit, if not very capable, for years, decades.

Out on the freezing beach she felt herself nodding. She didn't feel proud, however. She'd been sucked into it, a pathetic little thing with no agency, no plan, just an addiction. Unlike Britt Hayes. Everything about her seemed purposeful. She'd probably been head girl at school, or the naughtiest, whereas Tatty had tried to be invisible, and avoid the bullying because of her accent, her name. Yet was she in such a different position to Britt Hayes now? For both of them it was too late. There was only one direction they could go in. 'I understand you've made choices. Are you saying you regret them?'

'Don't get me wrong. I'm a damn good copper, when I want to be,' Hayes said. 'Policing requires many skills. Not everyone would agree with my tactics. But I do what I feel is right. I always looked after who I needed to. Money's never been my aim, let me make that clear.'

'What is, then?' asked Tatty, somewhat incredulously. 'Power?'

Hayes was shaking her head now. 'It's complicated,' she said. 'There's got to be a point to all this, hasn't there? A right way in a dark world. Nothing's black and white.'

Her eyes, Tatty could see, were taking in the sweep of the beach, the Golden Mile, the front shuttered for the winter, and out to sea where the cloud appeared to have stalled. It didn't look any more threatening than it had a few moments ago. Tatty felt disappointed. She wasn't sure whether she wanted to fight her way out of this mess or be crushed to death. What she definitely didn't want was further complications, or any bigger-picture shit. She just wanted clarity. 'Why are you telling me this?' she said.

'Like I said, for your own good.'

'Why should you care what's good for me?'

'Smart policing isn't about the law, necessarily. It's about what's right, and keeping the peace.' Britt Hayes's face shifted and she smiled.

Tatty didn't believe a word Hayes was saying. She had no idea what she was talking about. The world was black and white, good and evil – that was it. 'I'm going back to my car. You can't help me, can you? You're wasting my time.' Her teeth were chattering now. She didn't want to hear about some right or wrong way from this fruitcake. She wasn't sure morals even came in to it. Surviving was what it came to. She turned inland.

'I've already helped you – in far more ways than you have any idea of,' Hayes said.

Tatty kept walking, head down, wanting to shield her face, and mind, from the onslaught.

'Zach – how has he managed to evade arrest for so long? Please don't even get me started on what happened last summer, when his girlfriend and best mate were murdered. We didn't even question him. You do realise that, don't you?'

Hayes was making a very good attempt to be heard now, she'd caught up with Tatty and was striding along beside her, as if this were all in a day's work.

Tatty slowed, glanced her way. 'On the phone you said you could help me. Do you have any idea what's going on right now?' She couldn't bring herself to tell the assistant chief constable that her eldest son had been taken, kidnapped. It would make her seem so careless, so hopeless. She still had no idea why the woman would do anything for her anyway, except perhaps that she'd helped Frank in the past, had got involved in Goodwin Enterprises' wicked ways and was now stuck with the shit forever hitting the fan.

'I could have Frank arrested,' Hayes said. 'But do you think I want him talking? You never know how people are going to react in custody.'

Tatty resumed a good pace, eyes straight ahead. Yeah, she was getting it all right. Hayes didn't want Frank incriminating her.

'We've found three bodies in Breydon Water so far. My bet is Frank's behind every one of them. Then there are the two from last night. Executed while they sat in a car. Two bullets is all it took. That sort of violence, in a public place, was quite unnecessary. What did he think, that this would shift the attention away from the Breydon Water investigation?'

Tatty found herself nodding her head. Hayes was smart, that was for sure.

'Well, the opposite is happening.'

'But if you arrest Frank,' Tatty said, 'your position becomes far too precarious. You're scared of what he might say, aren't you?'

'I haven't finished with this part of the world yet,' Hayes said. 'Though you might want to consider how long *you* want to stick around for. The minute any of this gets a fraction closer to Goodwin Enterprises, say goodbye to your casino plans. Say goodbye to any legitimate business. You'd be finished, and that's presuming you're not arrested, and banged up for a good long while. Come to think of it – what did happen to Michael Jansen?'

'Ben, my eldest—'

'I know who Ben is.'

'He had nothing to do with those murders.' Tatty couldn't hide the shock from her voice. 'No, no way.'

'I didn't say he did.'

The concrete promenade still seemed a long way off, while the weather continued to stalk Tatty's back. 'Ben wants me to head up the Regeneration Committee.' She didn't know why she was telling a bent copper this. Because, despite the facts, the obvious, she was still trying to legitimise her business, her concerns, for her family as much as herself – maybe that was it.

'Some chance, but you never know. What I will tell you for free is that Frank is your biggest problem going forward,' Hayes said. 'Now, he shouldn't have done what he did last night.'

'You know it was him for sure? What about Winslow's crew? It's their patch.'

'Exactly,' Hayes said. 'You want to expand, don't you?'

'How do you know that?'

'Every business wants to grow.'

'There are other ways,' Tatty found herself saying.

'You're nowhere without trust,' Hayes said. 'Rivals can be dealt with. Insiders are far harder to handle.'

'What did you lot want with Zach, my youngest, yesterday?' Tatty said, wanting to change the subject.

Hayes shook her head. 'I've been doing my best to make sure he's left alone – for Frank's sake, believe me. That son of yours doesn't make life easy for himself, though does he?'

'Or me,' said Tatty. 'Two coppers came to the house yesterday evening – before that business by Gorleston pier.'

Hayes shook her head once more. 'Are you sure?'

'Yes. They were in uniform.'

'It's nothing I know about. I'll look into it.' She seemed genuinely surprised.

'Are you kept informed of everything that goes on?' Tatty asked.

'When it comes to your family, yes. I used to be head of Serious and Organised, until I was promoted. As you know, I've been looking out for Frank's interests for a long while. We helped each other.'

'Not any more?'

'He's lost his touch. He's getting on.'

'What about the new head of Serious and Organised then?'

'He's a guy called Kyle Neville – he answers to me.'

'You sure?' said Tatty.

'Absolutely.'

'Wouldn't mind meeting him in any case,' Tatty said. 'You never know when a new contact comes in handy.'

'Oh, you'll never meet him. He's not like me. He keeps a very low profile – out of the office. Thinks he's uncorruptible.'

'Don't they all,' Tatty sighed.

'The other thing is he's very short,' Hayes said. 'He doesn't think people take him seriously. But he's mean and calculating as hell, I can tell you.'

'Trying to make a point, yeah I get that,' said Tatty.

'Unlike Frank,' said Hayes. 'Who's more than gone to fat.'

'Don't be so rude,' was all Tatty could think to say. She looked ahead. Steps a short way on from the redundant jetty had materialised. Wellington Pier cut a brooding line in the beach further on. Beyond that the fading blue façade of the Pleasure Beach's big dipper sat looking tired and out of place, like a neglected child. Tatty's limbs felt like lead, her head numb. She hadn't eaten for she didn't know how long. Hayes appeared full of nervous energy, striding ahead. The detective was rattled, Tatty decided.

'Frank's time here is up,' Hayes suddenly said. 'Me and my partner used to respect his way of doing things. Not any more. You need to get him out of town, fast. Or take him out.'

Tatty took a deep breath. Stopped walking altogether. 'You want me to take him out? Frank? Who on earth do you think I am?'

Despite her outrage Tatty realised she wasn't wholly averse to the idea. There was a certain truth to what Hayes had implied. Frank had lost his touch. 'You're talking about my business partner,' she said, her voice tailing off. It even felt odd calling him her business partner. He'd never been that, not an equal partner, whatever she might have said to him.

'What sort of business do you think Frank knows best? You employ him.'

'It doesn't work like that. Plus I believe in loyalty.'

'If only others did. You deal with this correctly, and maybe you'll be able to carry on. Though none of this can get any closer to me, what Frank's been doing. I won't allow it.'

'You're not in control, are you?' Tatty said, thinking again of the coppers who had tried to pay Zach a visit yesterday evening, and that Hayes didn't know a thing about it. 'You're being squeezed, aren't you? By a new kid on the block? This Kyle Neville? That's usually the way. How quiet is he really? Maybe he doesn't keep such a low profile in certain company. Maybe he uses the fact that people don't take him seriously to great advantage.'

'No, you're all wrong,' Hayes said. 'As wrong as could be.'

Tatty wasn't sure she was. The woman was more than rattled. 'You're the one who's fighting to survive,' she shouted over her shoulder, into the wind, wanting to wound this woman further. Where was her loyalty, her respect?

'You have until Monday morning first thing to make Frank disappear,' Hayes shouted back.

Tatty strode on as far as the concrete steps, the esplanade, then paused, thinking fast. She waited for Hayes to catch up with her. 'OK. But before I do anything about Frank,' she said, 'I need to find my eldest, Ben. He was taken this morning. Dragged out of the Smokehouse by Winslow and a couple of his thugs.'

'Shit,' said Hayes, seemingly meaning it. 'I don't know anything about this. Retaliation, is it? I'm sorry. That's not good news. Why Ben?'

'Wrong place, wrong time.'

Hayes shook her head slowly. 'This is what happens when you lose our support. We're more powerful than you'd ever believe, the resources we have, the connections. Being watched by me, those closest to me, comes with a price, however. Frank knew that, then abused it, finally, last night. His fault.'

'Can't you do something?'

She sighed. 'Perhaps, if you do something for me.'

'You're police, it's your job. This is urgent, a priority. Please.'

'We all have different priorities.' Britt Hayes brushed past Tatty, determinedly not catching her eye, she sprung up the steps and appeared to be fishing for her phone as she strode away.

Tatty watched her put the device to her ear while increasing her pace. It was sleeting once more. It seemed to be getting dark as well. The days were meant to be getting lighter, lasting longer. This one had run out of all energy, hope, hours ago.

When Hayes was out of sight Tatty looked back out across the wide stretch of sand to the sea. The crushing wall of cloud had dissolved into a whitening flurry. She turned back to land, the Great Yarmouth seafront that had never been very good at facing up to the truth, and climbed the steps. She felt surer ground beneath her feet and began walking towards her car.

Put a gun in her hand, yes, she'd have no hesitation about shooting Frank in the head, if that meant Britt Hayes would help her find Ben alive. But she didn't think it would. Besides, she didn't have a weapon any more. She'd never felt quite so cold and lonely.

## 18

Something was in Ben's mouth. It felt like an old tennis ball. Grainy, scuffed fuzz, and without any real bounce left. He was trying to use his tongue to squash it out of the way so he could breathe more easily, because he couldn't breathe out of his nose. His nose, resting on the floor – a hard, concrete floor, he guessed – felt like a balloon so filled with hot that air it was about to burst. No, it was like a boil – the boil he'd had on his snout when he was sixteen, which his father had taken the piss out of remorselessly. *You've got bubonic plague, young man*.

Perhaps it was the whole of the side of his face he could feel – the enormity of it – which had swollen to incorporate his nose? Did he have a nose left?

He was alive, he realised with a jolt, though a good chunk of him wished he were dead. They hadn't tortured him, yet. They'd just beaten him, hard, he was remembering, and chucked him into a dark, cold corner of a garage. The other thing he was remembering, as he struggled to open an eye, was that they'd bound his hands and feet before the hardest strikes hit, which was why he couldn't move. At least he hoped it was why he couldn't move, and not because they'd broken his limbs, paralysed him, when he'd been unconscious.

The tingling numbness was suddenly interrupted by a stab of pain, which shot through him. This was quickly followed by another, which spread out from the base of his spine. At least he could feel something, he supposed. Paraplegics, quadriplegics, didn't feel a thing – neither had his father for that matter, not emotionally, the cold, ugly bastard. He suddenly wanted his sister – the only member of his family he could properly connect with, that he loved unconditionally.

It happened again. Someone was nudging him, kicking him. 'Fuck off,' he tried to say. But he wasn't sure any sound came out. He also realised that it wasn't a tennis ball in his mouth, it was his tongue. Something dreadful had happened to it. Like a rat had bitten it and it was now infested with the plague. Boil in the mouth. *Young man*. So fucked up.

'Get up,' a voice said. Another kick came.

Ben tried to move. 'Can't,' he said, or thought he said, while his right eye sprung open. Light was coming from somewhere, and was being swiftly sucked up by the rough grey concrete.

'Oi, up,' the voice said.

There wasn't a kick this time, though Ben felt his shoulders being pulled, squeezed, wrenched, not quite out of their sockets, because his hands, arms were tied together behind his back. This seemed to be keeping him whole, at least in body. His head then flopped, wobbled, flopped some more, as he was dragged into a sitting position, dragged across some acreage of concrete and left to slump hard against what felt like a breeze-block wall.

Gravity settled his tongue at least as his other eye began to open. More light hit his retinas. More connections were being made inside his head. Brain power was surging back, sparks were beginning to fly. He'd always thought of himself as the smartest in the family.

Shapes, figures, were coming into focus. Three men were in front of him, standing. Two were huge – he recognised them. One was Winslow, with a stain on his shirt, blood, and a thick nose – a thicker nose. Ben couldn't believe he'd headbutted him, then kicked him in the balls. Big mistake. The other man was the one from the back of the Hummer, the person who'd reached him first by the edge of the water. There didn't seem to be too much wrong with Ben's short-term memory.

He'd bottled it, of course, suddenly desperate not to drown like his dad. He'd been dragged back to the lock-up. He wasn't the bravest in the family, that was for sure. He thought Sam was, to be honest, the things she'd been through. Now what? At least Winslow hadn't killed him already.

'You know each other?' Winslow's henchman said, in that thick accent, pushing forward the man standing in the middle of the room. He was not like them. He was much younger, trimmer, Asian complexion. Smart rags, as Zach might have said – one of those puffa jackets, skinny trousers, trainers.

Ben realised he was being spoken to. 'No,' he tried to say, shaking his head. That was another mistake.

'Liar,' said Winslow. He then elbowed the fashionable young man in the ribs, who barely winced, however, and remained standing tall.

'You know him?' Winslow now addressed the young man, a snigger to the tone.

'Nope,' he said. 'Never seen him before in my life.' No fear there.

His accent was northern. Leeds? Mancunian?

'Do you want to tell Mr Goodwin over there who you work for?' Winslow said. He had his elbow ready, but he didn't use it. He didn't have to because the other thug whacked the young man on the back of his head with the pistol that he was still carrying.

Ben wondered whether it might in fact be unloaded, a replica. He'd had ample opportunity to use it and hadn't so much as let off a warning shot.

'Nope,' the man said once more, almost laughing, and rubbing his head, but nonchalantly, as if he'd barely been swotted.

Winslow growled. 'Fucking cheek. People like you, you don't know what's good for you. You don't belong here.'

'Boss,' said the henchman, 'he's the man.' He didn't sound like he belonged here, either. 'No mistaking. I waste him now?'

Their new prisoner barely flinched.

A phone began trilling – not a ringtone Ben recognised. Something vaguely familiar – from an old TV show? A cop series?

Winslow pulled a small black device from his pocket, stepped away. Started gabbing into it angrily, but kept walking until he was out of sight and earshot. The lock-up seemed to be compartmentalised with stud walling that didn't go all the way to the ceiling. Ben then tried to focus on the young man, wanting to pick up, by osmosis if needs be, some of his calm and confidence. Their sole captor for now didn't seem to know what to do with himself, so he pushed the man towards Ben.

'Get on the floor,' he said, waving his gun.

'Doesn't look too clean,' the man said. 'I'm not sitting on that.'

Ben could have laughed, out of sheer desperation. But he didn't have the tools. Or the guts.

'Get on the fucking floor.' He moved towards the man with the aggression of a one-horned rhino, and the man did move this time, slowly, nonchalantly, as seemed to be his mode.

He got to within spitting distance of Ben, not that Ben's mouth would have allowed him to spit at anything. There was a squeak from his trainers, as he crouched down, facing Ben. 'You all right?' he said.

Ben wasn't sure whether he managed to nod or shake his head in reply. He thought he made some sort of sound though. He wanted to cry.

A hand was placed on his shoulder, gently, and the man said, quietly: 'My name's Abir. I've been working with your brother.'

'How'd you end up here?' Ben managed to mutter. He wanted to talk, and not stop. He didn't want to be slumped here, awaiting the final curtain. Mind over matter, that was one of Avani's more annoying sayings. *Where there's a will there's a way*. She had a habit of making clichés sound fresh, fun. At that moment he missed her so much. What he'd give to see her one last time. 'Please take me back,' he'd say.

'I love you.' At that moment he might have missed her even more than Sam.

The thug was looking elsewhere, had pocketed his pistol, and was sparking up a fag. Ben hadn't smoked for a decade or so, but he could have done with a drag. Even some weed. Some of that industrial-strength stuff Zach smoked like fresh air. Avani hated smoking, hated weed, getting off her head, like Sam, which was why he'd never taken it up again when he was under so much stress, in London. Most of his colleagues took whatever was going – MDMA, coke, keta-mine. Not her. Or him.

'What?' He realised this person called Abir had said something else to him – too quietly.

'Set-up,' he said. 'Walked right into it. Your brother's a prick.'

'Yep,' Ben said. 'Where's he now?' The tongue was shrinking.

'Good fucking question.'

'Where did you get caught?' He could speak.

'Outside here, on the street. Walked right into them. I knew it.'

Ben looked over to their minder. He was smoking intently, staring back. He'd got his gun out again, and was holding it in his other hand, as if he didn't quite know what to do with it. Catching Ben's eye, he waved the weapon their way.

'Where's the other guy gone?' Ben said. 'The one in charge?'

'There're three of them,' Abir said. He leaned closer. 'They're making mistakes. Not working as a team. Amateurs, the lot.'

'Not what I reckon,' said Ben. 'Seem professional enough to me. What were you working with my brother for, anyway?' Abir didn't seem so amateur either. Yet he was in no better position than Ben. They were both fucked. Smart, and fucked – it didn't make sense.

'I never say no to a decent opportunity,' Abir said. 'You don't want to get stale – make too many enemies in the same place. Always good to move on.'

'Where're you from?'

'Leeds, originally.'

'I thought so. Is there really more on offer down here?'

'I didn't realise this place was stuck in such a time warp, I'll tell you that.' Abir looked over his shoulder. 'While working with your brother has its challenges.'

The thug flicked his cigarette end towards them, but it fell short.

'So where exactly is my brother right now?' Ben asked. 'Waiting outside?'

Before Abir had a chance to answer Winslow came trudging back into view. That bloodstain on his shirt made Ben wince. His father would have called him a bottler. The third thug remained out of view.

'Tie them both up so they ain't moving a fucking inch,' Winslow ordered. 'Our fun here has to come to an end.'

'There's no rope, boss. Nothing to tie them with.'

'Bash them on the head then. You've got a light on you, at least, haven't you?' Winslow asked his flunky. 'You know what to do. I don't want a fucking trace. I'm out of here. Give us a ten-minute head start.'

'You want a smoke?' the remaining thug said, slow on the uptake.

Laughing, Winslow stepped over to his man, slapped him on the face, not so playfully. 'Meet us in the usual place, and don't fuck up – you Albanian moron.' He then stepped over to Abir, and booted him hard in the side. 'The things I have to do.' He then swung his foot round, with surprising dexterity and poise for such an obese, old-school wanker. It was a move that took Ben by surprise. The crunch on the side of his head didn't take him by surprise however. There was nothing he could have done to protect himself.

Burning to death had to be worse than drowning, he thought in the split second before his mind switched dreamily to his bedroom in Gorleston. Not now, but when he was a little boy. It was like that time he had flu. He was sweating badly and he couldn't get the duvet off, and he was calling for his mother. He was screaming for her, but she didn't come for what felt like hours and hours. Finally, Sam appeared. She'd brought him a glass of water. She couldn't have been more than five or six.

## 19

'You don't have to stay, you know,' Sam said, once more.

They were in the kitchen. He was sitting at the dining table watching the dark fall onto the garden like the devil's cloak. He'd descended into the blackest of moods, knowing forces well out of their control were circling, pressing. The time for pretences, putting on a front, carrying on as normal, were well and truly over. It had been some ride, he supposed.

'Sam,' Frank said, 'I'm not going anywhere until your mum gets back. I gave her my word.' It was bad enough that he'd let Sam persuade him that she had to go home. They were meant to stay where they were – the Smokehouse, Frank maintaining that the gang wouldn't go back there a second time, not immediately anyway. The family home was a different matter.

Sam drove him, in her modest Beemer, while he'd sat there like the crippled passenger that he was. 'I don't know what's going on out there,' he'd said. It was about survival now, not that he was going to spell that out for her.

She'd remained by the kitchen island, fiddling with this and that utensil, though not venturing any closer to the fridge. She'd said she was hungry. He was absolutely starving. He couldn't remember when he'd last eaten. Breakfast? However, there was no sign of any food being prepared. He supposed Sam wanted to keep her distance, that she had no intention of sitting down at the table with him. He didn't blame her.

She had been generous enough to give him some super-strength painkillers, prescription only, as soon as they'd arrived back in Marine Parade. 'Any chance of a glass of milk?' he said now. He could feel the acids, the drugs, attacking the wall of his stomach. He didn't feel so uncomfortable sitting down at the moment, but knew that if he budged an inch he'd be rocked with pain.

'Sure, if there is any,' Sam said, moving over to the fridge. When she got there she turned back to face him without opening it.

'What did happen to Michael? He's dead, isn't he? Who killed him? You or Mum?'

'Are you going to get me that glass of milk?' He couldn't believe she wanted to talk about her old boyfriend.

'Not until you tell me the truth.'

He shifted in his chair – some harsh metal and wood affair. A product of Tatty's infatuation with a silly designer, who was more than happy to rip off well-heeled women with more money than sense – or was it taste? Nathan Taylor had a reputation that stretched back years. Like all of them, Frank supposed.

'It doesn't do to dwell on things – not in these parts, Sam,' he said slowly, desperately parched, knowing also that shortly before Michael had been killed, Sam had had a miscarriage. Double trauma. Triple if you included the recent murder of her father, whom she dearly loved. Except Sam didn't know everything. Who'd pulled the trigger, for instance, or even that Michael was definitely dead. 'You have to keep moving forward,' he said more sternly. 'The minute you stop to think, look back, you know this world is not for you. You should be elsewhere, Sam, making the most of your life. You're so young. Go abroad, have some fun.'

She was staring at him, tight-mouthed, as if she couldn't believe what she was hearing. As if she hated his guts.

'Or pick up your career again, why not?' he added. 'You were doing so well in London. Your father was proud of you.'

'Do you have any conscience?' she said.

He didn't know what she meant. 'What do you think your mum's going to do when all this has died down?' he asked, knowing it wouldn't die down happily. It was too late for that this time. Forces way beyond his knowledge and control had come into play and unleashed something brutally powerful, violent and unstoppable. There was no future here. Having shifted on his seat he couldn't get comfortable again, or stop the pain from spreading out from his hip. The painkillers couldn't have worn off already, could they? He needed to see a doctor. He'd busted something, that was for sure.

'How should I know?' Sam said. 'She'll do what she wants to do. Always has. What are you going to do, more like? You got us into this.'

He glanced out of the window again, not knowing what Tatty might have told her, or what she'd worked out for herself. It had got so much darker in the last few minutes. He couldn't believe it was still Friday. At least the weekend lay ahead – for some. The sleet had stopped, yet the cold was pressing against the glass. This was not the cosiest of rooms. Too many windows, hard surfaces, ill intentions.

In all the times Frank had been in the house he'd never been taken into the lounge, it occurred to him. The kitchen, and occasionally Rich's old study, were the only rooms he'd ever been reluctantly steered towards. He'd never been made to feel welcome here. He couldn't picture what the lounge would look like at all. Couldn't see Tatty sitting in there, feet up, a box set on the flat screen, surround sound booming, a glass of wine to hand, relaxing.

'You've got nothing to say, have you?' Sam goaded him.

'I'll do whatever I can to keep you safe. Goodwin Enterprises is a different matter.' He knew that he couldn't keep up with the lies, the pretence for much longer. He was no businessman. Tatty, and Rich before her, had understood that all along. He'd been promoted beyond his station, his use. He wasn't sure how he could keep them safe any longer, either. He could barely move. Howie was still not returning his calls. Neither was Britt. He'd been used, set up and was now being frozen out. What he wasn't sure of, however, was why. Why Britt and Howie had changed. Pledged allegiances elsewhere?

'Where have they taken Ben?' Sam was asking. 'He'll be all right, won't he?'

'I don't know, love, to be honest. I'm working on it.'

'Yeah? Doesn't look like it,' Sam said. 'You're just sitting there, twiddling your fat thumbs. Don't call me "love", either.' She opened a fridge door now. 'They haven't been in touch, have they?' she said, over her shoulder, 'the people who took Ben. Why can't we call the police?'

Frank looked at his phone, the blank screen. Sam was right about that as well. He'd been sitting there twiddling his thumbs, seeing as no one was getting back to him, and he'd run out of options, friends, contacts. He could have yelled in shame.

A noise out in the hall saved him from having to reply. Someone was at the front door. Opening it. Coming inside.

He couldn't get up to see who it was – head them off before they got too close to Sam. Her face was a picture of pure alarm. Leaving the fridge door open, he watched her move back to the stone-topped island, reach for the knife block and extract a gleaming Sabatier. She then hurried to his end of the kitchen. He didn't think she'd rushed over to protect him.

'It'll be your mum,' he said, trying to reassure her. 'Whoever it is has let themselves in. No worries.' He put his arm out, wanting to shield her. She flinched, with the knife in her hand. He thought better of the gesture. 'Or one of your brothers. Stay calm.'

'Ben?' she said. 'Back home?'

There was such hope in her voice. But whoever it was wasn't coming straight into the kitchen. Frank grabbed the side of the table, pulled himself to standing, struggling not to yelp with the pain. He needed opiates, morphine, smack. The whole of his lower body felt stiffer for having sat down uselessly for however long.

He hobbled to the island, clung on for a second or two, continued his trek to the kitchen door, with Sam following, close behind, the knife still in her hand. She could stab him in the back easily enough.

'Hello?' he called, stepping into the hall. Whoever it was had run upstairs. He could hear footsteps on the floor above, a door opening and closing.

'It's Zach,' Sam said. 'That's his room.'

'He could have said hello,' Frank said, breathing more easily.

'Zach?' Sam shouted up.

Frank hobbled to the front door, peered out into the night, saw Zach's motor, black against black. Remembered his own car, that the spanking new Lexus was marooned at the old caravan park. Right then he didn't care whether it was vandalised, nicked – if someone could bypass the immobiliser, understand the tech. The next vehicle he'd be driving around in was likely to be a mobility scooter, or a private ambulance – bagged up.

'His car's out here,' he said, dipping back inside and shutting the door against the eternal winter.

Sam was already heading up the stairs, having not let go of the knife, he noticed. He heard her cross the house, a door opening, though not closing. Voices raised, but not unfriendly. He looked about the hall, the door to the kitchen, the study, and the one to what had to be the lounge. He shuffled that way, opening it and stepping inside. It was not as he'd been expecting.

It reminded him of some stuffy old gentlemen's club, the original Goodwin casino. There was a lot of dark oak shelving, rows of embossed books, probably fake. Wine-coloured carpet. A studded, mahogany-coloured leather

182

suite. An old-style TV, and a fireplace with exposed brick-work and a copper hood protruding into the room. There was even a whiff of cigar smoke in the cold, still air.

Frank got out his phone, tried Howie's number again, lost for options. It went straight to voicemail. He decided to leave a message this time. 'Don't be a wanker. Ring me back. I need you.' He then rang Britt Hayes's number, readying himself for the message he was going to leave.

She answered, however, straight away. 'Have you found that boy yet?' she said.

'Who told you?'

'You think I don't know everything?'

'I know you don't,' Frank said.

'Like the names of those bodies we found in Breydon Water? We're working on it.'

'Why the hostility, after all these years?'

'Now's not the time, Frank. What do you want?'

'Where's Howie?'

'Out of town.'

'Still? How convenient. When's he get back?'

'We don't have that sort of relationship, Frank.'

He edged further into the room, but it was freaking him out. There was too much of Rich all over it. It was almost like a memorial. He couldn't believe Tatty had left it how it was. 'Any clues on where they've taken Ben, if you know everything?' he said.

'You made a big mistake, Frank. A lot of people are trying to pick up the pieces. If you know what's good for you, you'll go home, have a very quick think about your future, pack up and get the hell out of here.'

'You answered the phone to tell me this?'

'I got sick of you calling me. Insistent when you want to be, aren't you? What's it take for you to get the message?'

'We go back a long way, Britt. I don't think you're in any position to tell me what to do.'

'Nice talking to you, Frank – for your own good.'

'A young man's life is at risk. You know he's missing. How do you know this?'

'That's my business.'

'What the fuck are you going to do about it, then?' Frank was fast losing his temper. Silence came back at him. 'You've no idea where they've taken him, is that it? With all your resources, your surveillance?'

'Go home, Frank.'

'How do you know I'm not at home already?'

'I know where you are. I always know. Don't underestimate the constabulary, what we're capable of.'

'I just have.'

'Without me,' Hayes was whispering, menacingly, now, 'you'd have been out of the picture years ago. And that family you love so much – they'd be nowhere. Right now, from where I'm looking, they'd be better off without you. Home truths, Frank, sorry. But it's for your own good. Call it for old times' sake.'

'I get it.' And he did. His eyes scanned the dismal room. He was failing to picture Rich sitting in an armchair, puffing on a Montecristo, shouting for Tatty to top up his brandy. That's because he wouldn't have been sitting here for long. He'd have been out, playing the game, wreaking havoc, destroying lives. 'Here's a home truth for you

184

– your outfit's rotten through and through.' He wanted to laugh, but he was wincing with the effort of standing for so long. 'You're the one who's being played,' he continued, 'whose job, career, future, is on the line. Being a bent copper is one thing – being caught another. You protect my back and I'll protect yours – that's how it's always worked. We fed each other useful information, didn't we? To keep Yarmouth clean. I kept Howie gainfully employed, and out of the wrong kind of mischief. Don't forget that.'

'Like hell. Don't bring him into this.'

'Bit late, isn't it?'

'No it bloody isn't. You leave him alone.'

'You're being fingered, aren't you? That's what's happening. So you and Howie have had to support another network, another organisation. Not Winslow's lot – they're too stupid. But something else, with a better-placed insider.' But she'd hung up, and Frank was suddenly aware of someone behind him. He turned.

'What are you doing in here?' It was Sam. She was by the door. Her face, Tatty's face, full of thunder and loathing.

'What goes on in here?' he said.

'No one ever comes in here.' Her face melted a little. 'Dad wouldn't let Mum touch it, and after he died I think she couldn't be bothered.'

'Or she liked the memories, what it stood for,' Frank said. 'Your dad wasn't all bad. He loved you.'

'I don't want to talk about him. Zach's being weird,' she said, quickly changing the subject. 'He won't tell me anything.'

'Where's he just come from?' Frank walked out of the room and closed the door, respectfully, he thought.

'He didn't say. He's looking for something in his room. He didn't want me to see what. He's in a hurry.'

'He's not going anywhere until he's had a word with me,' Frank said, not that'd he'd be rushing up the stairs after him. His mind was still trying to digest the call with Hayes, and what other corrupt bastards she was now working with. They always had links with Serious and Organised. Kyle Neville, the guy who took over from her when she was promoted to assistant chief constable, could it be him? Though, more to the point, who was paying them? Who was behind it?

'Zach,' Frank shouted up the stairs, 'you coming down?' He was getting impatient, knowing that his time was fast running out.

'I don't think he wants to talk to anyone,' Sam said. 'Let alone you.'

## 20

The first thing that caught her eye was Sam's car, then Zach's, under the yellow light being thrown casually onto the forecourt from the nearest street lamp. Pulling up, she felt warmth like heroin flow through her veins. It had been a long time since she'd taken heroin. Track marks slowly disappeared with the ageing process – one of the benefits.

She parked the Merc, making sure she blocked both vehicles in. Her kids were forever telling her that she was useless at parking. She didn't think that was the case. She used to take great satisfaction from making sure her car was in Rich's way – either to stop him from being able to park exactly where he wanted when he came home late, or to stop him from bolting off after another piece of skirt. She was the ditzy housewife, shit at everything except spending money. His line, followed by a slap.

It was Rich who'd been useless at parking, because he'd been so careless, inconsiderate – with everything.

Climbing out, making for the front door, the ghost of heroin trickling through her veins turned to mercury. Ben's car wasn't there. It was still at the Smokehouse, waiting for its owner to be returned. From where?

Getting her house keys from her bag, she gulped at the night air. Gusts of Arctic chill were coming in from the sea and blowing over the upper esplanade, the old bowling greens, the trendy new children's play area, a couple of revamped tennis courts, large patches of municipal grass where her kids once kicked footballs, ran free. She blinked, trying to stem more tears.

In the time it had taken her to return to the Smokehouse, read the message from Sam saying she'd gone home with Frank, and gather her thoughts, before making her own way to Gorleston, there'd been no more communication from the bent copper. She supposed she wasn't expecting any. Hayes was waiting for her to make the first move. Where were the proper police? Where was Ben? Who'd been looking out for him? Not her, not any of them. Maybe this was what hurt the most.

Frank was meant to have kept guard over Sam at the Smokehouse, kept her safe there, because he'd thought that was a better place for them to be than the Gorleston home. The law of diminishing returns, he might have muttered. Yet he hadn't even been able to do that for her. At least they were here, plus Zach. Safe and sound, she presumed, but for how long?

'Hey, watch out,' she said involuntarily. The front door had moved with a force that wasn't all hers, while a stringy being of bone and scraggy muscle thumped into her. 'Ow.'

'Sorry. Sorry, Mum,' Zach said. He frantically pushed her aside.

'Zach, you need to listen to me right now,' came Frank's voice. But he wasn't rushing after him. He was at the back of the bright hall, Tatty saw, clutching the door to the kitchen. Looking ludicrously overweight, old and red-faced.

His bloody hip, Tatty remembered, stepping into the house. Some security, some muscle. But easier for her to deal with.

'Zach,' Sam said, 'don't be stupid.' Sam was hurrying past her now, shouting into the dark. 'Come back.' Sam stopped short over the threshold. 'It's freezing, fuck him.' She returned inside and shut the door.

'What the hell is going on?' Tatty said, looking at Frank. 'Where's he off to now?'

'He won't tell us,' said Frank. 'He turned up here a short while ago, went for something in his room and has now headed back out. I did my best.'

Like fuck, Tatty wanted to say. She made her way to the kitchen, having to squeeze past Frank. 'Do you mind?' She dumped her bag on the island, went to the fridge. The wine rack was not quite empty. She grabbed a bottle. Back at the island she opened it, poured herself a large glass. Took two large sips.

By now Frank had shuffled to within striking distance, and was looking at her sheepishly. He also looked scared. She'd never seen such an expression on him before. Was he scared of her? Or the moment, what everything meant, the lack of a future?

'Mum?' Sam said, entering the kitchen but keeping her distance. 'Don't you care?' She looked Tatty straight in the eye.

'No need to shout, darling,' Tatty said.

'Now Zach's gone,' Sam practically wailed, walking over to the dining table and collapsing onto a chair.

'Not far,' Tatty said, taking another sip, smiling to herself.

'He's got something and he knows something,' Frank said.

'He can tell us what, then,' she said, calming. Sure enough she heard the front door opening, hurried footsteps across the hall, and then watched as Zach charged into the kitchen.

'Your car's in the fucking way, Mum. Don't you know how to park? Useless woman. Move it, now.' Hands clenched into tight balls, he was glaring at her.

Slowly she put her glass down on the counter, careful not to spill any. She was enjoying the wine. Crisp and dry, and perfectly chilled. She stepped into Zach's way, swung out her arm and slapped him hard on the cheek – where he'd been hit already. He buckled, shielding his face, before he stood tall, drawing back a fist.

Frank stepped forward, fast for an invalid, blocking him. 'Don't you dare.'

'What the hell?' Zach said, caressing his cheek.

'You don't talk to your mother like that,' Tatty said. 'Or any woman.'

Zach turned, making for the door, but Frank beat him to it again.

'Go and sit down,' Tatty said, pointing to the kitchen table, where Sam was staring back at them, aghast.

'Do as your mother says,' Frank said.

'Fuck you,' Zach said, without much conviction and continuing to hold his cheek. He wandered over to the table, nevertheless, and perched at the far end, not looking at his sister.

Tatty hadn't hit him hard. It had been a loving slap. If she'd meant business he wouldn't be standing. Her father used to knock her to the floor. Rich too. She knew what real force felt like. She followed Zach over, sat at the head, keeping her eyes on him. It was a large table and he was a long way away.

Tatty looked behind her, nervous of the confrontation ahead, and of what truth might finally come out. Frank was making ground, slowly, shuffling awkwardly around a row of chairs, eventually lowering himself into a seat somewhere between Sam and Zach. Tatty wished he wasn't here – wished he'd disappear of his own accord. She guessed he'd always clung to the family like a limpet. But she knew he wasn't without information or use for a short while longer, and Zach did seem to do as he said. She would miss that.

'Where were you going in such a rush, Zach?' she said, realising that she hadn't brought her wine glass over with her. She could have drunk the bottle in one.

'Where've you been?' Frank chipped in. 'Where's Abir?'

'We're in the middle of a crisis, if it hasn't escaped your attention,' Tatty added.

'Nothing to do with me,' said Zach. 'That's your business. I've only ever tried to do my own thing.'

'Look where that's got you,' Frank said. 'I've tried to keep as much of this as possible from your mum, but you don't help yourself, do you?'

'What happened to your face?' Tatty asked.

'You hit me,' he said.

'Before. Has this got anything to do with Ben being taken? You turned up in a right mess this morning, and still haven't explained yourself properly.'

'No,' Frank interrupted. 'We know why Ben was taken, don't we?'

'Your fault?' Tatty said, looking at Frank.

'You might have wanted to claim back some territory, the Gorleston basin,' Frank said. 'It appears someone else had a similar idea.'

'You what? You're now trying to blame others for the biggest mistake of your life?'

'The biggest mistake of my life was getting involved with Rich, you, your family.'

'The things we've done for you, Frank. You ungrateful bastard.'

'The things I've done for you.'

'Stop bickering, the two of you,' Sam said, leaning forward. 'This is getting us nowhere.'

'I think I might know where Ben is,' Zach said quietly. 'I was in Lowestoft, on a run. Abir smelled a set-up, but he's a twat and what's it to me if he walks right into it?'

'Abir's OK,' said Frank. 'Fine fellow, smart. I don't know why he got mixed up with you, though.'

'New scene?' said Zach brightly. 'The pull of the Golden Mile and all that?' He paused. 'To be honest he was trying to lie low, and dumped me in it – to the tune of ninety K. Fucking unbelievable.'

'We don't need to hear this again,' said Frank.

'Is that right?' said Tatty.

'I'd every right to kick his arse out of the county. But no, I'm a charitable soul and gave him a second chance, which he fucked up as well. He walks down the street, for the meet and greet, and doesn't reappear. Now, either he's done a runner or he's been snatched. He deserved it, if you ask me.'

'Slow down,' Frank said. 'Where was this? Lowestoft?'

'Yeah, some industrial park, near the water. I have a large and varied customer base, getting bigger all the time, I'm proud to admit.'

Sam sighed, began shaking her head.

'No one's told me about Winslow's Lowestoft base. Must be a new set-up,' Frank said.

'Strikes me, no one's telling you much about anything,' Tatty said.

'Stop it, you two,' Sam shouted. 'What does any of this mean for Ben? I don't understand.'

'Who drives a white Hummer, shiny grill, polished side-plates – super twat ride?' Zach said.

'Why can't you talk normally?' Tatty said. 'Even your grandfather had a better grasp of the English language. I can't understand what you're saying half the time.'

'You saw it?' said Frank. 'He's making it that obvious?'

'I'd be lying if I said I hadn't glanced it,' Zach said.

'And you just left Abir there?' Frank said, rising from his chair with such force that the fancy steel and wood contraption was sent flying backwards onto the stone floor. Limping heavily, he made swift progress across the kitchen and out into hall, before Tatty heard a desperate cry of pain. 'Ah, shit,' he shouted, breathlessly. 'Tatty, you'll have to drive.'

'I'm coming,' said Sam, standing.

Tatty paused by the island, her head swimming. She tried to focus on Sam's chair, which had remained standing, like some stupid dream of metropolitan chic and civility she'd once had. 'No you're not,' she said. 'It'll be far too dangerous. You can stay here with your brother. Where were you going anyway, Zach?' He had remained in his seat, and no longer seemed in any hurry to be out of there. He was shaking, head in hands.

'Getting away,' he mumbled, 'from you. From all this.' He sniffed, spluttered, finally looked at her with tears streaming from his eyes.

'Sam,' Tatty said, grabbing her daughter's arm, stopping her from running into the hall. 'Please stay here and look after your brother.' Tatty had never felt so torn, her heart sinking.

'He can look after himself,' Sam said. 'He's old enough. I'm coming. I need to find Ben. They took him, when they could have taken me instead. But I hid and he didn't, because he went to confront them first. He was protecting me, Mum. Unlike you.'

More tears, more guilt. A flood of them, a surge. A storm surge. Tatty couldn't stand it. But there was a glimmer – at least she might not have to kill Frank just yet.

## 21

'You'll get stopped, driving like this,' Frank said.

'What'd you want me to do, thirty miles an hour?'

'That's the speed limit.'

Tatty kept her eyes on the road, which was dripping with yellow-tinged street light, and flaked with frost, as another mini-roundabout suddenly loomed. 'We all know you stick to the law,' she said. The main roads – or what constituted main roads in these parts – weren't straight for long. Frank had insisted they stick to the A12 and not the old Gorleston Road, saying they'd get snarled up the other way, at this time of Friday evening. What did he know? What did he ever know?

The traffic management in Lowestoft was even more circuitous than in Great Yarmouth, whichever bloody way, she reckoned. Maybe he wanted them to take as long as possible, and was having second thoughts. She couldn't see how he'd be capable of putting up much of a fight. She didn't think he was armed.

'For God's sake, slow down, Tatty,' said Frank, clutching the sides of his seat. 'You're doing sixty-five in a thirty. It's not going to help matters if we're pulled over.'

Maybe he was armed. 'I don't believe what I'm hearing. This is a fucking emergency. My son's life is at risk.'

'They won't do anything that stupid,' he said. 'He'll be all right.' He didn't sound convincing.

More illogical road lay ahead, making the Yarmouth one-way system look a doddle. Not that she could see herself engaging with those blasted roads again in a hurry. Traipsing over the old Haven Bridge, winding along South Quay, past the Historic Quarter. Commuting to the Smokehouse. Day after day? Then sitting down at her desk, putting the finishing touches to the super casino plans – calling the lawyers, the accountants, the architects, builders, suppliers, protectors. Keeping the backers happy, with their increasingly outrageous demands. Putting her hand up at the council, getting her rightful place at the head of the Regeneration Committee.

Forget it. Forget it all. Her priorities had shifted. Everything had changed. Family first.

'If they dare harm him,' she said, sharply.

She should have been driving Frank to the nearest stretch of open water, or a high bridge. No, a multi-storey car park, that'd do it. Push him off the edge. That's what Britt Hayes wanted her to do. But Tatty had never been very good at taking orders from those in authority.

She went straight over the next roundabout, barely feeling the bump. Caught Sam collapsed on the cramped back seat in her rear-view mirror. Her daughter hadn't said a word for the whole brief journey. She currently had her eyes tightly shut, though she wasn't sleeping, Tatty knew. No one could in the circumstances. Tatty wondered whether she'd ever be able to sleep peacefully again.

She wished Sam had stayed at home – though she couldn't expect her to look after Zach, any more than she could expect Zach to do anything useful to protect his sister. At least her daughter was close by. How could she have left Ben and Sam in the Smokehouse when the Hummer had turned up, loaded with scum? She would never forgive herself.

'Slow down when you get to Oulton Broad Station,' Frank said. 'It's the first left, straight after, sharp turn. I've been here before, yonks ago. Rich was interested in an old depot.'

They passed an unlit park, then some shopfronts, also unlit, shuttered. The street lights were not making a sterling effort.

Tatty overtook a car at a junction taking its time, swung onto the wrong side of the road, went the wrong way round a traffic island, rejoined the right carriageway, at pace – the Merc's diesel finding form.

Another roundabout, and Tatty didn't have to be told to slow down by Frank. She didn't have any option. Ahead the road was blocked. A police car was slung across the street just on from the train station. Another police car was positioned the other way, a staggered effect. The blue flashing lights were dazzling. There was no way she could get past without swiping either vehicle. 'What are they doing?' She stamped on the brake.

'What's happening?' screamed Sam from the rear of the vehicle, eyes open, alert now. 'There're police everywhere.'

'Back up,' said Frank. 'It's a roadblock.'

Tatty felt paralysed.

'Back up,' repeated Frank. 'We need to get out of here. Come on, Tatty, turn this thing round. There's no way forward.'

She didn't feel paralysed any more. She sprung herself free from the seatbelt, opened the door and climbed out, having forgotten that it was winter, that air could be so chilling. Or what it was to be alive and breathing. Pulling her mac tightly around her she made for the nearest police car, next to which was standing a copper in full high-vis gear. 'I need to get through,' she said, approaching him.

'You'll have to use to the other bridge, by Lowestoft Central,' he said. 'Follow the one-way system back round, and look for signs to the A12.'

'You don't understand,' she said, 'I don't want to cross the bridge, I want to go left before the bridge, to the industrial estate.' She tried to see beyond him and the flashing lights, but she wasn't sure what she was looking for, how obvious, how sharp the turning was. Maybe she could discern more flashing lights in the distance. 'Man's Way,' she added, remembering the name of the street Zach had revealed.

The policeman's radio, pinned to his chest, was blurting away. Another patrolman, who'd been standing across the street, walked over. 'You need to move your car, and leave the area immediately,' he said to Tatty. 'You're blocking the road. Emergency vehicles need to get through.'

Tatty was about to say something about how it was them, the police, who were blocking the road. However, she could see, amid the frantic blue light, that their cars had been carefully positioned, to let key vehicles zigzag through.

'She wants to get down to Man's Way, the industrial estate,' the other officer said to his colleague.

'What's she want to do that for?' He looked at her. 'There's been an incident. No one's going down there.'

'What incident?' she said.

She became aware of a siren, sirens, then a dark car swept into view, coming fast down the road, the way they'd come. It was not a marked police car, but a saloon with blue flashing lights embedded in the grill. It managed to get round her car easily enough, and barely slowed for the sentries, who had stepped well back. There was one occupant, driving – a woman, a woman Tatty was sure she recognised.

'You need to clear the area,' the more vocal of the two policemen said harshly. The strobing light hitting his high-vis jacket was blinding.

'Please tell me what the incident is, what's happened. Is it an accident? I have business down there.' She didn't know how else to put it. *Ben? Business?* How dare she.

'There's been a fire, some casualties, we believe. Emergency services are doing all they can.'

Tatty looked behind her, back at her car. Frank hadn't budged from his seat, not surprisingly. She couldn't see Sam in the back.

'There's nothing you can do, except get out of our way so we can do our job.' It was the other one talking, though not so officiously. 'If you're worried about your property, I can tell you that the incident has been contained. Full information will be made public in due course.' He turned to his colleague, conversation over.

'Contained?' Tatty said. 'What about the casualties?' She didn't see any ambulances hurrying to and fro. Or any fire engines. Shane came to mind, but he was stationed in Yarmouth, not here.

Both policemen had begun talking into their radios, moving back towards their patrol cars. For a second Tatty considered making a run for it and slipping down the side road. But she'd never been a fast runner, sporty. She felt sick. Her heart was in her mouth. Her life felt like a sham.

Slowly, she walked back to her car, swallowing hard, not sure she'd be able to keep everything down. She was becoming aware of other vehicles behind hers, and a few people on the pavements. A crowd was gathering. She opened her door and got in, trying to shrink from view.

'What is it, Mum? What's happened?' Sam's voice was pure fear and panic.

'The big brass have arrived,' Frank said much more calmly. 'Must be serious.'

Tatty stared at the steering wheel, the dash. She couldn't speak. She shook her head.

'Mum?' said Sam.

She turned, looked at Sam. In Sam's face, reflecting the flashing blue lights, she saw some of Rich in her set jaw, her anxious but determined expression. Sam didn't give up on things lightly. She'd always proved herself. Tatty swallowed hard again and something dislodged. Maybe it was the sense that she couldn't keep anything from Sam, ever again. Besides she didn't know how many children she had left. 'There's been an incident, a fire.'

'Another fire?' sighed Frank. 'Haven't we had it with fires around here?'

'There've been casualties,' said Tatty, still looking over her shoulder at Sam, and thinking of Yarmouth, Lowestoft, the whole area ablaze. Was this why she'd made a lunge for Shane? Because he could somehow save her from all this? She wasn't that clever, that calculating. Stupidly, she'd been trying to be something she wasn't.

She wanted to get into the back of the car with Sam, hold her tight and never let go. But she didn't, because she was still meant to be in charge, needed to set an example. Except what was she boss of? A crumbling empire that had only ever been a charade, bluster, front.

'Ben?' Sam said, faintly.

Ben had had a plan, ambitions to take them to another level, and he'd only been working for her for week or so. Perhaps he'd have been able to pull it all around. Why was she thinking of him in the past tense? She stopped looking at Sam, and settled into the driver's seat. 'I don't know,' she sighed. 'They weren't saying more. I'm not sure I can take it. Everything's happened so fast. I'm sorry, I've failed you all.'

'Why didn't Zach do something earlier?' Sam wailed. 'If he knew where Ben might be?'

'Don't blame Zach,' Tatty said. 'It's my fault. All of this.'

'You need to move this car,' Frank said, calmly. 'Let's get back to Gorleston, and Zach. Who's to say this is related anyway? Let's hope not, hey?'

'Hey?' She couldn't look at him. Of course it was related. 'Is that all you can fucking say? Get out of the car. Do something useful for once.'

'I've done my hip in, Tat,' he said. 'I need to get to a doctor, the hospital.'

'Out of the car. And don't you dare come crawling back unless you have good news.'

'It's freezing,' he said.

'Get out, Frank!' Sam screamed from the back.

## 22

It took Sam a moment or two to work out what the blinding light was. Sunshine, it seemed, was cascading onto the pillow next to her. A fluttering in her chest was becoming more apparent, while her eyes adjusted, grew accustomed. She felt heat on the back of head, and slowly realised it was the sun also. She must have eventually gone to bed without pulling the curtains and conked straight out. However, she'd taken a couple of sleeping pills with half a bottle of Sauvignon blanc.

Tatty had produced an unused blister strip. Sam hadn't questioned her as to where she'd got it. They both knew that she shouldn't have had any such pills in the house. Her mum had been banging on about being clean for months. The lies were never going to cease.

Sam lifted her head, her upper body, feeling that chemical heaviness. She was surprised that the sun felt so warm, shocked that there was any sun at all. Just as she was beginning to enjoy the heat, the idea of a clear blue sky, a beautiful day, more reality hit.

She flung the duvet off, leapt out of bed, grabbed her dressing gown from the back of the door and stepped onto the landing in bare feet. She paused, patting the pockets.

Quickly she returned to her bedroom, got her phone from the bedside table and, checking the screen, ran downstairs. Nothing. She slowed as she heard voices, raised, strained, coming from the kitchen. She tiptoed the rest of the way to the closed door. The kitchen door was never shut.

Trying to stifle her breathing, she put her ear to the wood. She didn't recognise the female voice. Nor a male voice, which was louder, and saying clearly, 'I'm deeply sorry.' She heard her mum cough. She knew that cough. It had become a nervous tick. Her uncle used to do something similar. Not that Simon or her mum were blood relations.

'Where is he now?' her mum then said clearly.

Sam didn't hear the answer. She threw open the door. Her mum was sitting at the dining table with two other people. A man and a woman. The woman was in uniform, the man not. Her mum looked over. Her face was ashen, despite the bright winter light bouncing in from the back garden. 'Ben?' Sam said, rushing round the island, towards the table.

Tatty shook her head. Sam stopped. They were all staring at her, as if she shouldn't have been there, had walked in on some secret meeting. Another scam, this one involving the police, whoever else. She looked down at her bare legs, bare feet, feeling very exposed.

When she returned her gaze their faces were melting with concern. The woman in uniform looked Mediterranean – Greek Cypriot? From an old Yarmouth family, Sam expected, hoped for some reason. Comfort in continuity, or something like that. Her mind, only recently pulled from a deep slumber, was now travelling at a hundred miles an hour. She didn't want to halt it, so she had to think, take in what was being suggested, presented.

The man was thin, skeletal, creepy. He was looking at her mother. 'Would you like to talk to your daughter alone?' he said.

Sam couldn't work out how they knew who she was. That seemed presumptuous. But who else could she have been? Plus these two were familiar. They weren't the coppers who had come round the other evening wanting Zach. Though she suddenly knew that they'd been to the house before. After her dad had died. That was it. The woman was the local family liaison officer.

Her mum was now walking towards her. 'Yes,' she said. 'Sam, let's go in the lounge.' She took her by the arm, gently but forcefully, and led her out of the kitchen, straight across the hall and into the cold, unused front room.

'I hate this room,' Sam said.

Letting go of her, her mum closed the door, shutting them in. 'Sit down, darling, please.'

'For God's sake, just tell me what it is.' Sam couldn't judge the tone of her mother's voice. There was some composure to her, at least. But she wasn't going to sit down and brace herself. She was getting far too used to bad news. That was all that ever happened here. Who'd died? Confirmation that Ben had been in the fire in Lowestoft? That something had happened to Zach, who hadn't been at home when they'd got in last night?

The little fucker had disappeared, yet again. There was no sign of his car, and his phone only was going straight to voicemail. Why hadn't Frank put a tracker on it, or the car? It was the twenty-first century. No one should be able to disappear for long. No one who you didn't want to disappear. Who you loved. Her mind was flying. She didn't want it to settle, to concentrate on the present. Though she had no option.

'It's your aunt,' said her mum.

'What?'

'Jess – who was married to your dad's brother, Simon.'

'I know who Jess is – she disappeared. Ages ago.' Sam was staring at the dismal fireplace, with its dull copper hood. She couldn't remember it ever having been lit. Couldn't remember the last time she'd actually sat in this room, though Frank was snooping around in here yesterday.

'Her body's been found,' her mum said. 'They've just identified her.'

'Where? Where did they find her?'

'In Breydon Water. You know, the police have been digging around in the mud, following the discovery of a corpse.'

'They've found Jess?' All Sam could think was that nobody had ever liked her, not even Simon. 'She had an affair with Dad, is that right?'

'They believe she was murdered. They've found a number of bodies – she was one of them.'

'When? When was she murdered? Recently?' Sam's mind switched to Zach. However infuriating he was she still loved him. He was breaking her heart, all of their hearts. She couldn't have something happen to him, as well as Ben, even though she loved Ben more. He'd always looked out for her, and she him a little bit, maybe. They were closer in age, that'd made a huge difference when they were growing up.

'They haven't put a date on it,' her mum was saying. 'They're doing tests. But they reckon she'd been in the mud for a good while.'

'Ooh. She wouldn't have like that.' Sam didn't know what she was saying. She was trying to picture Jess, in all her tarty finery, being dumped in the mud. How could her dad have fucked her? That's what Zach reckoned had been going on. She'd been stick thin with pumped-up tits and lips. It would've been like fucking one of those sex robots. But that's what men liked nowadays, wasn't it?

She'd barely known the woman – wasn't sure it was possible to ever really know people like that. No one had ever liked Simon anyway, including her dad, his brother. 'Why are they here, telling you?'

'She doesn't have – didn't have – many relatives.'

'What else?' said Sam.

Her mum was holding something back. Both of them seemed on the verge of smiling, laughing, nevertheless. For a long dreadful moment or two she'd thought they'd been talking about Ben. Similar thoughts must have gone through her mum's head when they'd turned up. The police never brought good news. How come her mum had even let them in? Wasn't there a rule? The hypocrite.

'They're looking for Simon.'

'Good luck to them,' Sam said. 'Can we renovate this room?' She was looking out of the windows. There were two, facing the front, and a wall of grey sea, despite the light, the low winter sun slanting onto it this morning. It should have been blue. Mediterranean blue. She turned back to her mum, who smiled. This was the first time Sam had seen a little lightness in her mother's face for a long while.

'They say they want to inform him personally – thought I'd know where he is. I think they suspect he has something to with it,' she said. 'He's a person of interest, was their phrase. Maybe they'll be able to track him down if they put their minds to it. I wouldn't mind a word with him myself, if they do.' Tatty walked over to the nearest window, stared out, tapped the glass. 'Do you think you'll want to stay here?'

'Why can't they track Ben down?' Sam said. 'That's far more urgent, isn't it?' Sam felt her stomach heave, something in her chest go.

'It's complicated, even discussing it with them.'

'You can't mention him to the police, can you, because of all your other nasty business, and how it might incriminate you?' The true horror of the situation was slapping her in the face once more. 'Even at that roadblock last night you wouldn't have said that your son might have been down there, which would have meant they had to let you through.'

Sam turned away from her mother, took in the dreadful room again. It was beyond renovation, modernisation. Apart from everything else, it was in the wrong town. Her mum was right, she didn't want to stay here. The sea would always be the most deadly battleship grey, despite the sun doing its best. Only suitable for a war zone. There'd always be the memories as well, embedded in the sand, the sodden turf, the damp brick.

'I should get back to the kitchen, the police,' her mum said, not addressing the issue of Ben. 'I want them out of the house.'

'You're helping them with their enquiries, are you?' A glint from outside, a sharp reflection, suddenly caught Sam square in the eye, making her wonder whether she might go back to being a lawyer. Shift from corporate to criminal. She wanted to help people – people who were afraid to go through the proper channels, who were afraid of the police. People who'd been mistreated, or ignored, by the state, its corrupt apparatus. She could practise from experience. Tell clients that she knew all about collusion, the abuse of power, family dysfunction.

Glancing outside, at the big wide world, which looked so flat and pitifully grey, made Sam think that she couldn't lose all faith, even if legal solutions didn't always exist. The opposite, in fact. She had to fight it, the system, and do something she'd never done before. She wanted to help people who truly deserved it, not assist rich wankers to get richer. She'd made enough mistakes in the past, falling for the wrong people.

'I'm getting them off my back,' her mum said finally.

'You're still not going to mention Ben to them, though, are you? They must know something.' She didn't care if she blew the whole scummy operation apart. She hated Goodwin Enterprises and everything it stood for. She hadn't yet checked the news, the media today, she realised. What might have been in the public domain. Who else had been found dead.

'There's no point,' her mum said. 'It'll be different investigations, teams. Different police forces as well – Suffolk and Norfolk.'

'What about the NCA? Regional chiefs?'

'I've been talking to people, Sam, believe me.'

'Who are you still trying to protect? Yourself? Frank?'

'You,' she said, leaving the room.

'Don't bother,' whispered Sam, her pulse quickening. The only person who'd ever tried to protect her was Ben. And maybe her dad in his warped and twisted way.

## 23

'Tea please, four sugars.'

'I'll bring it over, love, seeing as it's you.'

'Cheers.' She was an ever-friendly face on a cold bend of the docks. Frank pushed himself off the sticky counter and hobbled to the nearest table. The River Café was not table service. He was being cheeky enough asking Beth to do the sugar for him.

'I can see you've been in the wars, Frank,' she called after him.

'Wouldn't you believe it,' he said, sitting slowly. He needed all the physical help he could get. He hadn't been exaggerating as he'd made his way to the table. 'I'll tell you what, love, can you do me a bacon butty as well? Plenty of red sauce.'

'Coming up.'

'Cheers,' he said again, knowing it wouldn't be coming up anytime soon, despite the place being practically empty. It was mid-shift for those who had proper jobs nearby, and Beth took her time at the griddle. He used to come here in the old days. Beth hadn't got any younger, or lighter. None of them had. His doctor would kill him for what he was about to eat and drink. But his doctor could go and fuck herself. Try and get an appointment? Forget it.

He'd spent half the night in A&E as it was, only to be told that there'd be a further wait of up to four hours for an X-ray. No, they didn't have any beds, any room on a ward, they were in the middle of a flu epidemic. He'd have to wait in the corridor. They'd said it nicely enough, and he didn't doubt that it was someone else's fault – the lousy, under-funding, incompetent government and associated bureaucrats. The country was full of them, most on the take. Which was why he and Rich had set out on the path they had, all those years ago, so he'd liked to think.

'Where've you been? Haven't seen you in yonks,' Beth said.

She wasn't any less talkative, he was pleased to find. He needed to hear a perky voice. See a red, smiling face. Plus he needed a witness – witnesses – in any case. Safety in numbers for once. 'Nowhere special,' he said.

Before getting a taxi to the James Paget he'd hung around by Oulton Broad North train station trying to keep warm. He hadn't been able to get any closer to Man's Way, the industrial unit, the incident. What was he meant to do, crawl there, Glock in pocket? The emergency vehicles soon stopped charging about as it was. There was nothing more he could do there. He had no good news for Tatty. No news at all.

The café windows were dripping with condensation. He was staring at the beads of water, watching them slowly slide to the bottom of the glass. He was not going to call Tatty. He had nothing to say to her, ever again.

It might have been bright out, but it was colder than yesterday, with a ferocious wind whipping in from the sea.

This end of Yarmouth, this end of the world, the wind chill got you by the balls, and twisted.

He looked at his watch. Howie was late. At least he'd acknowledged his text, said he'd be coming. That was news of sorts, he supposed, but for him only. He sunk his head into his hands, closed his eyes for a second or two. Better to know exactly what was heading your way than be taken by any more surprises. So what that he was armed? He wasn't going to shoot Howie, or anyone else. The only person he was thinking about shooting was himself.

'Frank – knock, knock, anyone home?' Beth slammed a steaming mug in front of him, without spilling any. 'Four sugars, as requested.' Dextrous she was, despite the bulk. Experienced too.

'Thanks. Sorry. Yeah, I've been up all night.'

'Who hasn't?'

'You were on last night as well?'

'Weather like this – I don't like to think that the girls have got nowhere to warm up.'

'There shouldn't be any girls coming in here.' Frank tried to sit up. 'What do you mean?' He was paying attention now all right. He'd moved them into houses off South Quay, before Tatty had effectively disbanded that end of the business. There were only a couple of establishments left, and these were shortly to be closed and the occupants, the more vulnerable girls, moved to the Merchant's House across the river, Tatty's idea of a women's refuge. 'Well, it's got to pay its way, somehow,' she'd said, smiling. He was going to miss that, the odd moments of lightness, warmth, irony.

'They're back,' said Beth, 'far as I can tell. Have been for a while. None of them are in a good way. They use my toilets to shoot up.'

'You don't mind?'

'I'd rather they had something wholesome to eat.'

'Who's running them?'

'To be honest, I thought you were, Frank.'

He took a sip of tea. It could have been sweeter still. Checked the other customers once more – a couple of guys in filthy blue overalls, and a paunchy, middle-aged man, wearing a cheap suit, glasses and with thinning, badly cut hair. He was pretending to read the newspaper, a red top. 'No, Beth. I'd never let our girls out in that state, or in this weather.' That might have been true now.

'That's why I haven't seen you around then.'

He smiled and nodded back, suddenly feeling more comfortable, at home, than he had in a long while. 'Yeah, one of the reasons. Anyone else new been turning up?' He flicked his head towards the man in the cheap suit. It was a dark brown. Rich used to wear pinstripes. Frank couldn't remember when he'd last worn a suit, what might have happened to it. He wasn't sure he'd ever worn a suit.

'He's working with the Port Authority,' Beth said.

'Doing what?'

'Why don't you ask him?'

'I thought you're the one who likes to chat.'

'That's all he's told me.'

On secondment, Frank reckoned. Either from Border Force, or the NCA. The man seemed to be doing his best to ignore them. He'd chosen this café for a reason, however. 'You haven't been getting lonely, then?' Frank asked.

'Three Chinese men were here yesterday,' she said. 'Haven't seen them before. Their English wasn't too good. They were with a small white fellow. Not much older than a kid. He'd seemed to be showing them around.'

Frank glanced to his side, trying to see out of the window. While the café was little more than a breezeblock and corrugated-roofed hut, stuffed with every electric heater imaginable, it had survived all manner of storm and flood, and did command a spectacular view of the harbour mouth. Nothing coming into the port, day or night, would be missed from here.

'What'd they eat?' he asked.

'They didn't eat. They all had a Coke. They did ask me who the owner was, though. Not what people normally ask me.'

'What did you say?'

'Told them to mind their own business.'

'They might have been looking to make you an offer, Beth.'

'What would they want this old shack for?'

'You and I both know the answer to that.'

Rich had toyed with the idea of grabbing the land and turning the café into a proper restaurant and lookout, although he'd had a soft spot for Beth and didn't want to upset her. He'd eventually decided that he didn't want this end of Yarmouth, the port, to be prettied up, anyway, fearing others might get ideas above their stations. If he wasn't going to do it, no one would. He'd have blocked all and any requests that would have come through the council, the Regeneration Committee, as well as making his views personally, and violently, very clear indeed.

'How long have I been here?' Beth asked.

'Beats me.'

'Thirty-four years. I'm not going anywhere.'

'No, of course you're not.' He tried to look outside again, beyond the condensation. The brightness had dimmed. Cloud was thickening. He had no idea what the forecast was. 'Though isn't there someone you want to leave something for? We know what this spot's worth.'

She laughed. Not a smoker's laugh, because as far as Frank knew she didn't smoke. Nor a drinker's laugh. But an eater's laugh. It was thick with pork fat. Frank loved crispy rind, crackling, bacon, sausages, black pudding. Realised he hadn't eaten for over twenty-four hours.

'I don't have any family any more, Frank,' she said more softly. 'This is my life, for a little bit longer, I hope.'

The sound of the front door opening against swollen wood, coupled with a sudden drop in temperature, and then the sound of it being rammed shut again, made them both look up.

'It's your friend,' Beth said.

'Let's see,' said Frank.

## 24

Howie appeared equipped for a polar expedition. He was wearing the thickest of puffas, the woolliest of hats, sturdy Red Wings, skiing gloves. Beth quickly got out of his way as he sat straight down across from Frank.

'Fuck me,' he said, 'has the shit hit the fan. I shouldn't be here. Britt would do her nut. I've got about thirty seconds to hear you out. Smart of you to make it public, but not that public.' He swung his head towards the man who'd told Beth he was working for the Port Authority. 'I know who he is. We don't need to worry about him. Talk.'

'It wasn't me,' said Frank. 'I'm not saying the thought hadn't crossed my mind. Or that I wasn't in the vicinity. But I didn't kill those two dealers.'

'They know you were there.'

'They? Serious and Organised? And not just you and Britt, who happened to be out for an after-dark dog walk, along the Gorleston seafront?' Even as he said it he knew that it hadn't been Howie and Britt together. Britt wasn't that slight. Frank could feel his head shaking. It did it on its own nowadays, like one of those nodding dogs in the back of cars.

'Do you have any idea what sort of electronic surveillance equipment that department has at its disposal nowadays?' Howie said. 'All funded by the likes of you.'

'No need to treat me like an idiot. I know how things work. I know my way around.'

'Sensitive today, aren't we?'

'Hungry,' said Frank. 'And pissed off.' He shifted on his seat, trying to relieve the pain.

'I'm the one who should be pissed off,' Howie said. 'Going behind my back on such ventures. Jeopardising everything we've been working for. Britt's tearing her hair out.'

'She should stop worrying about me and start looking at her colleagues more closely. You were tipped off, were you? Or were you there of your own accord, working to some remit that you haven't dared share with me? And with who exactly, if not Britt?'

Howie pursed his lips, shook his head. He had narrow eyes, to go with the thin lips, a sharp nose and a strong jaw. All hard edges and angles, except Frank knew he had a soft heart somewhere, for Britt, and for Baz. Once upon a time for himself as well.

'What went on by the Ocean Rooms, Thursday evening?' Frank said. 'The two scum getting it.'

'You could have warned us, Frank,' Howie said. It didn't look like he was going to remove his hat or coat, or gloves.

'I tried to reach you. But someone else got to you first, didn't they, which is why you must know it wasn't me. I'm telling you again.'

'That logic doesn't stack up. Besides, Britt was nowhere near Gorleston beach on Thursday evening.'

'But you were? Who were you with? I'm asking again.'

'I know what you were planning. Distract an ongoing investigation with something much more explosive.' Howie paused, quickly checking out the lone man, whom he'd implied he knew all about. This one anyway. He returned his attention to Frank. 'I've got to hand it to you. The audacity, my friend, and right on Tatiana Goodwin's doorstep.'

'Don't call me your friend, unless you mean it,' Frank muttered, picturing the bloody mess on the inside of the Mondeo.

'Well, you're not my enemy, yet. Britt thinks differently, however. Can't blame her, where she's coming from.'

'Who she's been talking to?' Frank muttered. 'How long have you known me?' he said more forcefully.

'Getting on for a decade?'

'Have I ever misled you?' Frank sat back as Beth approached carrying a large white plate and a bulbous plastic tomato of sauce. The outside could have done with a wipe – drying, crusty ketchup had all the wrong associations.

'Sorry to interrupt,' she said, plonking them on the table and swiftly backing away.

'In desperate times people do desperate things,' Howie said. 'You were up against the wall, history closing in – I can see that. Now, though, you've got twice the trouble, with that showy wanker in his Hummer after you as well. You should never have done a deal with Winslow.'

'Where's Baz?' Frank asked, looking at his food and wondering whether standards had slipped. Did Beth really want to spend the rest of her days here? She should sell up, take herself off to a Costa.

'He doesn't like the cold. Bad for his rheumatism.'

'He didn't mind being out the other night, though. Come clean, Howie. What were you doing there? Who tipped you off? Who were you with?'

'I could say mistaken identity, Frank. We all suffer that from time to time, don't we? Unfortunately, for you, we all know that you were there.'

'I guess Britt and her team have been listening in. Is the Smokehouse bugged?'

'The new guy, Kyle Neville, he's pretty resourceful, I will say that.'

'Leaving you and Britt no option? Never met the guy, by the way. Still, they can't frame me for this.' Frank paused, made another mistake by looking across to the lone man, who was now looking their way. 'They were already dead. Two shots, one to the head, the other not so clean – that's what I saw. It couldn't have happened much before I got there. But then you know that.'

'You really don't want to know what I know, Frank. Believe me.'

Frank exhaled. 'How did it get to this?' He shifted in his seat, never having felt so uncomfortable. 'Ow.' His fucking hip. 'Who were you with that night, if it wasn't Britt? Don't just sit there stony-faced. The things you and I have been through. Kyle Neville, is that it?'

Howie glanced over to the man, looked back at Frank, smiled menacingly. 'OK – here's what you don't want to know. There's a new outfit wanting to make inroads here.

I'm not just talking county line stuff. International players, with serious connections.'

'Serious and Organised connections.' Frank sighed, sniffed. 'Now I'm getting it. What is it with this place? The weather? The amusements? Everyone wants in.' He was getting a bloody cold on top of everything else. 'The market's crowded enough as it is, if you haven't noticed.'

'They want the port. These are not amateurs. It's a consortium that stretches all the way to China.'

'And you and Britt are doing what you're being told to do by these guys, right?'

'Me and Britt have always been our own people. But we're operating in a radically new environment now. Times change. This is way out of your league.'

Frank sighed, feeling a pathetic breath of air slowly escape his lungs, his chest. He used to be so strong. Physically and mentally.

'They've got freight in mind, chemicals, container loads of the stuff. Kyle Neville is in the middle of a balancing act, building a case with the NCA while lining his pocket and going up the greasy pole.'

'How did you two fall into such a trap?'

'Your past activities haven't helped. He's worked stuff out. Has a hold. He's a ruthless fucker, as well, as are so many men of that diminutive size. Likes a good show. You might want to ask him where he was Thursday evening.'

'With you? He was in on the hit? So I'm right?'

'I've said enough.'

'I'm now collateral. You were trying to set me up?'

'You've been getting in the way, Frank, for a long while. It'd be a lot easier for everyone if you were out of the way. You know too much – you do now, anyway.'

'Maybe that's the only currency I have left,' Frank said.

'You're not going to strike a deal. You know that, mate. We don't do that, do we?'

'Fuck off.' What Frank didn't know was how many people Howie had killed in his career. He'd never asked. It would have been impolite. He wondered how many of them had received the look he was getting now. Howie had always favoured his hands, or knives, to shooters. Other means too, so he'd implied, such as throwing people off bridges, buildings, boats. Out of fast-moving cars. Far less messy and incriminating. 'I'll talk to whoever I want.'

'No,' said Howie. 'Not this time – whether voluntarily or if you're pulled in. We can't afford the risk. Everyone cracks eventually. What you're going to do is disappear. Fast. See, I am offering you a way out.'

Frank looked at his bacon butty. He could have done with two. He shook his head in disappointment. 'This is why you agreed to meet – to tell me this?' A side of chips wouldn't have gone amiss either. Big fat greasy chips, smothered in salt and vinegar.

'I'm way out on a limb here – I only came for old time's sake. See, I'm not a total bastard.'

'Yeah?' said Frank.

Howie pushed his chair back, pulled his beanie over his ears, looked set to leave. Frank couldn't believe that this was it, after all this time, and what they'd been through together. He didn't like abrupt endings, he realised. He'd never got a chance to say goodbye to Rich.

'Your food's getting cold,' Howie said, a gentler tone creeping into the assassin's arsenal.

Frank picked up the ketchup container. He lifted the top off his sandwich, squirted a jet of red, watery sauce onto his bacon, two pale, flaccid rashers. He kept squirting the sauce onto his plate, shifted his aim to the table, the space directly in front of Howie. Squirted some more, trying to squeeze the living daylights out of the container. 'I reckon your and Britt's days are numbered here, as well,' he said. 'Where are you heading?'

'None of your fucking business,' Howie said, standing, looking like he was ready to trek to the North Pole. He'd have to go that far to escape the mess they were in. They all would.

Frank struggled to stand, clueless as to where he was heading, what was left for him. He looked down at his food. The bacon wasn't nearly crispy enough. He wasn't going to send it back, complain to Beth. He never complained about anything. Just got on with it. 'Wait up,' he said, hobbling after Howie.

Howie paused at the door, stared back at him, a look of disgust unmistakably crossing his face. 'What's up with you?'

'Busted my hip. Haven't been able to get to a doctor. When did you last try to get an appointment? It's impossible.'

'I don't see doctors. Haven't been in years. I'm fit as a fiddle.'

Frank didn't doubt it. Out of the café, the wind was swirling round South Denes, getting under Frank's jacket, trousers, slapping his head, chilling him to the core. He was not equipped for this, never had been. There was no traffic this time of the day, the weekend. 'I thought you said Baz didn't like the cold, that you'd left him at home.' The dog was suddenly at Howie's heels.

'Did I? He must have followed me here. He's got a good nose. Loyal as anything, aren't you, boy?' He leant down and patted the dog. Baz became increasingly excited.

'Glad you can at least count on your dog,' Frank said. 'Give us a lift, will you? I'm fucked.'

'Say that again,' Howie said, a smile breaking out on his tight, thin lips.

The thing was, Frank had a feeling Howie wasn't going to kill him just yet. Maybe he really was delivering a warning, giving him a chance, telling him to get the hell out of there – as an old friend.

The café didn't have a parking area, as such. Customers left their cars on the side of road, which was without a pavement on this stretch of South Denes. There were only three vehicles in sight: a newish Merc, a red Transit and a Citroën C3, with the ludicrous plastic moulding on its flanks.

Across the road was a new metal fence – thick, grey, chest-high strips, topped by sharp points. Behind this were two massive rectangular warehouses, covered in corrugated steel, neatly grey also. They'd recently been done up. There was a long loading bay. No trucks in sight. No signage anywhere. The new owner of this depot wanted to keep an anonymous profile. Frank didn't know who the owner currently was, or what the warehouses were to be used for. Chemicals newly imported from China? Maybe this was the real focus of the lone man in the café's attention. He hadn't asked Howie who he was. There was no point.

'Where're you heading?' Howie said.

'The office?' said Frank.

'Is that a good idea?'

'I should clear my desk out, gather my personal belongings.' Frank could have smiled, but the cold and the pain in his hip were making it impossible to express anything other than pain, hopelessness.

'Where's your car?' Howie asked, backing away.

'Long story. I got a taxi, here. They're not easy to book nowadays. Had to wait for over an hour.'

'No one to drive you? What about that kid, the young Goodwin? Actually, I know. Here's another piece of advice. You need to forget about him, the whole family. They're all toast, and more work for me today. Go on, get the hell out of here.'

'Are you going to give me a lift some of the way, then?' Frank was suddenly concerned for others, not just himself. Old family allegiances could not be dismissed just like that, of course. More lives were in peril. Those he really loved.

'We're on foot. Better for your heart. See ya.'

Useless, Frank watched Howie walk briskly away, with Baz trotting loyally along beside him. They crossed the road, turned right on Hartman, which went towards the sea. Howie didn't look back, and Frank didn't shout after them again, though he thought of the first time he came across Howie, or rather Howie had come across him. He'd approached him in the street, Regent Road, outside the club. Howie must have been watching him for a while. He appeared to know his movements. For a second, Frank had thought that he might have been making a pass. Wanting free entry. He'd such a glint in his eye.

'I used to kill people for a living,' he'd said by way of introduction. 'I'm retired now.'

'You look too young to be retired,' Frank had replied, he remembered all too clearly. Yeah, he'd fancied him immediately.

'That's what I was thinking. If you ever need a hand let me know.'

He hadn't left Frank with a number, an address, any way of letting him know how he could be contacted. But he popped up again, soon enough, eyes bright. Just when Frank happened to need his services, as well. It was some time later that Frank realised Britt Hayes and Howie Jones were an item – had always been an item. There was no such thing as a coincidence in this game, only a doddery old fool willing to be played.

Turning his head, he looked across to the blank-faced depot once more – a new front making its steely presence known. He felt in his pockets for his phone, found his right hand had stumbled on his Glock 17. His fingers tightened around the handle.

He should have shot Howie when he had a chance – though that would have meant shooting the dog as well. He couldn't have done that. He'd gone soft. He pulled the gun from his pocket. No one else was around. No vehicles heading his way. The only sounds, he realised, were seagulls squawking, and maybe, in the distance, the chug of a ship shifting down the Yare. He was far enough from the café to be sure no one could see what he was doing. Not that he especially cared.

It was a well-weighted piece, which had cost him £2K, in used twenties. Better balanced than the Glock 19. No wonder this was most law enforcement agencies' gun of choice. There were eight rounds in the magazine, space for another ten, including one in the chamber. More than he'd ever need. He raised the gun, at arm's length, pointed it towards his face, stared down the barrel.

Out in the middle of the street, at the sharp, narrow end of Yarmouth – end of the world, it might as well have been – the wind had picked up and it felt like he still had grit in eyes. They were watering like mad. He couldn't focus on the barrel. It was impossible to see inside, from this distance. He brought it closer to his face. The hole was still too small, too dark, to be defined, to give any clues as to what might be inside, what answers. Where it would lead.

## 25

Zach wasn't hiding quite in plain sight. However, there was a broad view, a vantage point, and something like a parapet, even if it was made of glass, thicker than your thumb.

He could have done with a vat of boiling tar, to tip onto any marauder trying to make it up the hill. Yarmouth had a medieval history, that much he knew. It still felt medieval. Fire and brimstone and all that shit. He didn't think boiling water would have the same effect as tar. It would probably turn to ice before it dropped more than a couple of metres. Ice, though, a big enough block, could do some damage. Or one of those stalactites – an ice stalactite, ripping through a chest and piercing a heart. He'd read somewhere that it happened occasionally – in Siberia, maybe Switzerland, a ski resort. A dagger of ice falling off a building, stabbing someone, and then the ice would melt and no one would ever know how the person was killed. No prints or DNA on a knife, for instance.

Couldn't they just look up, work it out? Though he knew that not all the authorities saw the obvious, or were the smartest kids on the block. To accept those wages?

The sun had been out earlier, blasting through the endless windows, knocking him into consciousness. There was no electricity, which was why he'd not been able to activate the blinds. Now the clouds were pouring in from the sea, across Yarmouth, the pointy end of the spit, making the river look like lead. It was a poisonous stretch of fucking water, that was for sure. Couldn't see why his uncle had wanted to build such a house, with such a view.

Look at me, I'm the king of the castle, or some such bollocks, Simon would have said. Zach, meanwhile, shook a fist at the world, triumphant – in his failure. His arm fell by his side. His hands were freezing, so were his ears and head. The pain was ice-cream cold.

He left the balcony, turned his back on Yarmouth and stepped inside, then spent an age and all his strength trying to shut the sliding doors. Salt and rust were playing havoc with the runners. He didn't think anyone could have been in the building for months.

Had the electricity not been cut off, and the backup batteries run down, he supposed the alarm would have gone berserk when he broke in. As it was there wasn't so much as a peep. Nor a smidgen of heat. The concrete box was brutally exposed to the elements. So much for twenty-first-century insulation. He didn't think that Simon would have given much of a shit about the environment when he commissioned the house. The statement, the position, would have been all he cared about.

Endless corners would have been cut, reams of legislation ignored, because Simon was a Goodwin. Zach laughed, and his jaw ached, and he surveyed the empty master suite.

Someone had done some tidying up, clearing out, on behalf of his uncle. There wasn't even a fucking blanket to go on the bed – not that he could find.

He'd yet to have a proper snoop round, however. Last night he was in no state, being powerless, and powderless. Didn't those concepts go together well. Except gear never lasted long enough, even the synthetics. Perhaps power didn't, either.

He checked the time on his phone, ignoring the messages, the missed calls log, ignoring the temptation to check into social media, check any media. He didn't want to know what was going on out there, in the cold, cruel world. What might have happened to Abir – and Ben. He knew he should have felt more for his brother. He felt bad about that. But, growing up, Ben and Sam were a gang, and he was the one left out. Had to find his own way, and at such a tender age, because it wasn't as if he had much of a mother to look after him, while his dad was just a prick.

He looked at his phone. It suddenly occurred to him that he shouldn't have left it on. He could be traced. What a dimbo.

The coppers who'd turned up at his home the other evening, looking for him, they'd have the know-how. Their superiors, anyway. He pressed the power button hard, turning the thing off. He should have flung it in the drink. Picked up another burner.

Staring at the blank screen, in the concrete fortress high on Ferry Hill, he felt like he was in some kind of prison already. They were after him, weren't they? He knew they'd get him one day. Dealing class As from the back of

Range Rover? An accessory to this and that. Some jealous fucker had probably dobbed him in.

Man, prison would be lonely. Though not necessarily drug free, from what he'd gathered. Still, right now he could have done with some company, preferably female. He wasn't so good on his own. Where was Clara when you wanted a chat and a cuddle, no strings? There were always strings. Sian's beautiful, tiny face popped into his mind. Would the pain of losing her so violently ever cease? The weird thing was he didn't think he was that into her when she was alive.

Maybe it was Clara's mum he needed now, Nina the cleaner, to help him tidy up the mess he'd got himself into. She'd worked tirelessly for his dad, hadn't she? He took off, skipping down a flight of polished concrete steps, his mind focusing on a new business idea. A jingle popped into his head. *No murder too large or small, no scam too wide or tall, we hide your traces in the most unlikely of places.* Though wasn't this Frank's job already?

Flying into the massive kitchen-lounge area, on the floor below, he quickly lost his bounce, and stood stock still in the middle of the room. He couldn't ring Frank yet, maybe never again. He sniffed, glanced about the place. There were acres of polished concrete, raw steel ageing fast, and bare wood planks with little shine. He sniffed again, wiped his eyes. He loved Frank – the only person who'd ever really cared for him. He shook his head, hard, trying to shake that moment of weakness away. Wiped his eyes again.

The counters were mostly empty, while the furniture looked like you wouldn't want to sit on it for long.

Everything was in the right place, but wrong, somehow. Maybe Simon hadn't quite disappeared into the ether. Certainly, there was unfinished business all over Yarmouth. Something his mum wasn't so keen on acknowledging.

The longer Zach stood there the more he realised that it didn't smell right in the large room, either. He peered into the sink. Last night he'd not been able to find a cup, a glass, and had to drink out of the tap – at least the water was still running. However, there was a glass standing in the middle of one of the sinks right now, trying its best to glint at him. There was a finger of water in it. He shook his head. He was losing it. Imagining things. Hallucinating.

Pacing the room, he sniffed and sniffed, until his nose hurt. Then he descended another flight of stairs and toured the ground-floor space. There was a cloakroom, a small gym and a games room – or den, he supposed Americans might have called it. There was a load of swanky equipment for people who had too much money.

Then he raced all the way up to the freezing top floor, where he'd kipped. He was struggling to understand why anyone would want a view of such a grey river, and drab grey roofs beyond, and a sky which was also grey. There were some shitty white turbines in the distance not making much effort to turn even slowly. He was finding it difficult to breathe, and had to run back out of the room.

Once on the main floor he found that the smell was becoming overbearing. It was a person smell, he decided. Unwashed body, though with something else. He lifted a chunk of hoodie to his nose, caught a whiff that wasn't appealing. He couldn't remember the last time he'd had a proper shower, put on clean rags. However, there was definitely more to the smell than his own rotten body.

He crossed over to the L-shaped couch, which up close was not pristine. There was a shade of dust and faint stains on two of the large, cream-coloured velour cushions, as if something dark, disturbing, had once been spilled. It hadn't been completely removed. He walked back to the kitchen area, peered at the glass in the sink and realised what the smell was. It was cologne, an all-too-familiar cologne. He was certain it was what his sleazy uncle Simon used to wear, which sort of made sense, given that it had been his house. Yet Zach didn't think such a smell could linger for that long, not like cigars, say.

Despite the temperature he wanted to open the windows, and for a blast of fresh air to blow through. He had no idea how to open them in this room, however. There didn't appear to be any handles, catches, devices or a system. Maybe they were electronic, except the electricity had been cut off.

He had a sudden, overwhelming feeling that he was already in prison – for every sin that he and his family had ever committed – despite the largeness and airiness of the space. Freedom never really existed anyway, did it? It was just an illusion. Something people dreamt up to give them hope, aspirations. But reality would always get in the way. The chains shackling you to a way of being, history, family, endless laws that sucked.

He kept looking through the glass for some sort of sign. Shouldn't the day have been brightening, at this hour of the morning – Saturday morning, too, if he remembered correctly – not darkening? It had started sunny and bright enough, hadn't it? Nothing good lasted round here. Not for long. What was also becoming clear, as the sky now grew greyer, was that he wasn't the only person to have occupied this building recently. Simon was back, was all he could think. There was no escaping your family, your upbringing, your past. Even in Ibiza he'd felt haunted by it, then weirdly compelled to return. He'd missed Frank – that support, that help, that bond – truth be known.

Besides, he wasn't the only young Goodwin to have snuck back. Both Sam and Ben had given up their London lives and returned, hadn't they? And so, it seemed, had Simon, once again. This was too freaky. Unless he really was imagining things – his mind fucked by years of pharmaceuticals, and a morning in someone else's crib, all on his lonesome. What he desperately needed now was a toot and a pill, and a long, quiet smoke. Nothing doing here, of course. He was completely out of gear, and out of cash and credit as well. Fucking Abir, wherever he was right now. It'd serve him right, that business with the Zees.

No, it didn't serve Abir right. Zach should never had abandoned him. He should be doing more to find Ben, as well. He was his brother, for fuck's sake. What were families, if they didn't stick together, fight for each other? Not *with* each other.

Zach glanced skywards once more, as if for inspiration. Why couldn't he be a better, stronger person? Frank at least had his code – never wavered.

These freezing new digs were fast losing their appeal. Zach wanted to get out of there. He'd tucked his motor behind a unit just off Riverside Road. The idea of the black chariot sitting there gave him some comfort. Except he had no idea where he could go in it, where he'd be safe – not just from all the dudes out to get him, but from himself too. Yeah, he never did himself any favours – that's what Frank, and his mum, were always saying to him.

Fine, he'd happily put up his hands right then and there, and admit that he was his own worst enemy. Yet, he was a Goodwin and Goodwins didn't give in, give up. Strength, boy, back bone – he could practically hear his father.

He found himself wandering across the room towards the stained couch. He collapsed on it front first. Maybe he was simply exhausted. It'd been some twenty-four hours. More shut-eye might help him think more clearly.

It took him a while to get comfortable, not just because of the cold, but also because the couch was rock hard. It was a stupid designer item made for gawping at, not dozing on. The fabric stank as well. Not of the Simon cologne smell, or dirty, unwashed bodies – like his own – but of cleaning product. Chemicals. He shifted his head, his nose away from the cover, and shut his eyes tighter and curled into a ball, pulling a cushion on top of him for heat. However, just as sleep might not have been far away, he heard a knocking sound. Thumping, more like.

Someone was downstairs, banging on the front door. Which must have meant they'd either scaled the solid steel, two-metre-high electric gate, as he'd had to do, or somehow opened it. Maybe with a key, or the correct passcode. But if that was the case then why were they then banging on the door? 'Fuck,' he said aloud, hauling himself off the couch. He ran round the room a couple of times, before creeping downstairs.

He kept as close to the walls as possible, despite the fact that the stairwell had no external windows. On the ground floor he tiptoed across the hard, square hall and slipped into the gym. The banging on the front door had stopped, but he had a feeling that whoever was there hadn't left the premises. He was right.

The gym had a line of windows above head height, so no one could see in, he guessed, as they faced the front yard and beyond that the wall and gate to the street. Having climbed onto a weightlifting bench, however, Zach could look out. A man and a woman were standing on the grey slate front path. They were not in uniform but they might as well have been. They screamed pig.

Zach immediately climbed down and exited the gym, and ran up the stairs as quietly as possible. Once back on the top floor he kept away from the windows, even though they looked the other way, across the river to Yarmouth. Things were not making sense. The police could not be after him – no one knew he was here. They must have been after Simon, meaning that they had information he was back. It couldn't just have been on the off chance, could it?

It didn't appear they had a warrant. They weren't busting the door down. Zach felt safe enough to retrieve his phone and switch it on. He couldn't spend the rest of his life running around this shell of a house, waiting for the pigs to return with a battering ram. The phone practically leapt out of his hand as one message alert after another beeped in. There was only one person he could call for help and advice. The one person he only ever called when things were desperate. And it wasn't his mum.

## 26

Since she'd last looked two more cars had joined the motors lined up facing the sea in the Marine Parade car park, a hundred metres away or so. That made five in total. It was hard to tell from where Tatty was standing how many people were in each car. Most would be occupied by lone pensioners, desperate men.

They kept their engines running for the warmth. Each car was puffing little clouds of exhaust. None of these cars was electric or hybrid. They weren't occupied by modern-thinking individuals. It was a scene that had been going on for decades.

Tatty thought of Frank. At least he now had a hybrid, of all people. Not that he could probably drive it at the moment, with his busted hip. But he understood aspects of the natural world, how and where plants grew best, even if he didn't understand human beings so well. As far as she knew he'd never had a partner, a relationship.

Where the hell was he? OK, she'd kicked him out of the car last night, but with strict orders. He was a man of resource. Had been. Loyal, too. The silence was killing her. All the local news was now saying was that there'd been a fatality in a fire in a warehouse in Lowestoft. No name would be released until next of kin had been informed.

*Next of kin?* Well?

One report suggested there were problems identifying the victim due to the intensity of the blaze. An investigation was ongoing. Yeah, right. The ACC Britt Hayes was also keeping quiet. She must have known something more than what was being released. That was the point of the police, wasn't it – such investigations? How they played the public. Except Tatty wasn't sure who knew what in that rotten force. The two in her kitchen earlier this morning were only fishing, even if they'd managed to create enough of a stink.

Tatty had a sudden urge to do something very violent to Britt Hayes. Nothing about her made sense. Her allegiances didn't stack up. Her boyfriend a former hit man? And what was it with the dog?

Tatty had never had a pet, never needed one living with Rich. He was all the animal anyone could ever have wished for. She moved away from her bedroom window, determined not to do Britt Hayes's dirty work for her. She didn't owe her, not personally, whatever Hayes might have implied. She wasn't sure Hayes had ever been much use to Goodwin Enterprises. The other way round, more like, with Hayes in her trim, outdoor, keep-fit gear, trotting all over fat, hopeless Frank, ever eager to spill the beans. So he got to do what? Pat a fucking dog.

Where was Hayes right now? Not helping to find Ben. Or identify him – his remains. No one was. Oh God.

Letting her dressing gown fall to the floor, she turned her naked back on the Gorleston seafront, Marine Parade, the losers in their cars, the few others out walking dogs, and headed towards her en suite. She'd already had a shower, but she needed another. The tears had long dried up, but she felt filthy inside and out. She didn't know how much scrubbing it'd take to cleanse her skin, herself, of all the misery that had cloaked her and this dismal part of the world.

The shower was as hot and hard as she could bear, and she attacked her skin and hair with every soap and cleanser to hand. Normally she'd be careful of the amount of products she used, having once read that water was the best possible cleanser to maintain the skin's natural moisturisers and her wonderfully youthful glow.

She didn't crave youth and good looks any more. She'd seen enough, been hurt enough, to know what was what. Punishment came with her territory. To varying degrees she was used to that, she realised, scrubbing more of her skin, her body, with ludicrously expensive products. Vengeance was now her priority, before escape. Before she gathered her family, whoever was left and willing, and took flight like a migrating bird. Birds knew naturally what was good for them, what enabled them to survive, against all the odds. Humans didn't.

Back in her bedroom, half-heartedly towelling herself dry, she surveyed the mounds of clothes on her bed, those that had spilled onto the footstool, those draped on the chairs and pooled on the floor. It had been a hurried excavation of her wardrobes, her summer clothes having been buried deep.

She couldn't see anything suitable to wear now, to go to work in. Except it was Saturday. She wasn't going to work. But she wasn't going to stay at home all day, either, waiting to be informed, *as next of kin*, of her eldest son's death in a terrible fire. Despite the damp, the relentless cold, fires were all too common in her world. It was such a basic way to cause maximum damage, to eliminate someone and any evidence. Not for the first time she considered Shane, her choice in men, their usefulness.

Unearthed with a clump of bikinis was an unused bottle of Chanel No. 5. She'd told Rich countless times that Chanel No. 5 eau de parfum was for sophisticated women of a certain age. Who the fuck did he think she was? Mademoiselle, maybe – though that was ages ago.

She lunged for it now, took aim and launched it at the wall just above Rich's side of the bed. The heavy glass bottle smacked the plasterboard with force but it didn't smash, falling harmlessly, intact, onto the pillows. Tatty screamed in frustration, anger, terror – finally falling to the bed herself.

Burying her head in her summer finery she continued to sob, feeling her whole body shake. As the sobbing calmed, and she gained some control, she began to beat the clothes with her fists, as if she were beating the living daylights out of Britt Hayes, Frank Adams, the members of the Hummer gang and every other low-rent Great Yarmouth criminal, fraudster and con, harder and harder, in the face, the neck, the solar plexus.

'For God's sake, Mum, what are you doing?'

It was Sam's voice, right behind her. Tatty hadn't heard her enter the bedroom. She didn't look over her shoulder, didn't dare, as she continued to beat the bed with her fists, the idea of all her foes, piling up, one after the other. There were too many. And the shame. Her hands were having so little effect. She was far too weak.

'What the hell are you doing?' Sam repeated harshly. 'Why're all these clothes on your bed? You do realise you are completely naked, don't you?'

Tatty stopped thumping the bed, but it was much harder curtailing the sobs, which had started up again. For years, decades, she'd never once cried. Now she was at it all the time. 'Packing to go away,' she spluttered. 'I've been looking for my summer clothes.' She gulped air. 'We all need to get away. I thought we'd just go to the villa.' She took another huge breath. 'The weather can be lovely in Ibiza at this time of the year. It's almost spring there.'

'Jesus Christ,' Sam was saying. 'You've gone mad. You just want to run away? What a bloody horrible mess there is in here – and out there. You need help, Mum. Oh, and by the way, there's a man downstairs to see you.'

'What?' At that Tatty rolled over, covering her nakedness with the clothes to hand. She then wiped her face, her eyes, with an old pair of fine, silk shorts. 'Who? The police? Again? Do they have news about Ben? Oh, please God, no.'

'No, it's not the police. Calm down.'

'Calm down? How can I? How come you're so fucking together?'

'We need more from you, Mum, than this. You have to be stronger, show us the way. Dad would have, even when he was under all that pressure. How do you expect us to behave if you're acting like this? You're fucking mad.'

Sam was right, of course. Tatty had to set an example – if only for them. They were what made life worth living. 'Who's here?'

'It's that fireman you've been shagging.'

'Shane? How the hell do you know about Shane?'

'Do you think I'm blind? That's always been your problem, and Dad's. You think we don't notice anything. Well we do. Everything. Me, Zach and Ben.' Her voice wobbled drastically. 'Are you going to put some clothes on, or do you want me to show him straight up?'

Tatty swung her feet off the bed. She was still clutching some clothes to her body, but not ones she would be putting on for a number of months, not anywhere near here anyway. 'No, don't let him up. Please. He can't see me like this.'

Sam stomped out of the room, leaving the bedroom door wide open. 'Thanks,' Tatty said to the vacuum, meaning it. At least her daughter was still here, though gathering her own things, probably – packing to go away, for good.

What the hell was Shane doing here? She thought she'd made herself perfectly clear when he'd suddenly appeared yesterday, outside the Smokehouse. She didn't want his help, or for him to be any part of this. Too many innocent people – her family – were already getting hurt.

She rushed over and slammed her bedroom door shut and returned to the mess on the bed to find something half suitable to wear. She quickly pulled on a singlet top and a silly wrap dress, neither bringing particularly happy memories. She spotted the Hermès shawl that had been a gift from Rich, one of his better offerings. She dabbed her eyes with it then flung it around her shoulders and left her room in bare feet.

It was only when she was halfway down the stairs that she realised her hair was still wet from the shower and that she didn't have on any make-up. She must have looked like she was dressed for the beach, a strip of Mediterranean paradise. Not some freezing stretch of sand and dog shit, lapped by the steel-grey North Sea. Her heart had never been in this part of the world – or her head. Who had she been kidding? Ever since Rich had died she'd been putting on the wrong front. There was no way on earth that she was ever going to head up the Regeneration Committee. Besides, Ben had asked her to do so, part of his big pyramid plan, and she was never going to see Ben again.

'Tatty, I'm sorry if I'm interrupting anything.' Shane was looking at her intently, oddly, standing in the middle of the hall. 'I thought you should know something. I've been trying to ring you.'

'I've been in the shower,' she said, as casually as possible. Sam had remained by the door to the kitchen. Tatty gave her a filthy look. Sam gave her the finger back. Tatty returned her focus to Shane. 'What is it?'

'Can we go and sit down somewhere?' He was slightly flushed, either because he was embarrassed or because he was wearing an enormous down coat, which was zipped tight. He glanced over at Sam. She smiled back this time, though sarcastically. Tatty knew that look – it was what stared back at her whenever she looked in the mirror.

'You've met my daughter then?' Tatty said. They were more or less the same age, although they hadn't been to the same school. Sam had gone private, and done very well for herself – as Rich used to say. It was a lie. She'd been bullied remorselessly, and had hated every day. Yet Tatty had barely helped her, because she'd been self-medicating with abandon.

'Yes,' Shane said. 'She let me in.'

'What does he know?' Sam said, looking at her mum. 'We are a family,' she added, turning her head. 'You can tell me as well.'

'Let's go into the kitchen,' Tatty said. The house might have been boiling but her feet were cold. There was under-floor heating in the kitchen and plenty of edges to grasp onto, if her legs were to give way. She pushed past Sam, and managed to reach the dining table. 'Do you want a coffee or anything?'

'I'm good, thanks,' Shane said.

'Well?' Tatty said, glancing through the windows. She couldn't look at him. The day had started so bright, but now it was back to its usual thunderous temperate grey. She glanced down at her colourful wrap, her bare feet. She should have shaved her legs. It was funny how your mind flitted from one banal thing to another at such times. The need to feel attractive, desired, would never go away she supposed. No one was going to sit down.

'Don't take this the wrong way,' Shane began. 'I know some things, which I thought you'd want to know.'

'What do you mean don't take this the wrong way?' Tatty said.

'What you're involved in – I know things, everyone does. I'm just trying to help.'

'Get on with it then.' Tatty felt blindsided. She wasn't used to people helping her, unless there was something in it for them – most commonly money, or sex. Except she had a feeling Shane really did want to help her, as a partner, as a lover. And he was only Sam's age. It was not appropriate. She couldn't handle it.

'The shootings in Gorleston on Thursday night are being linked to the fire in Lowestoft – according to a mate in the service, that is. The regional fire investigation team have been called in. They're working with the police.'

Tatty sighed. She thought he had something new, important to say. She watched Sam's face fall. 'So?'

'The same gang's believed to be involved. You've got nothing to be worried about.'

Tatty shook her head.

'Hardly,' muttered Sam.

'Yesterday, you were in such a state, Tatty,' Shane continued. 'I didn't meant to stick my nose in unnecessarily, but I thought I'd try to find out what I could, see if I could help.'

'As you keep saying,' said Tatty, deliberately not looking Sam's way and keeping her focus on Shane, who still hadn't taken his coat off. The truth was, he wasn't so great in bed. He was too considerate.

'The police talk to the fire service, and vice versa, in such scenarios,' Shane said. 'They believe that the people who were shot on Thursday and the person who died in the fire last night were from the same gang.'

Tatty's heart fluttered. Then reality hit like a heavy grey cloud. There were problems identifying the body because of the ferocity of the blaze. How would they know? Ben had been kidnapped, and probably Zach's driver Abir as well. 'Excuse me,' Tatty said. 'Even if they were from the same gang, someone must have been responsible for both incidents. Otherwise it doesn't make sense.'

'Like a turf war,' Sam chipped in.

'Yeah. But some infighting has been going on. Factions have sprung up, and the whole operation has started to implode – according to my sources.' Shane smiled.

This was too much knowledge coming from her toy boy, whichever way you looked at it. Tatty couldn't put a finger on the precise moment when she started to hate herself again.

'What if others got involved?' said Sam. 'Or got in the way somehow, and were dragged in, and killed?'

'Sorry if I'm not being clear,' Shane said, 'but the person who was killed in the fire last night was one of them, a member of this gang that apparently has been trying to spread its wings in Gorleston and Yarmouth for the last year or so. The one who died, he was foreign, they know that. Also that he used a lot of aliases. Plus the rest of his crew are not exactly helping the police with their inquiries – the ones they've arrested so far. As you'd expect.'

Suddenly feeling strangely proud of Shane, and proprietorial, Tatty sought out Sam's response. Sam was looking bemused, like it was taking her some time to compute what Shane had said. Then her daughter brightened, ran over to Shane, grabbed his arms encased in their puffy sleeves, stood on tiptoes and kissed him very briefly but squarely on the lips. 'I fucking love you,' she said, letting him go.

The only thing Tatty could think to say was, 'I hope you're bloody right.' She could see that a lot more explaining was going to be necessary if she were to continue seeing Shane. She looked down at the stupid clothes she'd thrown on. Then again maybe it wouldn't be necessary to explain anything to him. He'd never asked anything of her, and clearly knew considerably more than she'd ever let on. Perhaps it was better to leave things unsaid after all, and be accepted for what she was. Not that she knew what that was any more.

A pill was what she craved more than anything. Except those demons had to be kept at bay for a short while longer. She needed to get out of the house, keep moving, while she still had the strength, any sense of purpose. 'Let me put on some proper clothes, then I suggest we all go for a drive,' she said as calmly as she could, heading out of the kitchen.

Halfway across the hall she paused. Of course Sam didn't love Shane, though such a man, her age, wouldn't have been a bad bet for her, she couldn't help thinking. Plus he had no edge, no malice. He was straight up, strong, sensitive. What Sam deserved.

Being with him, Tatty realised, hadn't made her feel any younger at all. It had only made her feel older, and shown her what she'd missed out on.

## 27

'Sit tight, out of sight,' Frank said into his mobile. 'That's my advice, listen to it.' He wasn't such a doddery old fool, was he? He couldn't believe he'd had his finger on the trigger, was that close to topping himself. Now here he was, back behind his desk, administering advice. Maybe everyone needed to reach the very brink once in their lives, just to see that there was always one more choice. That life went on.

'What do you think I'm doing? Like I'm a sitting fucking duck here, Frank.'

'It's the cops, you say, not Winslow's lot. You've got nothing to worry about.'

'Who are you kidding? They'll be back, with a warrant, if they're not watching this gaff from the street. Besides, there's nowhere to hide in here. It's too fucking minimal. Can't even find a cupboard. Have you ever been in here?'

'Yes.'

'Doing what?'

'The last time . . .' Frank thought back. He had a vision of him and Tatty rolling a body into a blanket, then another blanket. They used rolls of duct tape, until the thing was wound tight like an Egyptian mummy. Tatty was hopeless with the heavy lifting, anything physical. Frank had to do all that. Down the endless concrete stairs and into the back of the Range Rover it went, in the dead of night. Surprising how such a flake could weigh so much. Must have been the bags of silicone. But he wasn't crocked then – was a couple of years younger as well. It felt like more than a decade ago. Too much had happened since. 'You don't need to know.'

Zach exhaled. Frank almost felt his rancid breath come through his mobile. 'No, I never do, do I?' Zach said.

'You rang me, Zach. I answered. I'm only trying to help.'

'I'm stuck.'

'As I said, sit tight. It's a Saturday. They won't be able to get a warrant that quickly. And if they are watching the place, then you're better off staying out of sight.' At least, Frank thought, I know where Zach is now. Best try to get him to stay there, even if the wrong authorities might have been circling.

'But what were they doing here?'

'Looking for Simon, I expect.' He certainly hoped so, because of the digging they'd been doing by Breydon Water. He glanced about his empty office. He'd come to pack up his things, but he'd never kept anything personal here, of course. He didn't know quite what he was doing in here, apart from stalling for time. Plus, he supposed, he couldn't have staggered any further in his condition anyway. There were no cabs available when you needed one, and there was no one left to give him a lift.

He tapped the loudspeaker icon on his screen, dropped the device onto the glass desk and rubbed his arms. It was cold and empty in the Smokehouse. The heating had not been programmed to come on over the weekends, except for the emergency frost stat. Apparently it wasn't cold enough for that. Could have fooled him.

'You still there?' Zach was saying.

'Yes,' he shouted, 'I am still fucking here, but not for much longer.'

'Can you come and get me? I don't like this house. It's creepy.'

'Creepy? Big boy like you? Come on, Zach. You need to grow up fast.' Frank rubbed his arms again.

'So you keep telling me.'

'Yeah, well, you won't have to listen to me for much longer.'

'Why, where are you going?'

'What can I say? My time in this town is just about up. I'm no more use to anyone. Least of all your mum.'

'You are to me,' said Zach faintly.

Frank felt his eyes immediately begin to pop and water, and he hastily rubbed them with his sleeve, thinking blasted sand and grit gets everywhere. 'Fuck's sake, I'm practically immobile, Zach. Good for nothing.'

'Where are you right now?'

'I'm at the Smokehouse, clearing my desk.' He wasn't sure why he added that last bit. He was the one who needed to grow up.

'That won't take you long,' Zach said.

Zach knew him better than the others, though Frank couldn't laugh, or even smile. He was too distraught.

'My car's still at the caravan park, even if I could drive it. There're no cabs available. Saturday morning shoppers gone mad, I guess. I can't come and get you, that's for sure.'

'You could swim across.'

It was definitely the shortest distance, as the seagull flew. Zach would have been able to see the roof of the Smokehouse from Simon's concrete box. 'Now a boat might not be such a bad idea,' Frank said, thinking aloud.

'It's not just the police,' said Zach, 'is it?'

'Winslow's lot would know better than to start poking around Simon's property.'

'If they've got Ben and Abir, they're not going to stop there. I'm next, must be. Or you, Frank. Or Sam, Mum?'

'They're not going to risk going after anyone else right now – not after the fire last night.' He wasn't going to explain the further complication of a police force in thrall to another master. There was quite some silence on the other end of the line. Frank wondered whether Zach had even clocked the news about the fire.

'That's not all,' said Zach, finally. 'I think someone's been in this house recently. It's like, really weird, but it sort of smells of Simon, his aftershave, or cologne, or whatever that spray he used was. You know that smell.'

'It's his house,' said Frank, 'seems only right.' Frank did know that smell all too well. It even managed to get onto Rich, via Jess, Simon's wife, when he was fucking her. Frank supposed it was like some sort of marker, and Rich had been too arrogant to care. Except he'd paid with his life eventually.

'When was he last here, Frank, in Gorleston? It's like it's fresh. Smells don't last that long. I thought he was dead, or

253

something. You and Mum promised he'd never show up again.'

'The drugs you take don't half play with your mind, Zach. You're imagining things. Are you in withdrawal? Hallucinating? Going cold turkey?' Frank thought of a boat again, a certain way out of there. He couldn't believe Howie, or Britt, would just let him drive off. Rare and Yare Yachts still owed him, along with the yard next to it. He wasn't yet sure, however, whether he'd offer to take Zach with him. He doubted the kid would like his idea of sunny retirement.

But he'd need a pilot. Zach had had experience on the high seas. How long would it take to get down to the Mediterranean, via the Bay of Biscay? Or maybe they could pootle through the canals of France. That had to be easier, gentler. More suited to his grand old age.

Frank took his phone off loudspeaker mode, put it to his ear and tried to stand, clutching the desk with his left hand. He yelped in pain. Reality bit.

'You all right?' Zach said.

'My hip. Look, call me if anyone else turns up. I need to get my car, somehow. I'll come by as soon as I can.' Frank wasn't going to risk asking Zach to come and get him. The boy would be nabbed, side-tracked – who knew what? Zach was such a liability. The thing was, Frank couldn't understand why he even cared. He needed to get the Goodwins out of his system.

'You won't just leave me here, then? said Zach. 'There's no one else I can call.'

'What about your mum? Your sister?' said Frank.

'I've put them through too much already.'

'You think keeping out of their way now is helping? You've run off one too many times as it is.'

'I thought you were about to bugger off.'

'They love you, you know,' was all Frank could think to say. He felt that grit in his eyes again.

'What I don't get,' said Zach, 'is why Winslow's lot are after us. They tried to set me up. I thought we'd done some sort of deal. Besides, we don't do dope any more.'

'Yourself excluded,' Frank said, livid for what the boy had put him, them all, through. If he'd been physically there, standing in front of him, Frank would have swiped him with the back of his hand. Rich used to hit his kids. He had a feeling that they wouldn't be behaving the way they did – Zach anyway – if he was still around.

'What do we do then – Goodwin Enterprises?' Zach asked. 'I've lost touch.'

'There's the super casino project still on the go, plus a few old ventures are still ticking over.' Frank was thinking of the protection and money-laundering vehicles, the smallest of prostitution rackets. A soft, nostalgic spot was opening up inside him. 'Your mother and I have been working hard, while Ben's been exploring offshore investment opportunities.'

Zach whistled down the line. 'Everyone doing their bit.'

'Yep, you could say that. Even Sam's been helping.' Why was Frank even telling him this? He hobbled towards the door, sensing that Zach didn't want to get off the phone. Until what? He got there in person? He could be so needy, plus he hated being on his own. He wasn't cut out for this business. Few people were.

'I've been trying, too,' Zach said. 'Just made a few wrong decisions recently. I'll get it right next time. I've been thinking . . .'

'So have I, Zach. This conversation has gone on far too long. Who knows who else is listening in? There are others out there after us, not just Winslow's crew. Switch your phone off. Lie low.'

'What if I need to get hold of you?'

'Send up a flare.'

'Don't disappear, Frank, please. I need you. You're the only person who's ever helped me, understood me. Frank?'

## 28

'Come on, man, wake up. We need to think.'

'I am awake,' Ben said, feeling himself being shaken again. He'd been conscious for a while, clarity beginning to emerge with the fact that he wasn't dead. He was in too much pain to sleep. He was in too much pain to move. The right side of his body was killing him, as was his head. 'Where am I?' He opened his eyes again. Took in the cool, friendly shape of Abir. He was in touching distance. They seemed to be in a small, cold space. He was freezing, he realised, though there was plenty of light. Light at the end of the tunnel, he couldn't help thinking.

'He's back,' Abir said, anxious as hell.

As his eyes and brain grew more accustomed to what he was seeing, Ben clocked that Abir was crouched by a window, lifting aside a small flap of dirty material, a curtain of sorts. 'Who's back?'

'The man with a dog,' Abir said.

Ben shut his eyes, but his head immediately started spinning. Opening them once more, he tried to sit up. 'Give us a hand, will you?'

'You want to sit up?' said Abir. 'Man, you look like shit. Here.'

Ben felt Abir put his hands under his armpits and attempt to lift him into a sitting position. Holding onto him with one hand he even managed to get a cushion wedged behind his back. Ben couldn't say that he was comfortable, and his head was still spinning, but he could see the window clearly enough, and see where he was. 'Who's caravan's this?'

'Who cares?' said Abir. 'Looked in better shape than some of the others.'

'You're kidding.' More of the interior was making its sad presence felt. Despite his nose being bunged with dried blood, Ben was starting to pick up a terrible smell of mould.

'Zach has plans to renovate these. Part of his club project – Bingo. There's going to be a big top, where the sounds will be, pop-up stalls for food and drink, pharmaceuticals, these old caravans for VIP accommodation. Has he told you?'

Ben shook his head, then regretted it. 'Zach's stopped telling us what he's up to. For good reason, I reckon. What a stupid idea. Lift that curtain for me, will you?' Abir pulled the edge away and all Ben could see was a flat rectangle of grey. 'Who'd want to spend a weekend raving here? It might have some currency as a holding centre for illegal immigrants, but I don't see anyone paying to come here, least of all VIPs.'

'There,' said Abir. 'See him?'

'I don't see anyone.' Ben tried to lean forward to get a better view out. Then he did see a figure, closer to the caravan than he'd been expecting. He was wearing a dark puffa and a beanie. 'I don't see a dog.'

Abir was telling him to shush, then whispered: 'It's by his feet, some sort of boxer. Mean-looking beast. His master doesn't look too friendly, either.'

'What's he want?' Ben asked, now struggling to keep his voice low. Getting his jaw, his tongue working was hard enough, without adding any subtlety.

'Shush.' Abir crept around the window, lifted more material, looked out from the other side. 'He's trying some of the doors.'

'For fuck's sake, no.' Ben tried to slump down on the narrow bench, but found he couldn't move. 'I don't think I can take any more beating.'

'Hard to tell whether he's chancing it or looking for something in particular.'

'Or someone,' added Ben. He could feel his heart beating fit to burst. He wasn't sure what sort of state it was in. Not its finest, the strain it'd been under.

'He doesn't look like he wants a place to doss. Seems too natty, well fed, clean-shaved.'

'Part of Winslow's crew?'

'Something tells me not.'

'Where's the vehicle?'

Having staggered halfway across the industrial estate, Abir had managed to get an old Citroen Saxo up and running. It was the sort of vehicle that Ben supposed wouldn't look out of place in the caravan park right now. He'd slipped into unconsciousness somewhere between Lowestoft and Yarmouth.

'I shifted it to the far end of the park, next to a burnt-out caravan, once I got you in here.'

'Cheers.'

'You're lucky you're still alive. We both are.' Abir glanced at Ben then returned his attention to the window.

'Lot of fires around here.' Ben sighed.

'Only way you can get warm, this time of the year,' said Abir.

'How did you do it?' Ben asked. 'How did you get us out of there?' He could remember suddenly being dragged out of the burning lock-up, but not much else.

'I guess I grew up in a tougher neighbourhood than that geezer. Plus he didn't know how to tie a knot.'

'You got one of them? Took him clean out? You certain of that?' The night was too much of a smouldering fog – maybe it was best if it remained that way. Anyway, neither of them had phones on them. There was no way of checking the news, messages, any streams, making contact with loved ones. Having taken an age to gain full consciousness, Ben was becoming increasingly anxious about what they might be facing, who exactly would be after them.

He could smell bonfire on his clothes. They needed to get out of their rags. He would have liked to put on his suit, pretend everything was normal, though he wasn't sure it would've fitted over all the swelling. Plus he had a vague memory that it was the weekend.

'The one with the accent, who lit the fire, yeah? I got him. The boss and the other one were out of there well before. Not a nice crew, to leave your mate like that.'

'You killed him?'

'He's back.' Abir was still staring out into the gloom. 'Shush.'

'You killed him?' Ben repeated, knowing that fog in these parts could last for days, blowing in from the sea, rising from the marshes, the water meadows. Thick and freezing, this time of the year. However, there were moments when it cleared, when you could see for miles and miles, across the vast, empty flatness.

'No, I'm no murderer,' Abir said, his eyes still focusing on the great outdoors. 'Self-defence it was. I had no option. Besides, he was the one who lit the fire. That's what would have got him in the end.'

'Not sure they'll see it that way – or the police.' Ben picked some blood from his nose. Eased an airway. 'Where's that man now?'

'Three caravans away. Do you think the dog can smell us?'

'That's what they do, isn't it? We never had pets.'

'That thing doesn't look like a pet. More like a weapon.'

'What's he want? Who the hell is he?'

'You can ask him, he's coming back this way. Shush.'

Neither of them said a thing for a couple of minutes. Ben could hear his breathing, and the soft wind outside. Maybe even the sea. Abir wasn't making a sound. He was so fucking cool. He'd also saved his life. Ben heard the crunch of boots on gravel, perhaps an excited dog kicking up pebbles. A blast of freezing air swamped the caravan as the door was flung open, and the whole structure shook violently.

'So here we are then,' the man said, though not in a totally aggressive manner.

Ben thought he was going to be sick, before realising that he must have been sick endless times last night – wretched his damn guts up. His top, Zach's blasted hoodie, felt crusty, must have stunk. There was nothing inside him except fear, and he thought he'd had his fill of that for one lifetime.

'Who the fuck are you?' Abir said, not calmly. 'You and your dog are on private property.'

'Yeah?' The man stepped up into the caravan, shaking the flimsy construction further in the process, and grunted loudly. 'I'm a local.' He spoke slowly, though not sounding like a local, and continued to look around.

He was taking up an awful lot of space in the so-called living area, even though the front door remained wide open. Ben had never spent a whole night in a caravan before. He wasn't planning to ever again. He doubted you'd ever get properly warm or feel remotely secure in such a thing.

'You're still trespassing,' Abir said, trying to sound calm.

'Got any tea?' the man said. 'It's bloody freezing out there.' Despite wearing a coat fit for a polar exploration, Ben reckoned, he stamped his feet and rubbed his hands as if to make the point.

Inside the caravan it felt like an earthquake had started up. Ben was amazed these things managed to stand their ground in such a park as North Denes. It wasn't just the ferocity of the weather, having blown all the way down the North Sea and over the scrubby sand dunes, but the sea that was forever threatening to surge over the sand, and creep round the back of Yarmouth, via the Yare and the Bure. At that moment Ben would have welcomed a natural disaster, as the man-made ones weren't letting up.

The man made an attempt to reach for the tiny kitchen area. Opened a cupboard. Slammed it shut. The caravan shook dangerously again. 'Don't see any tea bags,' he said. 'I'm guessing you two haven't spent a lot of time in here. New digs?' His voice wasn't so authoritative now. It was becoming angry.

Abir had been forced to move closer to Ben and was practically sitting on top of him. Ben didn't mind so much as he felt shielded from the intruder's view. He was trying to keep his eyes on the horrible brown speckled flooring as it was. He didn't want to see or know what was coming next.

'We don't have any fucking tea, mate,' Abir said, getting angry also. 'What do you really want?'

Ben could hear the dog sniffing and padding around. Abir had taken out one man very successfully not so long ago. However, this person seemed a different proposition, hound or not.

'Any water?' the man said. 'My dog's thirsty.'

'The water's not connected,' Abir said. 'You'll have to fuck off and get it elsewhere.'

There wasn't so much conviction in Abir's voice to go with the anger. He must have been exhausted, spent.

'What to do you want?' Ben croaked. He had to do something.

'Frank's motor is up by the lodge,' the man said. 'I'm wondering what it's still doing there.'

'I don't know no Frank,' Abir said, in an accent that Ben was growing rather fond of.

'Everyone knows Frank,' the man said. 'You – what's your name?'

'Abir.'

'Thought so. And you, trying to hide at the back, I know who you are you.' The caravan shook as the man came further inside, trying to get a better look. 'There's no hiding in this part of the world, I can tell you that. Not from me.'

'What do you want?' Ben said, increasingly certain that this person wasn't part of Winslow's crew. They wouldn't have been given any more chances.

'Oh, hello – you've been in the wars, haven't you?' the man said. His accent was as flat and non-descript as Halvergate marshes. 'Your whole family, I reckon.' He turned, slammed his hand down on the tiny ledge by the sink. The dog yelped. 'I honestly don't know what to think. Whether you lot are just lucky, or very stupid. Maybe both.'

He turned back to glare at Ben. 'You're the elder boy, aren't you? The elder Goodwin. Wasn't sure to begin with. A lot of people will be very interested to know where you are. And you,' he nodded at Abir, 'you're a good driver, so I hear.'

'Cheers,' said Abir coldly.

'Yeah, I'm Ben Goodwin,' Ben said, trying to lean forward. 'So you know then that this is our land. The park's currently shut. You should not be on site, let alone storming into others' property.'

'Can't help it if my dog picks up a scent. He's bit of a free spirit, this one.' The man leant down and patted the dog, who was trying to find more space for itself in the caravan. 'Doesn't like the cold too much though.'

'Who the fuck are you?' Abir said, sounding like he was running out of patience and might do something stupid.

'I'm a friend of Frank's.'

'So that makes you a friend of ours,' Ben said.

'Not any more. Things have changed.'

'Look, we don't want any trouble,' Ben said.

'You've been enough trouble, you and your blasted family, for years. Where's your younger brother? I don't see his car here. He's who I came looking for – but you'll do. This is his operation, isn't it?'

'I guess,' said Ben. 'But I've no idea what he's got himself involved with. Me and Abir, we're just taking a breather, trying to keep out of trouble.' For a moment Ben thought he was going to lose it again. He was beyond caring whether he sounded scared. He'd never been very good at putting on a show.

'What an organisation. Goodwin Enterprises?' The man shook his head, removed his beanie. 'It's become a rotten joke, stale as hell.'

For some reason Ben thought he'd be bald, or close-shaved. But he had a fine crop of sandy-grey hair, neatly trimmed, conservatively so. He suddenly looked a lot less threatening, like an accountant perhaps, or someone in middle management, who kept in good shape. He had oddly thin lips, however, that were mean, disturbing.

'You – you work for him, don't you?' he continued, addressing Abir.

'I used to do some errands for Zach Goodwin, if that's what you mean,' Abir said. 'But no, I don't work for him, not any more.'

'He'd be impossible to work for,' Ben said, brightly. 'I do know my brother. The thing is he doesn't mean any harm. He's just a royal fuck-up.'

'That's not very respectful, is it?' the man said. 'So where is he?'

'As I said, I have no idea,' Ben said.

'Can't you call him? Either of you?'

'What do you want with him?'

'I'm tying up loose ends,' the man said. 'Running all round Yarmouth. Wouldn't normally mind the exercise – but time's tight.'

'We've got no phones,' said Abir.

'They took them,' Ben added, immediately regretting it.

The man was looking at him quizzically, and shook his head once more.

'You're not with them, are you?' Ben said. He couldn't stand not having his phone, he realised, not being in contact, or knowing what was going on in the outside world. What if Avani was trying to contact him? What if a tidal surge was on its way? What if World War Three had broken out? It might as well as have done.

'No,' the man said. 'I'm not with any outfit you'd have

heard of, or even thought about. Never does to be part of a crew. I've only got time for my best friend.' He looked around for his dog, put his beanie back on. 'You need to watch out for yourselves. You're not safe here, even from those you think you can trust.'

He stood, catching Ben's eye again. 'Families, they're the worst. Get out of town, while you can. There'll be no more warnings.'

He moved towards the door, stepped outside. 'Come on, Baz.'

'Oi,' Abir shouted after him, 'you still haven't told us who you are.'

'Why are you even telling us this?' Ben added, as loudly as he could.

'Call it my civic duty,' the man shouted back.

'Fuck's sake,' Abir said, getting up from the bench and watching the man go from the doorway. 'What a weirdo.'

'I think he was trying to help us,' said Ben.

'What makes you say that?'

'He didn't kill us, did he?'

Abir sighed. 'You think he looked the type?'

'I reckon it's those who don't who are the most dangerous.'

'Now what, then?'

'I think we should do as he says. There must be enough people after us, including the police.'

'How?'

'That car you nicked last night, that'll get us somewhere, won't it?'

'With every force and crook in the land looking for us, I don't think so,' Abir said. 'A fucking knackered, lime-green Citroën Saxo? There're not exactly many routes out of Yarmouth by road as it is.'

'You got a better idea?'

'Maybe.'

## 29

Tatty caught a smattering of the old town wall to her left as she accelerated along Priory Plain. The dark medieval flint looked cold and slippery under the suddenly brightening sky. Impenetrable too – centuries of fortification going to waste.

It was turning out to be one of those days where the weather couldn't decide what to do. Neither could the car in front. It was wavering from one lane to the other. She thumped the middle of the steering wheel, hearing the Merc's horn loud and clear. She immediately regretted it, with passengers on board.

The car, a Nissan of some sort, wavered some more, then went straight through a red light by the Euston Road fork, veering right and sticking to the one-way system towards the town centre. There were two people inside, old and small. Tatty supposed she'd panicked them into breaking the law. There was a pattern there. Another thing she wasn't proud of.

Tatty didn't shoot the light, however, and dutifully brought the car to a stop, and glanced at Shane in the front passenger seat. He was looking straight ahead. Beyond him she saw some more medieval wall shielding the Market

Place, which was an old burial ground, as Rich had once gleefully told her. 'This town has a right bloody past,' he used to say. 'I'm only keeping up the tradition.' He'd then invariably add, 'It's not as if you and your lot are a peaceful bunch.' Meaning those of Polish descent. Then he'd bang on about the Second World War, having very little grasp of the facts.

There were chunks of the wall all over the centre of the town, and a couple of round towers, one that was used as prison, as Tatty had always believed. The council had been pushing the heritage trail for years, pumping in huge amounts of Lottery cash. She wasn't sure such history was worth preserving. It couldn't have been a lot of fun in those days. She doubted it was much better now. They all needed to look to the future. Be more open, accommodating, tolerant, loving – that would have been a start. Lessons were never learned.

'Mum,' Sam said from the back, 'the lights are green.'

Tatty looked up, focused. Sam was right, of course. She eased forward, but then veered left at the last moment, taking Euston Road.

'Why are we going this way?' Sam said. 'Weren't we heading to the Smokehouse?'

'I've had a better idea.'

'Thanks for telling us,' Sam said.

'I just did.'

'So where to now? I don't believe this. You took long enough getting ready, and now we're taking another age to get anywhere that matters. We still don't know where they are, Ben, Zach – my brothers, Mum.'

'You don't think I don't know that? What do you think we're doing?' Tatty said. 'Looking.'

'Fuck's sake,' said Sam.

'You're not the only passenger,' Tatty said. 'Mind your language.'

'From you?' Sam said. 'Fuck off.'

Tatty kept her eyes straight ahead. She thought Sam had stopped being so livid. Shane hadn't said a word since they'd left Gorleston, and Tatty suddenly had a memory of driving Sam and a friend of hers into town, years ago, when the kids were teenagers. Maybe it was Sam and one of her brothers. They were always in a sulk. Always embarrassed by their mum, yet always expecting to be ferried around – even though it wasn't a regular occurrence. Tatty missed it, being needed like that.

Ashamed at her driving, her temper, being a useless mother and a hopeless lover, she kept well within the speed limit as they passed the Yarmouth NHS mental health facility and the East European corner shops, a boarded-up pub, some tatty terraces – late Victorian on the right-hand side of the road, 1970s on the left. The seafront loomed into view, a block of grey that could have been sea or cloud. Some gulls were twirling in the air, big and almost prehistoric looking. Tatty had never been very keen on seagulls, the way they swooped and scavenged.

A car forced her to slow before North Drive, by the back of the old theatre. Another Nissan, if Tatty wasn't mistaken. A model with a name she couldn't pronounce. She looked over towards the 'Gentleman's Club', a not-so-discreet entrance. Forbidden Fruit it was called. The name had always made Tatty wince. Shane was looking that way too. There was a scruffy poster of a puffed-up brunette in a tiny purple thong clasping onto a chrome pole. She was sticking her arse out, at Yarmouth, at the world. Tatty didn't blame her.

'Go often?' she asked Shane, who was still looking. He shouldn't have been looking at that, of course, but paying attention to her – something she realised right then that she both did and didn't want. It was far too late for any of that, she told herself. Get a grip.

Shane sat up in his seat, swung his head her way. 'We had our Christmas party there, as a matter of fact. All the squad not on shift.'

'Fun, was it?'

'Look, the people I work with need to let off steam now and then. They work hard for the community. They're prepared to put their lives on the line. They're a good bunch of lads. The commander thought it'd be fun, seeing as we all know how to swing down a pole.' He huffed a brief laugh.

'At the expense of others' dignity?' Tatty shook her head. 'Those poor women.' What the hell was she saying? What was he saying? Unbelievably, he'd told her he loved her only yesterday. But he wasn't so rash, so uncool, except for perhaps that moment.

'Since when have you cared about that sort of thing, Mum?' Sam said from the back. 'Don't we own a load of brothels?'

Tatty could sense her daughter shifting in her seat, leaning forward. Certainly she could feel her daughter's breath on the back of her head, hot and angry. Sam was trying to embarrass her in front of Shane. She didn't blame her. 'For your information,' Tatty said, 'I'm in the process of setting up a women's refuge, in the old Merchant's House in Gorleston. Didn't I tell you? I'm working with Nathan Taylor on the renovations.'

'I'd been to school with half the girls,' Shane interrupted. 'They seemed to be enjoying their dancing. I found it a little tricky being there. I remember them in the dinner queue. The other half were from Eastern Europe. That place is part of a chain, I think. There's one in Norwich, anyway. Does really well, apparently. If you ask me, I don't think it's that exploitative. I mean, they're earning good money, and that's not so easy in this neck of the woods even if you've got qualifications. Not many people did so well at my school.'

Tatty wasn't sure she'd ever heard Shane say so much in one go. Wasn't sure what he was getting at. Maybe he regretted having told her he loved her – was having second thoughts. Of course he was having second thoughts. He'd seen more than enough in the last twenty-four hours to understand what she was about and where she came from. 'I doubt the money they're getting is that great,' she said.

'They earned a lot of tips the night we were there,' Shane continued. 'We thought we'd do our bit.' He sort of laughed again.

They'd earn a lot more working for her, out of the Merchant's House, Tatty thought crossly. It was only ever going to be a refuge of sorts. She might have insisted on safety, dignity and respect, but nothing in life was free.

Those girls still had to pay their way. She pulled out onto North Drive, heading away from the Golden Mile. She was so full of contradictions, she wasn't sure she could even drive straight. When she'd used her body to earn money all those years ago, the pay had been dismal, the beatings worse. The only hope was nabbing a rich punter. And look where that had got her.

'It's not just about money, anyway,' she found herself saying, as if the Merchant's House really was to be a going concern, all plans back on track, and that the last twenty-four, forty-eight hours simply hadn't happened.

'No,' said Sam from the back seat. 'It's a massive, disgusting hypocrisy, that's what it is.'

Tatty heard herself in her daughter's voice. It was odd how your children could do that to you. Sam wasn't without her contradictions, either. But she'd forgive her anything.

'I don't mind about Shane watching strippers with his work mates,' Sam continued. 'That's what all men his age do. It's natural. But pimping out young women, many far from home, and probably here through coercion – that's not acceptable. I know what you're really planning, Mum, with that sleazy Nathan Taylor. I know what you and him got up to, when Dad was still alive.'

Tatty slammed her foot on the brake. Not for the first time recently she realised that it was impossible to hide everything from your kids. Anything.

They were by Marine Crescent, the sad semis lined up in a fat curve behind a couple of patches of grass, where dogs were let out to shit with abandon because their owners either couldn't be bothered to walk them any further or weren't able to. Across the road was the end of the boating lake. She couldn't see whether it was frozen solid. Maybe it had been drained, for ever, and was waiting for redevelopment. There weren't enough young children in Yarmouth any more. Or any civic money for such regeneration.

She turned and looked at her daughter. But before she had a chance to say anything, Sam had opened her door. 'I'm getting out,' she said, half on the pavement already. 'This is stupid,' she shouted. 'All of this.'

'Ring me when you calm down,' Tatty said, feeling her stomach give way, 'and I'll come and pick you up.' That was how it used to work, when, as ever, she was to blame. She was Sam's mother, for God's sake. She shouldn't have stopped the car. She should have remained calm, loving.

'Don't bother,' came the reply, as Tatty was expecting, along with the rear passenger door being slammed shut. The seatbelt buckle must have caught because there was a nasty clang. She didn't blame Sam one bit. It was better that her daughter was out of there.

Tatty glanced at Shane, who was biting his lips. She couldn't believe she'd been kissing those lips. She wasn't totally without feelings, understanding – she wasn't Rich. 'You can get out as well,' she said. 'Go on.' It would be far better for him if he did.

'Sure,' he mumbled, hurriedly undoing his seatbelt and opening his door.

Relieved, Tatty felt a fatal blast of air coming straight off the sea, over the shingle bank and the redundant boating lake, and straight into the expensive interior. It was primeval, eternal.

Shane firmly shut his door too, though there was no added clank this time, and suddenly the silence was overwhelming, along with the heat. Tatty could feel her cheeks burning and perspiration breaking out on her forehead. She avoided looking at her daughter and Shane on the pavement, or her flushed self in the rear-view mirror, and pulled straight out, only to hear a long, loud blast of a horn. A car swerved around the Merc and slowed. The driver was shaking his fist manically, before pulling quickly away.

'Sod you,' Tatty said, before looking in her rear-view mirror. Sam and Shane hadn't moved far, possibly because Shane was giving Sam a hug.

Tatty accelerated slowly towards the caravan park. She hadn't thrown one of her children out of the car for years. It used to be a regular occurrence. After twenty minutes or so she'd always gone back for them, until the time Zach disappeared, eventually finding his way to his dad and the then Goodwin Enterprises headquarters. They must have been in Yarmouth, shopping. Zach couldn't have been more than nine. Rich beat them both that evening.

She'd never thrown a boyfriend out of the car before, or Rich. Frank yesterday, she supposed, but that was different. However, Shane was no longer her boyfriend, she had to remember that, as well as the fact that Rich was no longer her husband because he was fucking dead, though not before time. Where was she really heading? Too fast towards a lonely old age. And it was her own fault. How could she ever make anything right again?

Beyond Barnard Road, and then Jellicoe, and the faded signs for the racecourse, the far end of North Drive was completely deserted. The Coastwatch station sat boarded up, while the stretch of dunes, wider here than anywhere else along the front, appeared to be without dog walkers. The wind turbines a little way out to sea were rotating with some purpose. A few ships, supply vessels and a tanker were sitting where a horizon might have been.

She'd forgotten how large the caravan park was. Just because it was at the far end of town, where this time of the year no one ever went, didn't mean that it was without potential. She'd seen plans Rich had had drawn up for a massive hotel complex. An auxiliary facility for the super casino. Prime land in a certain climate.

She and Frank had simply let Zach do what he wanted with it. They'd thought it would keep him busy, out of trouble. Couldn't have been more wrong.

She glanced at the weather again, sitting heavy and uncertain over the North Sea, as though trying to squeeze the ships off the horizon and out of the way for good. It was not a view you'd pay an awful lot of money for, even if there was a glittering casino within striking distance.

She passed the entrance to the caravan park and reached the turning circle at the very end of North Drive. Slowly she eased the long Merc round the tight corners until she was facing the route back along the front. It went all the way to the Golden Mile and Salmon Road, which lead to the Smokehouse. There were so many plans still in the pipeline.

That was all Rich and now she were ever any good for. Dreaming up schemes, and fleecing investors and money launderers along the way. Frank was right. They should have stuck to the traditional operations. The dirty, small-scale street dealing, prostitution, protection and extortion rackets. Cash and carry. But that was no world for her and Sam, as Sam had made clear. Or for Ben and Zach.

It had only been a few minutes since she'd left Sam on the pavement. Tatty would have gone back for her at that moment, had she not been in search of her other two children, who weren't currently being hugged by a strong, handsome fireman. Right then, presuming they were both still alive, they needed her more. She needed them, too – for love and forgiveness. Not that she yet deserved it. That was going to take some doing.

Ahead, two, three hundred metres away, she could see someone out on the dunes. They were well bundled up in a fat puffy coat and beanie, and quickly striding away from the Coastwatch station, back towards the Golden Mile. She could see a dog scampering along behind them.

Maybe that was all you could do, that was all that was expected from a mother. Care and attention. You didn't have to build an empire, a legacy for your kids. You just had to give them a bit of time, and love.

Tatty eased the car into gear and edged forward, pulling down lazily on the wheel, her mind on an alternative, gentler past where family really did come first and business second. They should have got a pet. The children would have loved a dog. Maybe it wasn't too late. But what sorts of dogs liked the Mediterranean? She had no idea, and felt a wave of heat, or perhaps shame and regret, shoot through her.

Something near and fast caught the corner of her eye and she pressed on the brake, gripped the steering wheel tighter.

A small car shot out of the caravan park, virtually clipping her grill and accelerating hard down North Denes. No one hooted, and she watched the vehicle until it was out of sight, not sure how many people were inside.

Joyriders, she assumed. They were always burning rubber at this end of North Drive. Must have been doing some off-road manoeuvres around the old caravans, churning up the paths, what was left of the lawns, the communal play areas. God, she hated this place, especially since she'd learned what Rich used to do here in a dismal caravan. He had no class, no conscience.

She took a moment or two to calm her breathing and shift the most horrendous thoughts from her mind. Then she pointed the Merc towards the entrance of the caravan park and drove slowly and cautiously inside. She wasn't surprised that there was no gate or chain blocking the way, announcing that the park was currently closed. The place was a free for all. No wonder kids would tear around here in stolen vehicles, committing acts of wanton vandalism. At least it gave them something to do. And Zach too, had been the thinking.

How wrongly kids were brought up, neglected, let down – the world over.

## 30

Tatty pulled up in front of the lodge, spotting Frank's Lexus. Still sitting there since yesterday, she supposed, following his little accident, the great, clumsy oaf. There was no sign of Zach's car, however.

Her phone announced two missed calls and one message. The calls were unknown numbers, while the message said, *Have news for you, ring me on this number*. It was signed Britt Hayes. Tatty rang the number. It rang and rang and just as Tatty was expecting the voicemail to kick in it was answered.

'There's something you should know,' Britt Hayes whispered straight off.

'Yes? Have you found Ben?' Tatty said, trying to remain calm. She was looking at a reflection of her car in the large main window of the lodge. She could see herself, small and inconsequential, behind the steering wheel. She'd forgotten that she was wearing her Hermès headscarf and shades, trying to look unrecognisable. The effect was doing anything but hide who she was. No one dressed like her in the vicinity. That had been another of her mistakes. No wonder her children had always been so embarrassed to be seen out with her, on those rare family occasions. Rich had always looked like any other badly dressed businessman.

'Your brother-in-law's back in town,' Hayes said, 'according to our intelligence.'

Another thing Tatty hadn't been expecting. 'Just as your lot finally want to question him about the disappearance of his wife? Why would he pitch up now?' Her silk scarf couldn't contain the rush of thoughts inside her head – not in anything like a sensible order.

'We're watching his house, on Ferry Hill.'

'I asked you whether you've found my son, Ben. I don't give a shit about Simon.' She couldn't believe he could be back. Their intelligence had to be wrong, which wouldn't have surprised her. Fuck him, anyway.

'You have two sons, don't you?'

'I hope so,' said Tatty. She pulled the scarf off her head with her free hand and threw it on the passenger seat. Shook her hair loose. Things were no clearer, freer.

'We know where one is right now,' Hayes said.

'Yes? Who? Which one? Where?' Tatty's heart skipped more beats, as she remembered visiting the morgue at the James Paget with Sam. Seeing Rich's corpse on the metal tray – his bloated purple body. Sam had screamed.

Catching her reflection again – a dishevelled, menopausal woman in an old Mercedes Benz – Tatty felt her heart continue to beat an irregular rhythm. None of this was good for her health. Gone were the days of lounging around in spas, when the most strain her cardiovascular system had to take was walking down stairs, getting into her car, sitting in a sauna, plopping into a jacuzzi, being fucked by a monster. The drugs she was on meant that she barely felt a thing, while nothing penetrated her mentally.

She was as cold and closed off as the North Sea. That's what Nathan had once said to her. Before he'd warmed her up, for a short while.

'Who? Ben, Zach?' Tatty shouted, realising that Britt Hayes had gone quiet on her. 'Are you still there?' Tatty couldn't look at her reflection again. She looked down at her lap instead, but not before she caught something else in the window – movement, glinting, a car sweeping into the park. She instantly looked over her shoulder, panicking. It was a taxi, the livery loudly saying it was an Anglia car, local. She tried to slide down in her seat, wishing she hadn't removed her headscarf, not because it made her feel more secure, hidden, but because she could feel blood rush to her face once again. The horror of her age. She'd thought she could handle it, growing old disgracefully. But it just reminded her of all the time that had passed, all that she hadn't done and all that had gone wrong. She wanted her time again, not just for her sake but for her kids. 'Britt?'

'Sorry, I'm not in a good place to talk right now.'

'Ben or Zach?' Tatty shouted. 'Which one? Tell me.'

'The younger one,' Britt Hayes said quietly, and mildly out of breath. It sounded like she was walking.

'Zach?'

'Yes – the one who's always getting into trouble.'

'Give it a break. Where is he? Is he safe?'

'As I said, I know where he is right now, but I don't know whether he's safe. He's at your brother-in-law's house.

'Simon's? What the hell is he doing there? It's shut up, isn't it?'

'You tell me.'

'Are you sure?' Tatty didn't think her face could get any hotter. It was like insects were crawling under her skin. It was like withdrawal.

'We've been watching it for some time.'

'Why didn't you tell me this yesterday?' Tatty was aware of the Anglia taxi pulling up practically alongside her car. It was white and green. She couldn't look.

'You didn't need to know yesterday. I'm not in command of that investigation, anyway.'

'I thought you oversaw everything.'

'It doesn't quite work like that.'

'Kyle Neville is it, who's really controlling the shots?'

'I don't know what your son's doing in there,' Hayes said, clearly eager to move the conversation on. 'But he probably wants to get out, before either his uncle turns up or the police go in.'

'He's done nothing wrong,' Tatty said. 'He's a good kid, deep down.'

'I don't need excuses,' Hayes said. 'I was offering some advice, that's all.'

'Thank you,' said Tatty. 'What about Ben, my eldest, who was taken yesterday by Winslow's crew? Do you know where he is now? Is he safe?'

'There was a fatal fire in Lowestoft yesterday evening.'

'It's been all over the news.'

'We understand that he was in that building at some point yesterday. One body was found, though we don't think it was him.'

Tatty decided not to tell Hayes that she already knew this. There was a gentle tap on the driver's window. Frank was waving at her, signalling for her to lower the window. She signalled back that she was on the phone.

'We're having problems with the identification, though initial evidence and intercepted communications lead us to believe that it was one of their own, which would make your son of plenty of interest. We believe he was with an accomplice as well – might still be.'

Tatty thought of Abir, Zach's driver. What a mess. 'Ben wouldn't have had anything to do with the fire,' she said, feeling about ready to combust herself. 'He wasn't involved with that gang in any way. They took him, abducted him.'

'We don't know everything that then went on,' Hayes said. 'We could be talking first degree.'

'For God's sake, I have no idea where Ben is now. I've had no communication with him since he was taken.'

'I can help you with that as well.'

'Where is he?'

'I think I've already been helpful enough, Tatty. I'm not an endless free resource.'

This was the first time Britt Hayes had called her Tatty. However, she hadn't said it in the most friendly of ways.

'Please,' said Tatty.

'Why? Why should I? What have you done for me? I gave you an idea.'

Tatty had an idea that they were all scrabbling around in the weak winter light, looking for purchase. But the ground was too hard, too icy to go it alone. And that was before the thaw, after which nothing would be stable. Maybe, finally, you had to look inward, and that the heart was the only thing left to test, if it wasn't already broken.

'Because you might just be a half decent human being, that's why,' she said, not answering the second part of Hayes's question. It was also possible that she was in fact addressing herself, and not Hayes. She didn't want to think about what her answer would be.

'No, I'm not,' Britt offered, almost straight up.

'At least you're honest,' Tatty said, warming to the woman for the first time. Maybe they could have been friends, in a different life.

'I've been around for too long. I've seen too much.'

'Shouldn't that make you more human, more caring?'

'It doesn't work like that.'

'It can,' Tatty said, desperate not to acknowledge Frank's presence. Pleading with her better self as well, perhaps.

Hayes laughed quietly. 'No. But I'm still interested in a trade. That's how the world works. I can only help you further if you help me. We already had a deal, don't forget. I'll ask you again – have you met your side of the bargain?'

'It wasn't a deal, it was an ultimatum. Besides, I thought I had until Monday.'

Tatty now looked at Frank once more, out in the cold. He wasn't even wearing a hat. She mouthed, *Fuck off, I'm on the phone*. She watched the taxi reverse and pull sharply away behind him. Frank remained by her car, his face a battlefield of pain.

'Events have moved forward more quickly than I was expecting,' Hayes said. 'I'll give you until this evening.'

'Then what happens?' Tatty asked.

'Did I not make myself clear?'

'To you?' Tatty said. 'What happens to you?'

'Me? This isn't about me.'

'Really? How long have you got?'

'I've got as long as it takes,' she said confidently.

'I don't think so,' Tatty said. 'Your time's just about up as well, isn't it?'

'Here? Oh no, I'll go on for ever.'

'What about your partner? You're both indestructible are you?'

'Something like that. You have until this evening.'

'You haven't told me where Ben is.' Frank was tapping on the driver's window once more. Tatty was surprised that he hadn't smashed the glass with his elbow. 'Please, and then I'll think about hurrying up with your order.'

'You're in the caravan park right now, is that correct?'

'How do you know that?' Tatty took a deep breath, felt her already broken heart crack some more. She couldn't trust anyone. The world was rife with betrayal.

'You need to believe in who I am, what I do. What I'm capable of. Faith, that's what you need, Tatiana Goodwin. That's what we all need, that and a reliable partner, plus a beautiful dog.' Hayes sounded like she was walking hurriedly somewhere again – trying to get out of someone's earshot.

Tatty suddenly got it – the man out on the dunes, Britt Hayes's watchman, security, lover. Who was hers? Frank? Hardly. What's more she now realised that Hayes must have given Frank orders to do away with her, just as she'd received the opposite instructions. She and Frank were meant to destroy each other, so a bent cop could keep a

286

cleaner sheet. Tatty wasn't meant to flee Yarmouth any more than Frank was. But please, not the kids as well.

'All this time,' Tatty said, 'you've been backing the wrong horse.' No, she could never have been friends with this person. 'Look, I know where Frank is right now,' she said sharply. 'I'll deal with him, I promise you – by the end of today. Just tell me where Ben is.'

'He's in a caravan, a couple of rows in,' Hayes said. 'He's not alone.'

'He's where?' Tatty said, looking behind her and seeing the larger statics, and the dismal rows of caravans behind, admiring Hayes despite herself for managing to control the situation from afar. What it would be like really to trust even one person, and a dog. 'In the North Denes caravan park?' Tatty asked, knowing the answer to this one. She'd come here looking for Zach, not Ben.

'Don't let me down,' Hayes said.

'He's still alive, though, tell me that?' She didn't want to see his body. She didn't want to see another dead body ever again. Another wave of anxiety flooded Tatty as she looked at the gearstick bulb and saw the car was in park. She didn't remember turning the engine off. She quickly looked up, at her distant reflection in the large window of the lodge, feeling tremendous heat building inside her once more. Her skin began to prickle. She'd need to reverse, then slam the car into drive and prong Frank that way.

'He was ten minutes ago, but I can't keep him alive for ever. That's your job.'

'Britt? Wherever you are you're not safe either. You can't hide in plain sight, not for ever. We all know that.'

But she had gone. Only silence came from Tatty's phone, and then the sound of rushing air and maybe the sea, because Frank had yanked open the driver's door. The blast of cold air was something of a relief, if Frank's audacity wasn't.

'Fuck's sake.'

## 31

'Leave me out in the fucking cold, will you?' Frank's hands had gone numb. He'd long lost the feeling in his feet, his legs. He wanted to grab Tatty by the throat and squeeze very hard.

'What the hell are you doing?' Tatty said. 'This is my car. How dare you. I was on the phone.'

Except Frank didn't think he could lose hold of the car door without toppling over. He hadn't seen so much disgust and anger in Tatty's face since the last time she'd yelled at him –which was only in Lowestoft yesterday evening. He could always shoot her, however. 'Who were you talking to? What are you doing here?' he said, trying to feel for his weapon in his jacket pocket with his left hand.

'Don't you fucking pull that on me,' Tatty said, gripping the wheel and stamping her right foot.

Frank let go of the car, tried to push himself away from the open door. He could see what she was trying to do. Nothing happened. The car didn't move either backwards or forwards. 'German cars for you,' he said. 'They're nothing like as reliable as they used to be. I swear by Japanese manufacturers nowadays. Besides, they're so much cleaner.' He tipped his head back, sniffed the sodden salty air. Coughed. Even his lungs hurt.

'Fuck you, Frank.' She practically collapsed onto the steering wheel

'Tatty, enough.' He wasn't going to shoot a defenceless woman. 'Truce?'

She was now shaking her head, not looking at him. 'Are you joking?'

'What are you doing here?' he asked again.

'I could ask you the same question.' She stopped shaking her head and slowly sat back in her seat.

'I've come to pick up my car. So I can go home, pack my bags and get out of this town for ever. OK?'

She turned his way and something like a smile crept out from the corners of her mouth. She was wearing lipstick and had done her eyes, and though she didn't look quite as immaculate as usual that smart steeliness was there. No messing, so he'd have liked to believe. He wasn't sure he'd ever realised what a beautiful pale green-blue her eyes were.

'I thought you loved this place, that you could never leave,' said Tatty. 'That's what you've always said. All that work on your garden, be a shame not to see that mature. And everything you've done for the local community, to make the streets safe, and provide real opportunities for those less fortunate. That's your line, isn't it?'

'I thought that was your line,' said Frank.

'The work you've done for Goodwin Enterprises, not

only on the super casino project – you want to miss out on the boom time just around the corner?'

Perhaps he'd never appreciated her sense of humour. There would never be a boom time in this part of the world. Far too much, for too long, had conspired against it. 'So what are you doing here?'

'Looking after my interests.' She smiled sweetly, then her face dropped.

If Frank had learned anything over the last three decades, he supposed it was that no one could keep up appearances for ever, not in Yarmouth.

'I came in search of Zach, but he's not here. Though apparently Ben is, somewhere.' She was now shaking her head. Her hair could have done with a comb.

'Ben is here?' said Frank. 'He's alive?'

'Yes,' said Tatty. 'I think so.'

'Thank God. This changes everything.'

'Yes and no,' said Tatty.

'Why's he here? How do you know?' He could feel the cold air reaching the bottom of his lungs, but at the same time some heat rose in his chest. This was good news, finally. He could have hugged Tatty, but she wouldn't have let him.

'He's not alone, apparently. He might be injured.'

'He must be with Abir, hiding out. Smart, given who'll be after them.'

'He's in a caravan,' Tatty said. 'There're hundreds of the blasted things.'

'Yeah.' Frank thought of Rich's stinking caravan, at the far end of the park, before he'd torched it with Rolly

Andrews and Graham Sands's corpses inside. He thought of what Rich used to keep in there. Emergency cash, passports, weapons. For years it'd been a forgotten corner of Yarmouth. Now nothing was forgotten. Too much was known.

'How are we going to find them?' Tatty said. 'Ben's phone's still going straight to voicemail.'

'Of course it is. They won't have their phones on them. They'd have been got rid of as soon as they were taken yesterday. Winslow's crew might be stupid but they're not that stupid.'

'One of them's dead,' said Tatty. 'One of Winslow's men.'

'Bloody hell – and Ben and Abir escaped?' He thought back to what Howie had told him. What Howie hadn't told him.

'Yes, it sounds like it.'

'Maybe Winslow's lot *are* that stupid.'

'That's what you said yesterday – to take us on.'

'Something went wrong, or Ben and Abir showed some serious nous.' Frank felt an old tinkling of admiration. 'Who have you been talking to?'

'Your friend.'

'Britt Hayes?'

Tatty nodded. 'Yes. She approached me.'

'You need to watch her. She's in a corner, she's dangerous.' Britt and Howie would have a plan. They'd outwit them all, two minds like that – and bodies. At least Tatty had told him she'd been speaking to her. 'Tatty, can I get in?' He needed to sit down. Neither his head nor his ticker could take it all in. 'I'm not going to pull anything.'

292

'How can I trust you?' She held out her hand.

'How can I trust *you*? You were going to run me over.'

'You were going to shoot me. Hand it over. Or you're not getting in this car.'

Frank sighed. 'You're just being stupid now.'

'Fine,' she said, starting the car.

He watched her put it into gear for definite this time.

'OK,' he said, letting go of the roof and reaching into the right-hand pocket of his jacket. Her tone had changed, softened. Everything had changed. Perhaps they could be friends again. His fingers were almost too numb to grip the pistol properly. Finally he managed to pull it from his pocket, by the stubby barrel. For the briefest of moments he contemplated twirling it round and putting a bullet in Tatty's head. He'd spent longer thinking about putting one in his own head. His fingers wouldn't have cooperated in any case.

She grabbed it from him, placing it on her lap. 'OK, get in.'

Frank zipped his jacket tighter and began hobbling around the car. He had to pause by the bonnet, take a breather, let the pain subside. He smiled at Tatty behind the vast, sloping windscreen. Hit and runs were far easier to cover up than plugging someone. She'd have known that. The car didn't budge, however, as he made his way around to the passenger side and opened the door. He took an ice age to lower himself into the seat. He was done with saloons for ever. Where he was thinking of heading a SUV was far more appropriate.

'You're sitting on my scarf,' Tatty said. 'Do you mind? It's Hermès.'

'Sorry,' he said, trying to shift his arse so he could pull the flimsy fabric free. It was impossible, because he could only put weight on his right leg, despite how hard he was pulling the thing. He used to be such a strong man. A bull of a man, so he'd been told by someone he'd once had sex with, who was no weakling himself. But that was a long time ago. Then the scarf came, along with a gentle tearing sound. A bit of the scarf. He was too embarrassed to hold it up. 'You can have it when I get out,' he said, crumpling it in his hand. 'There're more important things.'

'You've bloody ripped it, haven't you.' It wasn't a question. Tatty tutted. 'Unbelievable.'

He watched her reach for his gun in her lap, her fingers walk the grip.

'I said I'm sorry.' He didn't mean it. He was done with apologising. 'Are we going to sit here all day?'

'Did you have the gun with you yesterday, when we drove to Lowestoft?' She eased the car back, swung it round so it was facing the interior of the park, let it creep forward, before stamping on the brake.

'Yes.' The jolt hurt his hip like a whack with an iron bar.

'You could have been searched at that roadblock. Then where would we've been?'

'I stopped worrying about things like that years ago.' He didn't mention the fact that she'd kicked him out of the car, exposing him to closer scrutiny and the harshest of elements.

'How are we going to find them?' she said, calmer. 'Ben and Abir?'

Lined up along the front of the park were the larger statics. There must have been forty, fifty of them between the lodge and the Jellicoe Road perimeter. Rolly Andrews had been a hopeless landlord, Zach no better. Most caravans were now in a terrible state, the white plastic cladding having turned a grey-green. Regardless of whether the park was officially closed, at this time of the year he doubted any would have been occupied, by owners, leaseholders, squatters. The conditions were too severe. Any would be easy enough to break into though.

'Drive around,' said Frank, 'tooting the horn. If they see it's us, they'll come out.'

'I wouldn't be so sure,' said Tatty.

She rolled the car forward, slowly increasing the speed as they travelled between the front and second rows of caravans, the Merc's large diesel engine murmuring with lazy content. Combustion engines for you, Frank thought wistfully. If the last couple of days had told him anything it was that he was not a modern man. Tatty wasn't well equipped for this century, either. Nor her kids. Zach had started out so promisingly with his computer wizardry. But the moment he started taking dope dealing more seriously it quickly began to go wrong for him.

At the southern perimeter of the park Tatty looped round to the right and took the next lane back, which was between the second and third rows of caravans, bringing the car to a slow stop towards the middle. The further in from the once-prime spots on the front row the smaller and more numerous the caravans and staked-out lots were. At one point in the not-so-distant past holidaymakers had tried to claim every square inch they could. Guarding your territory was what came naturally to people. Frank knew that.

'Have you seen something?' he asked, as the car remained stationary. The grass between the caravans was long and shaggy, and not in a healthy way. Fat dollops of snow had begun to fall.

'Not a bloody thing.' She thumped the horn. 'He's my son. Why won't he come out?' She couldn't think about that question for too long.

'Can't see any vehicles, either,' said Frank. 'Why don't you drive down to the very end, by the racecourse? That'd be the best place to leave a vehicle. Abir would have known that. But are you sure they're still in the park?' He sniffed. 'Something's not right, I can sense it.'

'Britt Hayes said they were.'

'How did she know?'

'She'd sent her henchman.'

'Her lover,' Frank corrected. 'Of course. He's having a busy time running around Yarmouth this morning. Fuck.'

'It's what some people do for each other – people who love each other,' she said.

'Don't count on it. There are always other agendas, stories.' He looked up at the fallen sky. 'I suppose she also told you that Zach was at Simon's place on Ferry Hill.'

'Yes,' said Tatty.

He thought some more, knowing Howie, how he operated. 'Did you notice any vehicles on North Denes as you approached the park?'

'No,' she said, 'I wasn't here much before you.'

'Keep going,' Frank said, waving the way forward. 'Let's hope Ben sees your car, makes himself known.' Though he doubted it more and more the further into the park they went. The snow was not settling. The car, however, was making a grumbling sound as it progressed along the rutted, uncared-for track.

They got to the end of the row, which gave a view back towards the lodge. Tatty turned left, and left again, aiming to take another row before stopping the car with another painful jolt.

'Shit,' she said. She put the car into reverse and swung round at speed, before heading back to the lodge. The gun slid into the gap between her left leg and the centre console.

Frank contemplated grabbing it but he was clasping onto the sides of his seat, desperate not to put too much pressure onto his hip. 'What the fuck?'

She came to another stop back by the lodge. The giant widescreen wipers were making easy work of the snow falling lightly onto the windscreen. 'Do you think he's killed them?'

The man was an experienced assassin. Having survived Winslow's lot, only to be taken out by Howie Jones – what an end to a young life. But he didn't think so. They'd have been given their marching orders, something resembling a chance, like he had been. Ben and Abir were not players. Howie had always cautioned him against excessive and unnecessary violence. 'Restraint by force of will, Frank. That's how I've kept ahead of the law,' he'd once said. Frank wasn't sure he'd totally understood him.

'You sure you saw nothing else on your way here?' Frank asked. He was fishing for a chink of light. The sky seemed to be coming down with the snow, in shards, fractures. Where he was thinking of heading it'd never dip below freezing.

'Actually, yes – there was something else,' Tatty said. 'I don't know what's wrong with my mind, my memory. As I came into the park a car nearly hit me. It was coming the other way. I can't even remember what sort of car it was. I didn't get to see who was inside it. It was going too fast, on the wrong side of the road. Kids, I'd supposed. That's what they do at this end of the town – joyride, show off. That's what Zach used to get up to.'

'Not at this time of year, so much,' Frank said. 'Not in broad daylight.' He tried to look up, but there was so little space between the windscreen and the sky.

'Bloody lucky I didn't have an accident,' Tatty said, perhaps trying to make light of her foggy brain.

'You came here looking for Zach, knowing what else has been going on over the last twenty-four hours – might as well have been years – and this didn't strike you as like strange, connected? A car tearing out of the park? But it wasn't Zach, was it?' Frank shouted in pure frustration, and a terrible sense of time running hopelessly away. 'Because he's holed up in Simon's place on Ferry Hill. Have you ever paid any attention to what really goes on around you, to your kids?'

Tatty jolted in her seat, took a deep breath, kept looking straight ahead at the slush hitting the glass and as quickly being cleared away. Frank waited for her to reply, catching sight of the gun again, wedged between her leg and the centre console. She didn't reply, only shook her head.

'We can forget the park,' Frank said, running out of steam. 'My hope is they've scarpered – Ben and Abir. Warned away.'

'By your mate,' Tatty said. 'Some mate.'

She wasn't totally unobservant, Frank considered. 'He wants us out of town,' he said.

'They want you dead, Frank. Him and her. What a duo.'

'A trio, with the fucking dog,' he replied. 'They want us both dead.'

'I don't care about me – or you,' she said.

'But you care about your kids,' Frank finished for her. 'Well, so do I.'

'You tell me I don't pay them enough attention?' she said, tears slipping down her cheeks. 'I've tried. This, all this, was meant to be for them.'

'We need to get over to Ferry Hill, fast,' Frank said. 'Are you going to drive?' She continued to sit there, her shoulders shaking. 'Tatty, pull yourself together, woman.'

'Don't you ever say that to me again – that's what Rich used to say.'

'We need to get to Zach, before anyone else does.' He was ashamed, mortified. He shouldn't have said it. He watched her remove her sunglasses and wipe her eyes, then turn the Merc around and head for the exit.

The snow was easing. She accelerated down North Drive, quickly exceeding the speed limit. 'We need to keep this out of sight,' he said, retrieving the Glock and struggling to slip it into his jacket pocket.

'But to hand?' Tatty said, her composure coming back.

'There're enough people after us.'

'Where's Sam?' Frank asked.

Tatty swept straight across North Drive without slowing, turning right onto Jellicoe Road. There was no traffic. Most Yarmouth residents were afraid of such weather, especially the older folks. Despite the relentlessness of it, they failed to get used to it, and never stopped complaining about it. However, they weren't all stuck here, on this stinking spit of land, he reckoned. You just had to change your mindset. Clear your head. Open your eyes. Get out. Staring death in the face altered your perspective, that was something, he supposed.

'She's all right for now,' Tatty said. 'She's with Shane.'

They passed the entrance to the racecourse in silence. 'Good,' said Frank, trying to hide his surprise. 'I guess,' he added.

'I can't believe Simon's back,' Tatty said, perhaps trying to change the subject.

'If he really is,' said Frank, 'he must have cut a deal with them.' His mind was still half elsewhere, on a different theme. It was 14 February next week, Valentine's Day. He'd never sent or received a card – let alone a gift – in his life, although Rich used to send him off to buy and deliver stuff on his behalf – flowers, perfume, lingerie. None of it was ever for Tatty.

'With who? Winslow's lot, or the police?' Tatty asked.

'The police.'

'The good guys or the bad guys?'

'There're all bad.'

'In a good way – for us?'
'Those days are over.'
'So it's just night, from now on in.'
'That's one way of looking at it.'

## 32

'I don't understand why nothing's open,' Sam said. She was using her hands as an umbrella from the shit falling on her head. It was more sleet than snow. Wet and foul, and getting down the back of her neck. She was wearing the wrong coat, some cashmere thing from Bond Street. Proper Arctic equipment was what you needed, starting with a big puffy coat, like Shane's. She'd seen a number of men wearing them. All the rage, they were.

'The café on the front by the old theatre is usually open,' Shane said.

'You mean, the old theatre that's now a strip joint?' Sam said, cold and still livid, though not especially with Shane.

'It's hard to make a living here,' he said, dead serious. Dead boring.

'I know. Sorry,' she said. 'That was unnecessary. We've already had that discussion.' They'd hung about on the pavement for a while, not saying much, then set off because it'd got too bloody cold to be standing still. They'd passed a long row of large shut-up hotels and B & Bs leading towards the Golden Mile.

'So what's London like, living and working?'

'Busy; hard but fun. Seems like another lifetime I was there already.'

'You can't have been living there that long.'

'I went straight after uni.'

'It is open,' he said brightly, pointing. 'See – the place with the red and white awning.'

'I know that café. Zach and his mates used to rob it at night.'

'Entertainment has always been in short supply in this town,' he said.

Perhaps he wasn't so boring. Sam could feel herself smiling as they hurried across the road – not because traffic was bearing down on them, but because they were mercilessly exposed to the wind and the sleet. 'What are your plans, long term?' she asked.

'I have a good job, I'm lucky,' he said, as they neared the café. 'I feel I'm doing something important, at least. For now I'm happy. Though I'm still young. We'll see what happens – not that I'm in any rush.'

Sam had never heard such sentiment from any of her close friends or work colleagues in London. Everyone she knew was dissatisfied in some way or another. And the political situation exacerbated everything. Weirdly, it was easier to forget Brexit and all the Westminster bollocks when you were away from there and actually on the front line. No one talked about it in Yarmouth. Perhaps they were too busy trying to earn a crust, survive. Or score their next hit. She'd like to give up on the news entirely. She smiled with more conviction, straight at him, as they entered the café.

Once Shane had shut the door behind him, it was immediately warm and damp, despite the fact that the café was virtually empty. There were a couple of customers though, a middle-aged man, in, yes, an enormous puffa jacket and beanie, a big pair of Red Wing boots as well. He was with a man who looked about half his size and age. He was wearing a dark overcoat with a velvet collar, as if this would somehow lend him some gravitas. They were in the far corner, with a large black and tan dog lying at the larger man's feet.

'What are you having?' said Shane, at the counter. He'd unzipped his coat and was pulling his wallet from his back jeans pocket.

'No, it's on me,' said Sam, searching for her own cash. 'It's my fault. I got us into this row with Mum.'

'She can be very fiery.' He was smiling now.

Sam wondered whether he whitened his teeth. 'Tell me about it. What do you want?'

'It's not easy for her at the moment, though. She must be going through hell. There can't be anything worse than thinking you might have lost a child. A cappuccino would be great, thanks.'

Sam turned away, gulped, forced back the tears, trying not to put herself in her mother's position. As it was, she hadn't lost a child, but a foetus, the size of a broad bean. At least she'd never had to deal with the child's father. Gone from the face of the earth, like the bean. She was facing the misted windows, trying to see outside. She had a good idea where Michael Jansen, or whatever his real name was, had ended up, what exactly had happened to him, thanks to her mum. And she'd been doing her a favour? She shivered, turning back to Shane, and caught sight of the men in the corner. The smaller one was staring at her, not in a friendly way.

She ordered Shane's cappuccino and a hot chocolate for herself from the large woman behind the counter. She'd never liked hot chocolate, or chocolate of any sort, but she needed something warm and extra sweet, and she didn't think it'd look great pouring three heaped teaspoonfuls of sugar into a coffee. She didn't believe in artificial sweeteners. They gave you cancer.

They stood there awkwardly while the woman took too long to make the drinks. As Sam warmed up she could feel her cheeks and neck begin to tingle and she had the ludicrous feeling that she was on a Tinder hook-up where the conversation had run out already. When they finally sat down with their drinks, Shane looked at her with his sparkling teeth and ridiculously clear eyes. The only thing left to do, on such dates, was to say goodbye and scratch them from the contact list. Or go home and have sex with them.

'You should stay clear of my mother, if you want to know what's good for you,' she found herself saying. The hot chocolate was too hot and too watery, and she was still conscious of the men in the corner. The smaller one kept looking over – the creep. He was too clean-shaven for his own good. Maybe he didn't need to shave.

Shane smiled at her for too long. 'Your mum means well.'

'Not always. I'm not ringing her. I don't want her to come back and pick us up. I am a grown-up. Do you know, that's what she used to do when we were kids, when she was driving us somewhere? She'd suddenly stop and chuck us out of the car. I can't think how old we were then. Eight, nine. Or worse, for the boys anyway – she'd turn round, reach over and grab them by their hair and shake their heads. This was while she was driving. As you might have noticed, her driving is not brilliant at the best of times. She never pays attention.'

'It's OK.'

'No, it's not. She has a monstrous temper.'

This wasn't completely true, but it felt like it right then. Sam was unnerved by how handsome Shane was, and by the creep in the corner. She was the real wreck around here, clutching at straws, when she should have been playing her part, helping her mum.

'Don't be too harsh on her,' Shane said.

'I'm trying not to be. I guess I've seen a little too much of her recently. I should never have come back here last year. London's where I belong, or maybe somewhere else in the big wide world. This place is poisonous. I don't think London would be far enough away.'

'What about your brothers?'

'Sounds like they're all right. Alive, anyway. Not sure I want to see them much, either. Frankly, I could fucking murder them for putting me through this. Ben at least should have known better than to have got himself involved.' She tried to smile, but found herself dabbing her eyes instead.

'And your mum, she's got every right to be angry with the boys, if you ask me.'

He said boys as if he were somehow older than them. It was absurd. Ben had to be a good two or three years older than Shane.

'No she hasn't, not really,' Sam said. 'It's her and Frank, they're the ones who really got us into the shit. The only person my mother has any right to be angry with is herself.' There, she'd said it, and said enough. She wasn't going to waste any more energy on hating and baiting her.

She kept dabbing her eyes. Maybe over time she'd begin to love her again, and accept her failings, like she had her dad's. Somehow she'd never stopped loving him. Perhaps that had something to do with the fact that she seldom saw him, and he'd never changed. You always knew exactly where you were with him. Her mother had changed, and not for the better. That was the problem.

'Don't be upset,' Shane said, uselessly, and reached over and gently patted her shoulder.

'This hot chocolate's horrible,' she said, not expecting that physical gesture. She was almost embarrassed. 'There's virtually no milk in it.' She glanced at the woman behind the counter, and at the sad displays of old packets of crisps and muffins in cellophane, a chalkboard saying nothing, the decrepit machinery.

'This coffee's not great either to be honest. Though I've never had a real cappuccino,' he said. 'I mean, not in Spain. I reckon I'd love that.'

'Italy,' she corrected him, then regretted it. She kept saying things she didn't mean or want to say. He was disarmingly good-looking. God's sake. 'You can get half-decent coffee in London,' she said. 'Not just Starbucks, but cool, independent outlets. They've popped up everywhere. I miss them.'

'I don't get to London much, and I've never been abroad.'

'You're kidding.' She sat back in her uncomfortable white plastic chair. 'You've never been abroad?'

'No. Most of my mates have been. Lads' holidays. That's not really my thing.'

Really?, Sam couldn't help thinking. However, she managed to keep her mouth shut.

'One day, I expect, I'll fly off with the right person,' Shane continued, perhaps sensing her scepticism. 'I've got a passport and everything. So I suppose there's nothing to stop me. Except work.'

And my mum, Sam managed not to say. 'Let's get out of here,' she said instead, pushing back her chair. Both the men in the corner now appeared to be eyeing them up. Or glaring at them really.

'Sure,' said Shane, standing also.

She hurried outside and stood on the promenade in the shocking breeze that practically sucked the air out of her lungs, waiting for Shane, who was struggling to shut the café door, because the other men were also trying to get out, plus the dog. Sam watched Shane then hold the door open for them, closing it once they were all on the walkway. The dog was not on a lead. It looked well trained at least.

'Cheers,' the larger man said, nodding at Shane, then quickly glancing at his companion, who was buttoning his coat. He then looked straight at Sam. 'How's your mum?' he said stepping forward.

'Sorry, do I know you?' Sam said.

'Old friend of the family's,' he said. The other man had remained where he was, and was trying hard to look elsewhere. 'How is she?'

'Who are you?' Sam didn't think she'd ever seen him before. Either of them.

'I'll tell you who I am,' he said, stepping even closer to Sam. 'I'm bad news.' He laughed, then glanced over his shoulder at his mate again. His breath smelt of yoghurt.

'Piss off,' Sam said, beginning to shiver.

At this he smiled. 'It's lucky we've bumped into you,' he said. 'I did spot you back there on the pavement and wondered whether you might be heading this way. It was fortunate I had a business meeting already planned for here.' He looked over his shoulder once more. The other man seemed even keener not to be part of the conversation. 'It's the only café open anywhere near here,' he continued. 'There's one hell of a wind, isn't there?'

'I don't understand,' Sam said, trembling solidly now. Shane was not coming to her rescue.

'Put it this way – you don't want to be seeing us again. Steer clear of this town, this part of the world. I'm warning all you Goodwins. Better *I* get to you than any of the other people who are after you.' He didn't look over his shoulder this time. 'See ya.' He joined his mate and they walked briskly away, heading towards Britannia Pier, the dog dutifully following.

'Who the hell were they?' Shane said, stepping forward.

'How the fuck should I know?' Sam said. 'A right couple of weirdos. The guy who was doing the talking thinks he know us.' For a second she thought Shane might put his arm around her, but it would have been too late.

'Yarmouth's full of weirdos,' he said.

It was too cold to get her phone out to see what the time was, or to try to call a cab. She had no idea about buses. She couldn't remember the last time she'd taken public transport in Yarmouth. She wasn't entirely sure it existed. She wasn't sure where she could go, where it'd be safe, anyway.

'Where do you live?' she said. Maybe Shane could protect her for the next few hours, while she came up with a plan. She didn't think she had much of an option. Who she really wanted right then was Ben.

Shane was looking at his watch, a big chunk of sporty-looking plastic. No doubt it told the time to the hundredth of a second, with some GPS function locating his exact whereabouts, how fast he was walking, jogging, running. Except he'd never been very far.

'My place is off Admiralty Road,' he said.

'Can we go there? But don't get the wrong fucking idea.'

## 33

They were back, banging harder than ever. Zach got off the bed, stood, waited for the dizziness to go away and some feeling to return to his arms and legs. He'd given up on his hands and feet a long while ago. So what if he got frostbite? His phone was in his pocket, switched off as Frank had advised. There were no fucking distress flares anywhere in this stupid minimalist box, as far as he could tell. Not the sort of thing Simon would have kept in stock, anyway, unless he was planning on shoving one up someone's arse.

Zach crept out of the master bedroom and tiptoed down four flights of stairs, keeping as tightly to the walls as possible, until he was in the ground floor stairwell. It was dark. The door to the entrance hallway was shut. He supposed he'd shut it on his way up, when the cops were there the first time, trying to keep as much distance and as many barriers in place as possible.

Fumbling forward, arms outstretched, he got to the inner door feeling for the handle and gently turned, opening the door without a creak. Daylight had made its way into the hard, square entrance hall, courtesy of a row of glass bricks above the plain, steel-backed front door. The windows in the gym were a safer bet for peering out of, however, and he crept out into the hallway, heading for the other internal door.

Halfway across, another series of thumps on the outside of the door shook him to a halt. As the reverberations died down, he picked up the sound of his breathing, heavy and rushed as if he'd had a serious workout. Back to the gym with you, my boy, a voice in his head said. It wasn't his dad's. Sounded more like Frank.

He edged forward a step, noticed a spyhole in the door. He hadn't spotted that before, otherwise he wouldn't have clambered about in the gym, trying to look out of those windows when the cops were here earlier. If he ever built a house he'd make sure you could see the entrances from all floors. There'd be no balconies getting in the way. Or at the very minimum there'd be working CCTV all over the shop. He presumed there was, except what use was that when the electricity was out? You had to plan for all eventualities. The world was medieval, always had been.

He took another couple of steps forward and pressed his eye to the tiny magnified circle of glass, trying not to breathe. Even so, all he could hear was his breathing and his heart thumping. It felt like he'd snorted a couple of fat lines of ninety-nine. Bumpety-bump, thump, thump.

Two people were outside again, a man and woman. Except they weren't the cops. It was Frank, come to the rescue. Though Zach was not happy about who he'd brought along with him. Why was his mum here? He stood back, sighed, felt another breath right behind him. Then he was pulled backwards. An arm whipped round his neck, and something sharp was pressed into his lower spine.

'What the fuck?' he managed to say, not able to turn his head far enough to clock a look. His windpipe was being squeezed, while his war wounds from the Zee brothers were making themselves painfully felt.

'Open the door,' a male voice said, right in Zach's ear.

Zach caught an unmistakable whiff of the cologne again. 'Simon?'

'Open the door, Zach.'

'It's Mum and Frank,' Zach said. Simon had loosened his grip slightly.

'I know who it is,' Simon said.

'What the fuck are you doing?'

'Just open the door, Zach.'

'How?' The door was a metal barrier worthy of a castle. There were what looked like various keyholes, but no locks or knobs to turn on the inside. There was also a red switch just to the left of the door. When he'd broken in last night he'd climbed onto the first-floor balcony and eased a window open – a window he now suspected had been used for others to gain surreptitious entry.

'Here,' Simon hissed, his left arm reaching round Zach. There was a key in his hand, nothing like Zach had seen before, and he inserted it into one of the locks.

'Why's there no electricity?' Zach asked. 'It's fucking freezing in here.' Whatever had been prodded into his back was no longer there. The newfangled key? Simon's other arm was still around his neck, however.

'Why are you here, I could ask?' Simon said. 'This is my house. You broke in. What'd you expect's going to happen to you?'

'Everyone thought you'd gone for good. That the place was sitting empty.'

'They were wrong.' Simon pulled the door open for him. 'Hello, Tatty, Frank,' Simon said calmly.

The sharp object was back in the base of Zach's spine. Even if it was just a key, Zach didn't doubt it could do serious damage if enough pressure was exerted. Lost for words, thinking that if he squeezed his insides hard enough he'd be able to repel the object, he only managed to grimace at his mum and Frank. They weren't smiling. Even colder air rushed past them into the hall.

'Hello, Simon,' Tatty said. 'Thought we'd find you here.'

'Let go of Zach,' Frank said. 'Let us in and we can all sit down and have a chat.'

'Your son broke into my house, Tatty,' Simon said. 'He was using it as a fucking squat. That is not what I call respectful behaviour. I have every right to protect my property.'

Zach felt Simon nudge him forward. He would have stumbled had Simon's arm still not been around his neck.

'Families look out for each other, Simon. You might have forgotten that.'

'Not this one, Tatty. This one never has. Blame your late husband, if you want to blame anyone. He set the example.' Simon coughed and laughed.

Zach remembered that cough, it was like a nervous tick.

'Everyone knows you're back, Simon,' Tatty said.

'Really? Seems like I caught young Zach by surprise.'

'Let us in, you bastard, quick like,' Frank said. 'The police have this place under surveillance. They'll be watching every corner. You can't pull anything and get away with it.'

'Of course they do,' Simon said. 'Who do you think's paying them?'

'You what?' said Tatty.

'Not all of them,' said Frank. 'Besides, they're smarter than you.'

'Are we talking IQs, Frank?' Simon said. 'Look at you – you've gone to fat as well. Way past your sell-by date. The problem Rich had was that he didn't deal with you soon enough. I always told him you were a useless slob. That's why he's dead. No one to watch his back.'

'Let Zach go,' said Frank.

'Fuck off, Frank,' Simon said.

For a second or two Zach contemplated ramming his elbow backwards into Simon, maybe his head as well, catch him on the snout. However, Frank was shuffling forward, into the doorway, a black object suddenly in his hand. A shooter. Frank had pulled a bloody shooter. Except Zach wasn't being let go. Simon was only tightening his grip, and pressing the object harder into his spine, not giving any ground. It was suddenly a very crowded space.

'I said let Zach go,' said Frank.

'No chance,' said Simon. 'He's got a knife in his back. You've been lucky, Tatty. Your kids have been lucky. Honest to God. But this is where their luck starts to run out, all of them – Zach, Ben, Sam. And my patience. You want to test me? Go on. Look at you lot. Pathetic. No wonder this town has gone to the dogs.'

'Mum,' said Zach. It felt like the knife, or key, or whatever it was, had broken skin, was tearing through muscle and sinew, on its way to bone and his spinal cord. He didn't mean to sound quite so high pitched, scared. He couldn't help it. 'He's not kidding. It fucking hurts.' He couldn't stand the smell of Simon's cologne for much longer either.

Time then did something weird. It both slowed down and sped up, like he was tripping. Like he was removed from his body somehow and observing the scene as if he were a little CCTV camera, hiding in a corner of the ceiling. The electricity back on. Electricity shooting through his veins. Mushrooms, man.

The first thing he was conscious of happening was Tatty flinging her hand out and catching Simon on his cheek. Zach didn't know how she managed to get any power into it, but there was a loud slapping sound and Simon loosened his grip, reeled away. Autopilot kicked in and Zach managed to land that elbow in his uncle's chest after all.

They were then somehow all through the front door, with Simon tripping backwards and Frank falling on top of him. Muscle or not, Frank was still huge, could pin most people down and keep them there. It probably helped that he still had the gun in his right hand, and was waving it at Simon's head. It was a neat affair, not dissimilar to the shooter the Zees had pulled on him a couple of days earlier. Go on, thwack him one too, Zach urged. But Frank didn't bash Simon with it, because his mother stepped over and took the gun from Frank, professional like, and walked around Simon until she was pointing it at his head, steady as a rock, making no mistake about her intentions.

Zach had the sense that she'd use it in a blink. Go, the mother-lode.

Impressed, spurred on, Zach found himself shutting the front door and everything dimmed. In the half-light he saw Frank rolling off Simon, who was still squirming on the floor, bleating. He'd grown a goatee and clipped his hair tight, Zach noticed. He was wearing the same sleazy designer gear, though. A light tan leather jacket, a crew-neck sweater underneath, black jeans and expensive leather trainers.

'Tat,' he was saying, 'don't be stupid, we can work some-thing out. We always have.'

Frank was struggling to stand. Zach had forgotten about his hip; Frank obviously hadn't. The tumble on the hard concrete floor couldn't have helped. For a moment he felt crushed by his love for the big man.

'You've always been a fucking coward, Simon,' Tatty said. 'I'm going to enjoy this.'

'Tatty,' Frank said, 'you don't need this on your conscience. Let me do it. It's my job. He's got away from me twice in the past, but not this time. Besides, you've got your kids to look after, a future. My time's run out.'

Frank was propping himself against the wall with one hand. He was holding the other out for the gun.

'Let's get him upstairs, first,' Tatty said, not handing it over. 'There're a few things I'm still not sure about.'

'Is that door locked?' Frank said, nodding towards the fortified barrier.

'It's meant to be on some sort of electric mechanism, I reckon,' Zach said. 'But the electricity's out. Simon had the key.' He looked down at his uncle. Zach stepped over him, kicked Simon in the side. 'Get up, you bastard.' Zach didn't enjoy kicking Simon as much as he thought he would.

He was still family, his late dad's brother. Even Zach had been able to tell that Simon had been in awe of his dad. Jealous as fuck. Brothers for you. Not that Zach had ever been that jealous of Ben, he supposed. In many ways he always felt it was the other way round. He wished he'd got on with his brother better. Wondered whether he ever would. There was so much he'd like to say, apologise for. Zach was aware that he'd been an arsehole for far too long. He'd never listened, despite Frank doing his best. He wanted that time again. Another childhood.

'Up,' his mum was saying, waving the pistol in Simon's face.

It sort of suited her, Zach thought.

Frank hobbled over and tried to boot Simon in the ribs. It was pathetic. Then he bent down, tried to grab Simon by the shoulder, gave up almost instantly. Simon was right, Frank was way past his sell-by date. Except, all things said and done, Zach loved the man. He'd got him out of so many tight corners. No one could say he wasn't loyal. It actually pained Zach to see Frank so crocked. The man deserved a break, a sunny retirement.

'Whoah,' Zach found himself saying, as he watched his mum now bend down and clock Simon one on the cheek with the pistol.

Simon moved this time, getting to his feet double quick, advancing on Tatty ready to strike. She was being pushed into a corner. Frank wasn't so slow this time.

Zach stepped forward as well, though not so quick. He had to pull himself together, finally, get into shape. Maybe he would take up that place at uni after all. Sports science. Become clean and strong. The sound of the gun going off brought him straight back to the present. He could feel the reverberations in the small hard hallway, and in his head, until finally Simon's moaning and complaining took over.

'You've fucking shot me,' Simon repeated. He was clutching his chest, his right side, staggering on his feet.

Zach could see blood on his jacket, his hands. It didn't seem to be spurting out, though it was spreading quickly. This was the second time in under a year that he'd been in close proximity to someone who'd been shot. The last time there'd been a lot more blood and gore, and it'd been instantly fatal. Simon was still standing.

'Best listen to me the first time,' Tatty said.

'What now?' Frank said. 'He's getting blood every-where.'

'It's his house, do you think I care? Upstairs, Simon.'

'Why not just finish him here?' Frank said.

'Don't you want to know exactly who he's been talking to?' Tatty said. She looked Zach's way. 'Zach, make sure the front door's locked.'

'Why don't you just do as Frank says?' Zach said. 'Then we can all get out of here. The cops will back.'

'The pain he's put me – us – through, I want to get my money's worth.'

Maybe having a gun didn't suit his mum. What a mean bastard she could be. Childhood memories started to flood his mind before he spotted the large key on the floor. He didn't feel like locking them all in, he'd liked to have run away again. When the cops came back he supposed they'd have a warrant, a battering ram. He doubted that even the steel door would keep them out. But then again Simon had had the place specially designed, specced up. Perhaps the door was cop-proof. The house wasn't, though. He'd got in easily enough.

He picked up the key and worked out where it fitted and locked the door. There was a solid, satisfying click. Now he really felt like he was in a prison, a cell, banged up for a good long stretch. Except he hadn't committed the worst crimes that day, that year, that decade. Plus, he might just get out with a good chunk of his life left to live, and make amends. Unlike his mum and Frank. They were fucked however you looked at it.

'Move,' said Tatty, waving the gun at Simon again.

'OK, OK,' he wheezed.

The bloodstain on Simon's jacket was spreading, but he began shuffling towards the internal door to the stairwell like a good boy. He was leaving quite a bloody trail, however, his posh rags ruined. Zach desperately tried not to step in any blood, moving as close to the walls as he could.

Frank closely followed Simon, walking no more easily. 'Why'd you never put in a fucking lift?' Frank said, looking up at the short flight of stairs.

Simon had managed to climb onto the first step. 'Because I was never going to get old in this gaff, mate,' he said faintly.

'In this business,' Frank added gruffly. 'It's a young man's game.'

'Have you got a problem with women, Frank?' his mum asked. 'With women working? What do you mean it's a young man's game?'

'Right now I've got a problem with stairs,' Frank said. 'I'm not the only one. Tatty, is this such a good idea?'

'Jesus wept,' Tatty said. 'Bit late if not, isn't it?'

'There's another room on this floor,' Zach said. 'A gym, across the hall.' He pointed back the way they'd come. Simon didn't say a thing. He wasn't going to hasten his own death, Zach supposed. However, Zach was desperate to get it over with. Where had his life gone so wrong? When had it ever gone right? He was barely out of his teens. He should never have come back from Ibiza. It wouldn't be so far off spring there right now. Uni, up north, or the Balearics, with the bars and the beaches and the babes? What sort of option was that? Quite a good one, actually, if he'd ever be in a position to choose.

'OK,' said Tatty, 'we'll interrogate him down here in the gym.'

'Might be some equipment we can use,' Frank chuckled.

'What are you now, the fucking Gestapo?' Simon wheezed.

'You've earned this, Simon,' Tatty said.

'I need a hospital,' Simon said. 'I'm dying.'

'Not yet,' said Tatty.

Zach thought his mum was right, despite the blood. Simon wasn't dying. There was still colour in his face, with the goatee that didn't suit him one bit. He'd probably just been winged, a small chunk of belly sliced open. A lower rib splintered, maybe. There'd be a bullet in the wall somewhere out in the hall. Something else for the cops to get excited about.

'When we've finished with you,' his mother added, waving the gun with even more flourish, 'you'll be dying, believe me, and you'll know it, just as Rich did, in his last few moments.'

Yes, his mum could be cruel. But she could also be loyal, he supposed. She'd let him get away with murder, practically. Though now it was really weird and fucked up. Was he meant to let *her* get away with murder? He wasn't sure he'd want to see her again, whatever happened next. Frank, though, he'd miss like mad.

They were still in the stairwell, Simon and Frank moving like wounded snails. Zach felt his heart beating fit to burst and a soaring headache, like his brain was going to explode. How fucking long was this going to take? 'Can we just get on with it?' he said.

## 34

'We're here. You should get yourself to a doctor, a hospital,' Abir said, nudging Ben hard in the side as if he'd somehow dropped off.

Despite the overwhelming tiredness, it'd been impossible to sleep on the short journey. There were the appalling reverberations of the diesel engine shaking his wrecked body to the core, the fumes drifting through the windows that appeared never to have shut properly, and the constant yelling and chanting of the Norwich City supporters. The train had picked up more and more of them from the few stops along the way – Halvergate, Acle, Brundall.

Yellow and green was never a great colour combination. Set against the patches of freezing fog, sleet and the odd shock of sunny brightness occasionally visible through the train's smeary windows, it was enough to induce a further bout of nausea. The rolling stock didn't appear to have changed since he was a kid, since his dad was a kid. Never had Ben welcomed arriving at Norwich station more.

The doors opened with an old-fashioned hiss, and the hordes started to clamber out, Abir getting to his feet first then having to haul Ben up.

'I'm OK,' said Ben, shrugging off his friend and saviour.

'You're not,' said Abir. 'You need to get checked out.'

'Nothing's broken,' Ben said. 'Bit of concussion, I expect, but that'll go. We need to keep moving.'

They were practically marched off the train with the crush, and on up the platform. Never had Ben appreciated the pull of match day more, either, especially as it seemed to be a derby, according to the chants, Norwich versus Ipswich, otherwise known as Ipshit. *City till I die*. Unless those were always the chants.

The concourse was packed with police, some with dogs, no one looking out for two mild-mannered young men, not attired in yellow and green, or blue and white, even if their clothes were torn and faces bruised and bloodied. Besides, the plan was not to head through the barriers. As far as Ben knew they still didn't have any tickets, cards or cash. Abir was going to lift a wallet, a purse, when the opportunity arose. Ben didn't think that'd happened on the two-carriage train from Yarmouth.

There'd been no ticket inspectors at Yarmouth, and it'd been easy enough to squeeze through the barriers at the beginning of the journey. It was how they used to get around as kids, even when they had the cash.

'There's a London train,' said Ben, pointing. They were at the beginning of platforms two and three. The long London train was on platform two. The shorter Midlands train was on platform three.

'Didn't we settle on Manchester?' said Abir. 'I have better connections up north, I told you. It'll be safer.'

'I thought you were escaping all that – that that was why you headed down here.'

'Where's that train go?' Abir was pointing to the train on platform three.

'I don't care,' said Ben. He wasn't going to tell him that it went direct to Manchester and then onto Liverpool. 'I'm going to London.' London was bigger than Manchester – far easier to get lost in, he'd have thought. Besides, he knew it, and most importantly knew where Avani lived. However, he did want Abir with him, at least until he was safely at Avani's door, presuming she'd let him in.

Abir had slowed, though continued to follow him as they walked up the platform, the London train on their right and the Manchester train on their left. The chanting continued in the background, loud and aggressive, echoing in the cavernous space.

'Come on, mate,' Ben shouted. 'I think this train leaves at half past.' The London trains always departed on the hour or half hour. There were a couple of minutes to go. Ben stopped, waiting for Abir to catch him up.

'Sorry, this is where we part then,' Abir said, holding out his hand.

'You're joking,' Ben said. 'Come on, let's get on this train.' He nodded to his right. 'We can talk about it on the way to London. Besides, I don't have a ticket, any money. I can't be stopped. Pickpocketing is not my thing.'

'Needs must,' Abir said. 'You'll work out a way. Chat someone up.'

'Looking like this?'

'Maybe someone will take pity on you.'

That was what he was hoping once he got to London, to Avani's door, Saturday teatime. 'This is really it then, is it?' he said.

'For now,' Abir said, turning.

'I owe you one,' Ben said, realising that he hadn't even shaken his hand. 'For saving my life,' he muttered, his eyes watering, as he climbed onto the London train, not looking back.

The first carriage was cold and virtually empty. The second was not much fuller, but it was warmer. However, he didn't see any likely candidates in here. He kept going, knowing that the conductor began at the back of the train, moving forward to first class. Maybe that'd be where his best options lay. He'd have more time, at least, at the front of the train. If he bottled it he reckoned he could always disembark at Diss. He probably had until then. Maybe even Stowmarket. He had to get to London, though, just to see Avani one last time. Say how sorry he was, what a mistake he'd made.

The train was now moving, he realised, catching sight of the Norwich City stadium, a row of railwaymen's cottages and an old industrial building waiting for redevelopment, a steely flash of bright sky reflecting on poisonously still water, as the train rattled over a narrow river, before beginning to gather pace.

Maybe it wasn't Avani he craved. She'd dumped him – for what? For being himself. Sam had never been so judgemental. She'd always accepted him. When they were growing up they relied on each other almost entirely. They were the best of friends. Infuriatingly close, as far as others were concerned. But that was how it was, and then they'd grown up and grown apart. Where was Sam now, this minute? He didn't want to run away from her, for ever.

The next carriage looked more promising. But Ben had decided on first class, the very front of the train, and he kept going, using the seat backs for support, walking with his feet and hands. Fields were opening up beyond the train's dirty windows, while his mind had switched to business, and the lost opportunities there. He hadn't even managed a week in Yarmouth, working for his mum, for Goodwin Enterprises. He could have made such an impact, given a little more time. Though he knew he would never return to that sort of organisation. Besides, Goodwin Enterprises was finished.

If he had a corporate future he supposed it'd be abroad. London was just a stepping stone, should he even get that far. He wondered, briefly, whether his mum, and Zach, were safe, where they'd end up. Sam he hoped would be all right, always. She was tough and resourceful, when she needed to be. God, he loved her to bits.

The automatic doors let him into the plush quiet of first class. When his dad used to go to London on the train he only ever travelled first class. Of course he did. Growing in confidence, if not strength, Ben sat at a table for four. Felt his broken body collapse into the old plush seat. These trains hadn't changed for decades, either.

Two women were sitting opposite. He knew their type, middle-aged, provincial, neat – far more conservative and small minded than they'd ever acknowledge. Predictably they both recoiled, shrank back in their seats, despite the table being wide, the old first-class seating giving them plenty of space. He must have looked like a tramp, and smelt like one too.

The women reminded him of his mum, for all the wrong reasons. He probably needed to call her, get a message to her to say he was all right. Except he didn't think he was ready to speak to her. He didn't want to be mean, but how did he address the fact that his mother, and her business interests, had very nearly got him killed? This was going to take some time to come to terms with, to forgive. Not just his mum, but his rotten father too, and his lethal legacy.

Perhaps, however, he could have done with getting hold of Frank, asking him to bring some cash. Then again, he'd had it with all that, already. He had to be better off making his own way for the time being – something he'd never been that great at, or even expected to do. His dad, and then his mum, had always been in the background, pushing him this way or that. Then Avani. She was probably the hardest to please.

'I'm sorry,' he started to say to the two women, 'it's not what it looks.'

However, they were doing their best not to pay him any attention. He knew he was never going to be able to lift a wallet, delve into someone's handbag. He was not Abir, not that sort of criminal. He didn't want to be any sort of criminal, full stop. It was far too much hassle.

The train was pulling through proper countryside now. Winter in full swing. Dark ploughed fields, bare trees, air thick with mist and failing afternoon light, a few gentle hills taking the pain out of the hardness. It was easy to forget quite how flat Yarmouth and the surrounding views there were. He had a sudden craving for a jagged Mediterranean coastline, waves of pine trees and holm oaks tumbling down to a cerulean sea. Half moons of sand. A beach shack selling beer and *gambas a la plancha*. Ibiza, that's what he wanted. Didn't they have a villa there? But sharing it, with his family?

Ben struggled to lean forward, wanting to attract the women's attention. 'Sorry to bother you,' he said, trying to sound like the public school-educated boy that he was, 'but can I ask a favour? I need to borrow a phone and a bit of cash.' Everyone put on a front now and then, and sometimes that front wasn't so far from the truth.

## 35

Simon was still bleeding heavily, yet keeping shtum. Tatty stood back and looked at her watch, the flashy gold Rolex, once Rich's, of course. She was freezing. Little light was coming into the room from the thin strip of windows high up. It was early to be getting dark already. The weather must have taken another turn for the worse, the day never having had much of a chance.

Maybe night would provide them with some cover at least. She and Frank had buried Jess at night, out in the mud. And they hadn't even killed her. The man responsible for that was slumped against a weight-training machine, making a terrible mess on the floor.

Frank and Zach were sitting on a sleek, narrow bench across the room, letting her get on with it for now. She'd insisted. Maybe Simon was going to die, without revealing anything further. They could just leave him here. Cut and run.

She could barely look at her youngest son. Sam hadn't rung her saying she wanted to be picked up. What on earth could she be doing with Shane, at such a time? Nor had Ben managed to message her to say he was safe and sound, having escaped the caravan park moments before she'd got there – if Frank's theory was right. Maybe she'd never hear from him again. Or Sam. Could she blame them?

She took aim, pointing the gun in the vague area of Simon's right leg. 'Who's your cop?' she asked. 'This is your last chance?'

'Go to hell, Tatty. You're going to kill me anyway. Find out the hard way.'

The second shot was less of a shock to her system. She'd braced herself, held the gun how Frank had taught her, had gently squeezed the trigger, riding the safety. It took every effort not to let off another round, that was the thing with automatic weapons. This new one of Frank's was a joy to handle. Yes, she hadn't kept her side of the bargain, that promise she'd made to herself all those months ago, when her children's lives were on the line the first time.

She'd learned nothing, putting their safety, their very existence at risk once more. She looked at the weapon in her hand, Simon twitching on the floor. Maybe once you got a taste for such things all rational thought went out of the window. Killing was as addictive as temazepam, as heroin. It wasn't as if she could protect her children anyway.

'Fuck, Mum,' Zach was saying. 'You shot him again.' He'd got to his feet, as had Frank.

Frank was moving towards her, his hand outstretched. 'That's enough. Give me the gun, Tatty.'

'No,' she heard herself say. 'It's not enough. It'll never be enough.'

'Mum,' said Zach, 'do as Frank says.'

'Kyle Neville,' Simon said, more loudly than Tatty thought possible.

She looked down at him. The blood was spreading fast now, and Simon was making no effort to stem the flow. 'You what?'

'He's the cop – OK? He's working with a Chinese operation. Short guy, trying to make his mark.'

'He took out Winslow's dealers in Gorleston basin, Thursday night,' Frank said, resigned. 'He wasn't on his own.'

Simon nodded. He had gone very pale now. He was struggling to breathe. She'd only shot him in the thigh.

'I get it,' said Frank, looking straight at her and not Simon. 'This guy Neville, the new head of Serious and Organised, wanted us and Winslow's lot to drive each other out, so he could control the new arrangement, while hanging onto the casino plans, courtesy of Simon. Clever, almost. Except Hayes provided a complication. He's obviously been leaning on her – everything she knows.'

'Who's to say she hasn't recruited him?' Tatty said. 'That it's the other way around.'

'Not how she works. You'd be a fool to team up with someone in the force. I doubt he's quite decided what to do with her yet. Both as crooked as each other. He'll use her for what he can get. Though they'd have different agendas. He'll be after the money – and the power.'

'And what was she ever after?'

'Control,' said Frank. 'Same difference. But the skeletons piled up. It's the way it is.'

'She can't have long, either,' Tatty said.

'I wouldn't be so sure. She's resourceful,' said Frank. 'Has her handyman as well. I don't think he's half as rattled as her. He's a big, fit chap, that's for sure. Nothing scares him.'

'Why were the police round mine this morning asking about Simon, telling me they'd found Jess?' Tatty said.

'I told you, Hayes is resourceful. Maybe she's trying to blow Neville's plan out of the water before he's barely got started. They'd have different cop teams working for them.'

'What did they want with Zach, the day before?' She was not impressed with the double dealing, the endless going behind people's backs. That was not the way to run a business, let alone a regional police force.

'That'd be Neville's lot, I reckon,' said Frank. 'Perhaps trying to establish an alibi for what was going on in the basin. I don't know, but Neville was behind the shootings that evening. I'm certain of that, along with my old friend Howie Jones. Neville's way of commanding loyalty.'

'Britt Hayes wanted me to take you out, Frank,' Tatty said. 'That's her way of commanding loyalty?'

'Her way of getting others to clean up after her. We all do it, one way or another. She doesn't want you hanging around town any longer, either,' said Frank. 'We're a liability.'

'I know.' Tatty sighed. 'You always said you'd keep as much of the dirt away from me as possible, that was your prime job, but you've told me too much.'

'You've hardly taken the back seat.'

'I did, for all those years I was with Rich.'

'Then you thought you'd have a go?'

'It's not so easy, is it?'

'No. So what happens to Winslow, and his crew?'

'If he's got any sense he'll be well out of here by now. But he hasn't, so I suspect we haven't quite seen the last of him.'

Tatty shook her head, glanced down at Simon. 'What a fucking mess. There's no future, is there?'

'No, not here,' said Frank.

She tried not to think of the moment when she stepped in and it all started to go wrong. It was the morning she was informed of Rich's death. Of course she could run a business, an organisation – more efficiently, profitably, ruthlessly, than he ever could. That was what she'd thought.

For a second her mind wandered to Nathan Taylor. Then Shane. Both men were on the level, more or less. They'd seen something in her, as she had them. But it couldn't have been the future, because she'd been heading for disaster from the moment she was born. She didn't deserve to live.

'I guess this sort of business doesn't suit me very well,' she said softly, bidding for a tiny bit more time. 'I've failed. I've failed you all.'

'And you blame me for wanting to run my own line?' said Zach. 'This is some shit show.'

'Leave it out, Zach,' Frank said. 'Tatty, give me the gun, will you?'

She looked at Frank, his big, bald head. He was a good man, in his way. Though like her, things had gone wrong for him right from the beginning as well. It was only ever a matter of time. She looked at her youngest son. He certainly hadn't had the best start in life, the best role models, despite the money. She hoped things would come good for him, desperately so, and for Sam and Ben – once she was out of the way.

Frank could still play a part, be a father figure to Zach at least, if he wasn't banged up. He'd done his best playing the cops at their game, she supposed, hoped, but he wasn't a strategist. He could never see too far ahead. It had been a mistake making him her partner, even if it was only to be temporary. He had no vision beyond the street.

'Tatty?' Frank said, desperation and urgency in his voice. He knew her, but not as well as she knew herself.

'Mum,' Zach said, 'someone's banging on the door.' He started jumping up and down, trying to look out of the narrow strip of windows in the gym. His beautiful boyish body, which used to be so fit, purposeful. The hours he used to spend in the gym, with a safe, steady career mapped out ahead. 'It's the police, tons of them,' he was gabbling. 'Fucking hell. They're like all really tooled up as well. SWAT gear.'

'Go and let them in,' Tatty said. 'Go on, you and Frank. I'll stay here with Simon.'

'No,' said Frank. 'Give me the gun. There's nothing left for me. You've still got a job to do.'

'Yeah, what's that?' Tatty said. The gun really did feel very comfortable in her hand. She could hear the banging on the door. Someone shouting through a loudhailer. She could no longer hear Simon breathing. She wasn't going to look down at the floor lest it did something to her resolve.

'You know exactly what that is,' Frank said. 'Zach, go and let them in will you, before they start using stun grenades or whatever.'

'Go on, Zach,' Tatty said. There'd been so much she'd tried and failed to protect him from. So much she'd never

335

wanted him or the others to witness. They'd seen it all, one way or another, however. It was more than just failure. It was a disgrace. She was a disgrace. Yet no child of hers was going to see her final act. They didn't deserve that to be imprinted on their delicate minds. 'Zach – MOVE, NOW, PLEASE,' she screamed.

'I love you,' she said much more quietly, as he stepped towards the door. 'I love you and Sam and Ben.' Her wish, her last wish, was that they'd help each other, that they'd look out for each other. Love each other dearly. But she wasn't counting on it.

'Frank,' she said much more loudly, 'you can get out of here as well, RIGHT NOW.'